The
Young
Oxford Book
— of —
Timewarp Stories

The
Young
Oxford Book
of
Timewarp Stories

DENNIS PEPPER

OXFORD
UNIVERSITY PRESS

OXFORD

UNIVERSITY PRESS

Great Clarendon Street, Oxford OX2 6DP

Oxford University Press is a department of the University of Oxford.
It furthers the University's objective of excellence in research, scholarship,
and education by publishing worldwide in

Oxford New York

Athens Auckland Bangkok Bogotá Buenos Aires
Cape Town Chennai Dar es Salaam Delhi Florence Hong Kong Istanbul
Karachi Kolkata Kuala Lumpur Madrid Melbourne Mexico City Mumbai
Nairobi Paris São Paulo Shanghai Singapore Taipei Tokyo Toronto Warsaw

with associated companies in Berlin Ibadan

British Library Cataloguing in Publication Data available

ISBN 0-19-268167 7 (hardback)

ISBN 0-19-278189 8 (paperback)

1 3 5 7 9 10 8 6 4 2

Typeset by
Mike Brain Graphic Design Limited, Oxford

Printed in Great Britain

Contents

Contents

Introduction

This is a collection of stories in which time is important, either to the way the stories are told or to what they are about. There are ghost stories here—ghosts are, after all, adrift in time—there's a witch story, a love story or two, stories of time shifts and switches, of distortions to time, and of time travel itself.

I'm a traveller in time, and so are you. But this view of time—we are born, live for a while, and die—is not what interests the writers of time travel stories in this collection. They speculate about freeing ourselves from what anchors us in our individual time line to travel into the past or future just as we might travel to India or America. Come to think of it, this already involves us in some kind of time travel. We could, if we wished (and had enough money) travel in such a way that we need never see the sun set, never see today end. It wouldn't mean we didn't grow older though.

Writers have devised various methods of transportation which for the sake of their stories we are inclined to accept without asking awkward questions. But whatever their means of transport these travellers are out of their own time. They are anomalies, and potentially dangerous ones. If time travel were possible, if we could travel into the past or future, then what? One of Ray Bradbury's dinosaur hunters steps on a butterfly—and the world the travellers return to has altered significantly, and for the worse. Time tourists flock to Golgotha to see the crucifixion—it's educational, after all— in Garry Kilworth's story only to be confronted with their own responsibility and with the knowledge that it will be repeated 'for ever and ever'. In Harry Harrison's entertaining variation on the classic paradox (what would happen if you travelled into the past and killed your own grandfather before your father was born?) a lizardoid from the future—reptiles are the dominant species again— turns up in the present to rescue the proto-lizard from which their race began. Must he succeed, since he exists and has existed in the future, or is it possible he could fail?

In Steve Bowkett's complex story about sidestepping time to preserve essential knowledge, refugees from the horrors of the distant future are rounded up and imprisoned. Any objects they have brought with them as possible bribes are destroyed. Even what is in their heads may be dangerous. But the past is not always a refuge nor is knowledge from the future always seen as a threat. Poul Anderson takes a different line. His future civilization uses the past as a prison. Some criminals, those it wishes to be rid of, are transported into the past, the exact place and time chosen with care. But any knowledge they might have is disregarded: it would be largely useless because the conditions would not be right for its use. Gant, in Ted Thomas's story, is imprisoned in the past, not for any crime but because his time machine crashes and he can't return. He too finds that all his knowledge and training, his twentieth-century medical skills, are of little use when treating the primitive people among whom he is stranded.

Sudden *shifts* in time, into the past and back again, give depth and complexity to several stories, 'The Picnic' and 'Fire, Fire' for instance, that are not concerned with the implications of time travel itself. There is a time *switch* in Ken Cowley's '. . . And Three to Go'. The seventeenth-century warlock escapes a hanging by switching places with a twentieth-century researcher who happens to visit the pub where the hanging took place. It does not, we discover, provide him with the freedom he must have hoped for.

Then there are the ghosts. Most ghost stories direct the reader's attention to the hauntings and the (usually malevolent) activities of the ghost. I have chosen ones that focus instead on the bridge in time that exists between haunter and haunted. In 'Master Ghost and I' the ghost is, unusually, from the future, our present. It is only through his intervention in the past that the present he knows comes into being. There is some dispute, in 'The Silver Box', over who is the ghost—Carole, sick in her bed today, or the psychic investigators a hundred years hence—but the story is about their attempts to communicate across the intervening years and whether the future rather than the past can be altered when you have already seen what will happen.

But they are all stories, these and the ones I've not mentioned. I've chosen them because I think they are good, challenging stories, but also because, above all, I think you will enjoy them.

Dennis Pepper
July 2001

My Object All Sublime

POUL ANDERSON

We met in line of business. Michaels' firm wanted to start a subdivision on the far side of Evanston and discovered that I held title to some of the most promising acreage. They made me a good offer, but I was stubborn; they raised it and I stayed stubborn; finally the boss himself looked me up. He wasn't entirely what I'd expected. Aggressive, of course, but in so polite a way that it didn't offend, his manners so urbane you rarely noticed his lack of formal education. Which lack he was remedying quite fast, anyhow, via night classes and extension courses as well as omnivorous reading.

We went out for a drink while we talked the matter over. He led me to a bar that had little of Chicago about it: quiet, shabby, no jukebox, no television, a bookshelf, and several chess sets, but none of the freaks and phoneys who usually infest such places. Besides ourselves, there were only half a dozen customers—a professor-emeritus type among the books, some people arguing politics with a degree of factual relevance, a young man debating with the bartender whether Bartok was more original than Schoenberg or vice versa. Michaels and I found a corner table and some Danish beer.

I explained that I didn't care about money one way or another, but objected to bulldozing some rather good-looking countryside in order to erect still another chrome-plated slum.

Michaels stuffed his pipe before answering. He was a lean, erect man, long-chinned and Roman-nosed, his hair grizzled, his eyes dark and luminous. 'Didn't my representative explain?' he said. 'We aren't planning a row of identical split-level sties. We have six basic designs in mind, with variations, to be located in a pattern . . . so.'

He took out pencil and paper and began to sketch. As he talked, his accent thickened, but the fluency remained. And he made his own case better than anyone had done for him. Like it or not, he said, this was the middle of the twentieth century and mass production was here to stay. A community need not be less attractive for being ready-made, could in fact gain an artistic unity. He proceeded to show me how.

He didn't press me too hard, and conversation wandered. 'Delightful spot, this,' I remarked. 'How'd you find it?'

He shrugged. 'I often prowl about, especially at night. Exploring.'

'Isn't that rather dangerous?'

'Not in comparison,' he said with a touch of grimness.

'Uh . . . I gather you weren't born over here?'

'No. I didn't arrive in the United States until 1946. What they called a DP, a displaced person. I became Thad Michaels because I got tired of spelling out Tadeusz Michalowski. Nor did I want any part of old-country sentimentalism; I'm a zealous assimilationist.'

Otherwise he seldom talked much about himself. Later I got some details of his early rise in business, from admiring and envious competitors. Some of them didn't yet believe it was possible to sell a house with radiant heating for less than twenty thousand dollars and show a profit. Michaels had found ways to make it possible. Not bad for a penniless immigrant.

I checked up and found he'd been admitted on a special visa, in consideration of services rendered the US Army in the last stages of the European war. Those services had taken nerve as well as quick-wittedness.

Meanwhile our acquaintance developed. I sold him the land he wanted, but we continued to see each other, sometimes in the tavern, sometimes at my bachelor apartment, most often in his lakeshore penthouse. He had a stunning blonde wife and a couple of bright, well-mannered boys. Nonetheless he was a lonely man, and I fulfilled his need for friendship.

A year or so after we first met, he told me the story.

I'd been invited over for Thanksgiving dinner. Afterwards we sat around and talked. And talked. And talked. When we had ranged from the chances of an upset in the next city election to the chances of other planets following the same general course of history as our own, Amalie excused herself and went to bed. This was long past midnight. Michaels and I kept on talking. I had not seen him so excited before. It was as if that last subject, or some particular word, had opened a door for him. Finally he got up, refilled our whisky glasses with a motion not altogether steady, and walked across the living room (noiseless on that deep green carpet) to the picture window.

The night was clear and sharp. We overlooked the city, streaks and webs and coils of glittering colour, ruby, amethyst, emerald, topaz, and the dark sheet of Lake Michigan; almost it seemed we could glimpse endless white plains beyond. But overhead arched the sky, crystal black, where the Great Bear stood on his tail and Orion went striding along the Milky Way. I had not often seen so big and frosty a view.

'After all,' he said, 'I know what I'm talking about.'

I stirred, deep in my armchair. The fire on the hearth spat tiny blue flames. Besides this, only one shaded lamp lit the room, so that the star swarms had also been visible to me when I passed by the window earlier. I gibed a little. 'Personally?'

He glanced back towards me. His face was stiff. 'What would you say if I answered yes?'

I sipped my drink. King's Ransom is a noble and comforting brew, most especially when the Earth itself seems to tone with a deepening chill. 'I'd suppose you had your reasons and wait to see what they were.'

He grinned one-sidedly. 'Oh, well, I'm from this planet too,' he said. 'And yet—yet the sky is so wide and strange, don't you think the strangeness would affect men who went there? Wouldn't it seep into them, so they carried it back in their bones, and Earth was never quite the same afterwards?'

'Go on. You know I like fantasies.'

He stared outwards, and then back again, and suddenly he tossed off his drink. The violent gesture was unlike him. But so had his hesitation been.

He said in a harsh tone, with all the former accent: 'OK, then, I shall tell you a fantasy. It is a story for winter, though, a cold story, that you are best advised not to take so serious.'

I drew on the excellent cigar he had given me and waited in the silence he needed.

He paced a few times back and forth before the window, eyes to the floor, until he filled his glass anew and sat down near me. He didn't look at me but at a picture on the wall, a sombre, unintelligible thing which no one else liked. He seemed to get strength from it, for he began talking, fast and softly.

'Once upon a time, a very, very long time in the future, there was a civilization. I shall not describe it to you, for that would not be possible. Could you go back to the time of the Egyptian pyramid builders and tell them about this city below us? I don't mean they wouldn't believe you; of course they wouldn't, but that hardly matters. I mean they would not understand. Nothing you said could make sense to them. And the way people work and think and believe would be less comprehensible than those lights and towers and machines. Not so? If I spoke to you of people in the future living among great blinding energies, and of genetic changelings, and imaginary wars, and talking stones, and a certain blind hunter, you might feel anything at all, but you would not understand.

'So I ask you only to imagine how many thousands of times this planet has circled the sun, how deeply buried and forgotten we are; and then also to imagine that this other civilization thinks in patterns so foreign that it has ignored every limitation of logic and natural law, to discover means of travelling in time. So, while the ordinary dweller in that age (I can't exactly call him a citizen, or anything else for which we have a word, because it would be too misleading)—the average educated dweller knows in a vague, uninterested way that millennia ago some semi-savages were the first to split the atom—only one or two men have actually been here, walked among us, studied and mapped us, and returned with a file of information for the central brain, if I may call it by such a name. No one else is concerned with us, any more than you are concerned with early Mesopotamian archaeology. You see?'

He dropped his gaze to the tumbler in his hand and held it there, as if the whisky were an oracular pool. The silence grew. At last I said, 'Very well. For the sake of the story, I'll accept the premiss. I imagine time travellers would be unnoticeable. They'd have techniques of disguise and so on. Wouldn't want to change their own past.'

'Oh, no danger of that,' he said. 'It's only that they couldn't learn much if they went around insisting they were from the future. Just imagine.'

I chuckled.

Michaels gave me a shadowed look. 'Apart from the scientific,' he said, 'can you guess what use there might be for time travel?'

'Well,' I suggested, 'trade in objects of art or natural resources. Go back to the dinosaur age and dig up iron before man appeared to strip the richest mines.'

He shook his head. 'Think again. They'd only want a limited number of Minoan statuettes, Ming vases, or Third World hegemony dwarfs, chiefly for their museums. If "museum" isn't too inaccurate a word. I tell you, they are *not* like us. As for natural resources, they're beyond the point of needing any; they make their own.'

He paused, as if before a final plunge. Then: 'What was this penal colony the French abandoned?'

'Devil's Island?'

'Yes, that was it. Can you imagine a better revenge on a condemned criminal than to maroon him in the past?'

'Why, I should think they'd be above any concept of revenge, or even of deterrence by horrible examples. Even in this century, we're aware that that doesn't work.'

'Are you sure?' he asked quietly. 'Side by side with the growth of today's enlightened penology, haven't we a corresponding growth of crime itself? You were wondering, some time ago, how I dared walk the night streets alone. Furthermore, punishment is a catharsis of society as a whole. Up in the future they'd tell you that public hangings did reduce the crime rate, which would otherwise have been still higher. Somewhat more important, these spectacles made possible the eighteenth century birth of real humanitarianism.' He raised a sardonic brow. 'Or so they claim in the future. It doesn't matter whether they are right, or merely rationalizing a degraded element in their own civilization. All you need assume is that they do send their very worst criminals back into the past.'

'Rather rough on the past,' I said.

'No, not really. For a number of reasons, including the fact that everything they cause to happen has already happened . . . Damn! English isn't built for talking about these paradoxes. Mainly, though, you must remember that they don't waste all this effort on ordinary miscreants. One has to be a very rare criminal to deserve exile in time. And the worst crime in the world depends on the particular year of the world's history. Murder, brigandage, treason, heresy, narcotics peddling, slaving, patriotism, the whole catalogue, all have rated capital punishment in some epochs, and been lightly regarded in others, and positively commended in still others. Think back and see if I'm not right.'

I regarded him for a while, observing how deep the lines were in his face and recalling that at his age he shouldn't be so grey. 'Very well,' I said. 'Agreed. But would not a man from the future, possessing all its knowledge—'

He set his glass down with audible force. '*What* knowledge?' he rapped. 'Use your brains! Imagine yourself left naked and alone in Babylon. How much Babylonian language or history do you know? Who's the present king, how much longer will he reign, who'll succeed him? What are the laws and customs you must obey? You remember that eventually the Assyrians or the Persians or someone will conquer Babylon and there'll be hell to pay. But when? How? Is the current war a mere border skirmish or an all-out struggle? If the latter, is Babylon going to win? If not, what peace terms will be imposed? Why, there wouldn't be twenty men today who could answer those questions without looking up the answers in a book. And you're not one of them; nor have you been given a book.'

'I think,' I said slowly, 'I'd head for the nearest temple, once I'd picked up enough of the language. I'd tell the priest I could make . . . oh . . . fireworks—'

He laughed, with small merriment. 'How? You're in Babylon, remember. Where do you find sulphur and saltpetre?

If you can get across to the priest what you want, and somehow persuade him to obtain the stuff for you, how do you compound a powder that'll actually go off instead of just fizzing? For your information, that's quite an art. Hell, you couldn't even get a berth as a deckhand. You'd be lucky if you ended up scrubbing floors. A slave in the fields is a likelier career. Isn't it?'

The fire sank low.

'All right,' I conceded. 'True.'

'They pick the era with care, you know.' He looked back towards the window. Seen from our chairs, reflection on the glass blotted out the stars, so that we were only aware of the night itself.

'When a man is sentenced to banishment,' he said, 'all the experts confer, pointing out what the periods of their specialities would be like for this particular individual. You can see how a squeamish, intellectual type, dropped into Homeric Greece, would find it a living nightmare, whereas a rowdy type might get along fairly well—might even end up as a respected warrior. If the rowdy was not the blackest of criminals, they might actually leave him near the hall of Agamemnon, condemning him to no more than danger, discomfort, and homesickness.

'Oh, God,' he whispered. 'The homesickness!'

So much darkness rose in him as he spoke that I sought to steady him with a dry remark: 'They must immunize the convict to every ancient disease. Otherwise this'd only be an elaborate death sentence.'

His eyes focused on me again. 'Yes,' he said. 'And of course the longevity serum is still active in his veins. That's all, however. He's dropped in an unfrequented spot after dark, the machine vanishes, he's cut off for the rest of his life. All he knows is that they've chosen an era for him with . . . such characteristics . . . that they expect the punishment will fit his crime.'

Stillness fell once more upon us, until the clock on the mantel became the loudest thing in the world, as if all other sound had frozen to death outside. I glanced at its dial. The night was old; soon the east would be turning pale.

When I looked back, he was still watching me, disconcertingly intent.

'What was your crime?' I asked.

He didn't seem taken aback, only said wearily, 'What does it matter? I told you the crimes of one age are the heroisms of another. If my attempt had succeeded, the centuries to come would have adored my name. But I failed.'

'A lot of people must have got hurt,' I said. 'A whole world must have hated you.'

'Well, yes,' he said. And after a minute: 'This is a fantasy I'm telling you, of course. To pass the time.'

'I'm playing along with you,' I smiled.

His tension eased a trifle. He leaned back, his legs stretched across that glorious carpet. 'So. Given as much of the fantasy as I've related, how did you deduce the extent of my alleged guilt?'

'Your past life. When and where were you left?'

He said, in as bleak a voice as I've ever heard, 'Near Warsaw, in August, 1939.'

'I don't imagine you care to talk about the war years.'

'No, I don't.'

However, he went on when enough defiance had accumulated: 'My enemies blundered. The confusion following the German attack gave me a chance to escape from police custody before I could be stuck in a concentration camp. Gradually I learned what the situation was. Of course, I couldn't predict anything. I still can't; only specialists know, or care, what happened in the twentieth century. But by the time I'd become a Polish conscript in the German forces, I realized this was the losing side. So I slipped across to the Americans, told them what I'd observed, became a scout for them. Risky—but if I'd stopped a bullet, what the hell? I didn't; and I ended up with plenty of sponsors to get me over here; and the rest of the story is conventional.'

My cigar had gone out. I relit it, for Michaels' cigars were not to be taken casually. He had them especially flown from Amsterdam.

'The alien corn,' I said.

'What?'

'You know. Ruth in exile. She wasn't badly treated, but she stood weeping for her homeland.'

'No, I don't know that story.'

'It's in the Bible.'

'Ah, yes. I really must read the Bible sometime.' His mood was changing by the moment, towards the assurance I had first encountered. He swallowed his whisky with a gesture almost debonair. His expression was alert and confident.

'Yes,' he said, 'that aspect was pretty bad. Not so much the physical conditions of life. You've doubtless gone camping and noticed how soon you stop missing hot running water, electric lights, all the gadgets that their manufacturers assure us are absolute necessities. I'd be glad of a gravity reducer or a cell stimulater if I had one, but I get along fine without. The homesickness, though, that's what eats you. Little things you never noticed, some particular food, the way people walk, the games played, the small-talk topics. Even the constellations. They're different in the future. The sun has travelled that far in its galactic orbit.

'But, voluntary or forced, people have always been emigrating. We're all descended from those who could stand the shock. I adapted.'

A scowl crossed his brows. 'I wouldn't go back now even if I were given a free pardon,' he said, 'the way those traitors are running things.'

I finished my own drink, tasting it with my whole tongue and palate, for it was a marvellous whisky, and listened to him with only half an ear. 'You like it here?'

'Yes,' he said. 'By now I do. I'm over the emotional hump. Being so busy the first few years just staying alive, and then so busy establishing myself after I came to this country, that helped. I never had much time for self-pity. Now my business interests me more and more, a fascinating game, and pleasantly free of extreme penalties for wrong moves. I've discovered qualities here that the future has lost . . . I'll bet you have no idea how exotic this city is. Think. At this moment, within five miles of us, there's a soldier on guard at an atomic laboratory, a bum freezing in a doorway, an orgy in a millionaire's apartment, a priest making ready for sunrise rites, a merchant from Araby, a spy from Muscovy, a ship from the Indies . . .'

His excitement softened. He looked from the window and the night, inward, towards the bedrooms. 'And my wife and kids,' he finished, most gently. 'No, I wouldn't go back, no matter what happened.'

I took a final breath of my cigar. 'You *have* done rather well.'

Liberated from his grey mood, he grinned at me. 'You know, I think you believe that yarn.'

'Oh, I do.' I stubbed out the cigar, rose, and stretched. 'The hour is late. We'd better be going.'

He didn't notice at once. When he did, he came out of his chair like a big cat. '*We?*'

'Of course.' I drew a nerve gun from my pocket. He stopped in his tracks. 'This sort of thing isn't left to chance. We check up. Come along, now.'

The blood drained from his face. 'No,' he mouthed, 'no, no, no, you can't, it isn't fair, not to Amalie, the children—'

'That,' I told him, 'is part of the punishment.'

I left him in Damascus, the year before Tamerlane sacked it.

They Live Forever

LLOYD BIGGLE, JR.

Before he stepped out of his hut into the clear morning air, Mathews repeated his calculations of the night before. The result was the same. In Earth-time, this was the Day. And if it were not, if an error had crept into his records down through the years, this particular day was close enough. It would do.

He stood looking at the village below him, at the laboriously-cultivated fields on the lower slope, at the peacefully grazing *zawyi*, some of which were still being milked. From the village street the little chief saw him, and raised both hands. Mathews returned the greeting, and took the down path.

The chief approached him humbly. 'Is your Day of Days satisfactory?'

Mathews looked down at the breath-taking panorama this strange planet served him each morning with his breakfast. The haze of ground mist was shot through with riotous colours that drifted and spread and changed before his unbelieving eyes. Without warning the jungle would suddenly flip into the sky and hang above itself in a dazzling, inverted mirage. In the distance the broad surface of a mighty river mirrored the pink-tinted clouds of early morning. The sight awed and stirred Mathews as it had on thousands of other mornings, and as it would each morning as long as his eyes served him.

'The Day is satisfactory,' he told the chief.

The chief gave a little grunt of satisfaction, and shouted a command.

From nearby huts came warriors, eight, ten, a dozen. They carried an odd miscellany of weapons, and Mathews was responsible for many of them—spears, blowpipes, a boomerang, bows and arrows, and odd items that Mathews had invented. They were a resourceful people, these *Rualis*—quick, intelligent, and brave. They reacted with rare enthusiasm to a new idea.

Women came forth to approach Mathews with shy respect. They bowed before him with their gifts. He accepted a skin of sweet wine, bread cakes, and pieces of dried meat. A whispered request, and a small boy scurried into a hut and returned with a hoe.

'The Day waits,' Mathews said. He took the downward trail, and the *Rualis* marched behind him, singing lustily.

They moved quickly down the cool, sunny mountain slope, and the torrid heat of the jungle rolled up in waves to meet them. The natives moved ahead of him when they reached the jungle path. It was a custom, almost a ritual, that they should precede him into the jungle, to protect him from the nameless terrors that lurked there. Mathews had never seen these terrors, and frankly doubted their existence, but he never protested. His ability to yield graciously on matters that were really unimportant was one reason for his success with these people.

The Tree was their objective. It had been a forest giant when Mathews first saw it—fifty-eight years before, by his calculations. The Tree held some mysterious significance for the natives which he had never fathomed. They conducted ceremonies there, and their dancing kept a broad, circular track cleared. But they never invited his presence, and he never attempted to intrude.

The *Rualis* seated themselves in a circle about the Tree. They had removed their clothing, and perspiration glistened on their sun-tanned bodies. Insects swarmed around them. Mathews waved his hand in a friendly salute, and turned off the jungle trail. The path he followed was faint, overgrown, almost obliterated. The *Rualis* never used it, and it had been ten days since his last visit.

He moved a dozen yards into the jungle, slashing at the undergrowth with his hoe, and reached a small clearing. He seated himself on the ground, and drank deeply from the wine skin. Insects droned incessantly overhead, colossal insects, but they did not bother him. That was one of the many mysteries of this strange planet. The insects plagued the *Rualis*, but ignored the Earthman.

Back at the Tree, the *Rualis* continued their singing. The song tossed swingingly on the breeze, backed up by intricate thumping on a dried *liayu* fruit. Mathews suspected that they were a highly musical people, though he knew too little about music himself to share their extreme pleasure in it.

He pushed the wine skin aside, and chewed solemnly on a piece of meat, feeling a deep, relaxing peace within himself. It was his Day—his birthday, by Earth-time, as well as he had been able to keep it. It was also, by a coincidence he had often pondered down through the years, the anniversary of the tragedy that had placed him on this planet.

The ship had crashed on his sixteenth birthday. It rested somewhere in front of him, hidden by the impenetrable curtain of green. Long years before, the roaring jungle had swallowed it up in its clinging, rusting embrace. It had been years—decades, even—since Mathews had last hacked his way through to visit it. Now he was content to leave it undisturbed. There was nothing entombed there except memories, and the clearing had memories enough to satisfy him.

On the other side of the clearing were the graves—six of them, side by side. At one end Mathews had buried his grandfather. At the other end rested the mortal remains of old Wurr, the immortal man who was not immune to accidents. Between them lay the four-man crew of the *Fountain of Youth*.

'Seven is a lucky number,' his grandfather had said. 'Come along, and bring us luck.' So Mathews had come, and brought luck only for himself. Of the seven, he alone had survived the crash.

At the time the *Fountain of Youth* set forth bravely for the far reaches of the galaxy, he'd had little understanding of his grandfather's quest. The adventure, the excitement was enough. He hadn't particularly cared whether they reached their objective or not.

Now he was an old man, and he understood—too well. It was not an idle whim that led his grandfather to name the new

star ship *Fountain of Youth*. Grandfather Mathews quite literally sought the source of eternal life, but his objective was a planet of youth, rather than a fountain. He sought the home of old Wurr.

Wurr, the kindly old immortal! Mathews' memory could still search back over the years and bring him vividly to life. Bushy hair, black, twinkling eyes, low, husky voice, he never seemed anything but ordinary.

And the known facts about him were nothing less than staggering.

Wurr had survived a precipitous arrival on Earth when the space ship on which he was a passenger plunged into the Pacific Ocean. Wurr was found bobbing on the surface in a space suit, the only survivor. He was a mature man then, and from that day until he left Earth on the *Fountain of Youth*, three hundred and seventy-two years had elapsed. That much was documented history.

During those centuries he had not aged perceptibly. Doctors examined him, and X-rayed him, and studied him repeatedly, and their only comment was a rather frustrating shrug of the shoulders. He was an ordinary man, with a single difference.

He lived forever.

Ordinary man and immortal man, man of simple, unaffected habits, man of mystery. He was a sly and candid observer of the human scene. Historians sought him out—an eye-witness of more than three centuries of Earth's history. He submitted willingly to examinations, but he baulked at answering questions. He was no different, he said, from anyone else—where he came from.

Grandfather Mathews became acquainted with him, and reached a conclusion on a subject that had been giving rise to much speculation ever since Wurr had completed his first hundred years on Earth. Wurr's home was a planet of immortality, a planet of perpetual youth.

Supposing an alien, a native of Earth, were to visit that planet. Would he receive the gift of immortality? Grandfather Mathews conferred with Wurr. The immortal man was reluctant. He liked Earth. Eventually Grandfather Mathews convinced him, and the *Fountain of Youth* expedition was born. Earth had lately developed star travel, and Wurr knew with the exactitude of a skilled navigator the stellar location of his home planet in the Constellation Scorpio. Grandfather Mathews was confident.

Mathews understood, now, that the old man had not taken him along as a whim. He had frankly sought immortal life for himself, but he was a practical old fellow. He admitted the possibility that he might already be too old, too near to death, to be redeemed by the powers of that miraculous planet. But his grandson, only a boy in his teens—surely the planet could work the miracle for him!

That was the legacy the old man had sought for Mathews. Not wealth, not prestige, but immortality. Mathews gazed at the six graves with a searing pang of regret. Perhaps the bones had already dissolved in the moist jungle soil, but he carefully tended the graves as a lasting monument to his own loss, to a loss that seemed more tragic with each passing year as his life drew to a close, to the loss of life itself. But for the stupid accident, he might have achieved that which men of Earth had dreamed of for as long as there had been dreams.

And life was good. Even on this savage planet it was good. He had been too young when he arrived to feel deeply the loss of the civilized splendours of Earth. His very youth had given him much in common with the childlike *Rualis*. He had enjoyed love and laughter, the hunt, the occasional, half-coming tribal war. He had helped the *Rualis* to become strong, and they gave him lasting honour.

Life was good, and it was beating its measured way to the inevitable end, to the damp soil of the jungle. And it might have been otherwise.

Mathews got wearily to his feet, and went to work with the clumsy, stone-bladed hoe. He cleared the green shoots from around the headstones he had carved with such care so many years ago. The mounds had to be reshaped after every rainy season. The jungle was perennially encroaching upon the clearing. The open ground had been much larger in his younger days, but as he grew older he allowed the jungle to creep back. Now it seemed a struggle to hold the space remaining.

There were times when he thought he should remove the graves to a high, dry place on the mountain side. But this place seemed to belong to them, and they to it—here, where their quest had ended, hundreds of light-years from Wurr's planet of immortality, wherever it might be.

He could not work long in the savage jungle heat. He gathered up his things, and followed the faint trail back to the Tree. Still singing, the *Rualis* took their places behind him, and he led them out of the jungle.

The climb up the slope seemed harder with each trip. When he reached the village he was quite content to sit down and rest, and watch the children play, before he attempted the steep path to his own hut. He held a special affection for the village children, and they for him. Perhaps, he thought, it was because none of his wives had been able to bear him children, though when he gave them to men of their own race they always proved fertile. It was as though fate were not content with denying him physical immortality, but must also cut him off from the perpetuity that children could have secured for him. In his more bitter moments he believed that the six who died had been dealt with more kindly.

But he had to admit that life was good. The *Rualis* were an attractive, graceful, light-skinned people—small of stature, much smaller than he, but sturdy and strong. The children matured with astonishing rapidity. It was only three Earth years from birth to adolescence, and then, alas, perhaps another seven or eight years from maturity to death. The *Rualis* who reached the age of fifteen, by Earth standards, were rare. Mathews had watched many generations come and go, and he'd had wives from every generation, but no children. He had long since given up the thought of children.

When he had rested, he got to his feet and walked slowly down the village street. A child caught his attention, a girl, and even among the charming *Rualis* children her beauty was exceptional. With a smile, he stopped to admire her.

The mother appeared in the doorway of the hut, and turned aside shyly when she saw him. 'You have a beautiful child,' Mathews said to her. 'She is the image of her great-great grandmother. Or perhaps it was her great-great-great grandmother—I do not recall exactly. But she, too, was a beautiful child.'

The mother was pleased, but held herself apart with proper good manners. The child prattled excitedly. 'Today is my birth festival,' she told Mathews.

He said gravely, 'Today is also my birth festival.'

The child seemed startled. 'What is your age, Earthman?'

Mathews smiled wistfully. How was he to explain seventy-four Earth years to this child? And the *Rualis* had no number large enough to embrace the quantity of the fifty-seven day months they called years that Mathews' life had spanned.

'I do not know,' he said. 'I cannot remember.'

He turned, and sought the path to his hut . . .

The child watched him until he disappeared. 'Mother,' she said, 'why does the Earthman not know his age?'

'Hush,' the mother said soothingly. 'Age does not matter to the Earthman. Like the Tree, his kind lives forever.'

Timestorm

STEVE BOWKETT

The iron tongue of midnight hath told twelve.

A Midsummer Night's Dream

Red lightning burst on the West Hill without warning. Da Silva's team was the nearest, out on routine patrol near the field-perimeter—and staying sharp on Dr Carlson's orders, because there had been a lot of disruption in the area just lately that boded ill for refs coming through . . . Refs, and whatever else the future cast up.

An alert crackled out over Danny Bryant's helmet mike, the words badly distorted by static. Behind them, and beyond the harsh swishing of white noise, he could actually hear the boom and crash of Time's ocean breaking on the shore of the night. Eternity coming in with the tide. It was the most wonderful, the most terrifying, sound he could imagine.

Da Silva, the Team Leader, responded at once. He acknowledged Core Control's message and then snapped out his orders to his men—splinter manoeuvre, in buddy-pairs, around the base of the hill and then in a twist pattern upwards. That should allow them to mop up incoming refs with minimum fuss or danger.

'Copy. Moving,' was all Danny needed to say. Fifty metres away through the summer-rich maples he could see his team buddy Kane. Or at least, he could see the recognition lights glinting on Kane's armour; a pattern of blue and gold sparkles that marked the man out immediately.

Danny got going. He spoke into his mike, giving orders to the weapon strapped to his back. It was a standard pulsegun that could do anything from raising goosebumps to shattering rocks. The settings shifted now to heavy stun: Danny swung the gun round off his shoulder and broke into the easy lope that brought him out on the track to West Hill. Kane soon joined him from a side path and they jog-trotted together heading for Zero Point.

'Whatcha think,' Kane said, 'sols or civs?'

Danny grinned. Soldiers or civilians? This was leading to one of Kane's bets and another chunk out of Danny's pay. 'I can't afford your gambling, man,' Danny came back, chuckling, 'but I reckon civs.'

People from the future, using time travel to escape the evils of the world yet-to-be. The scientists, the big brains, should have realized that chronotron technology would be used and abused like any of Man's grand inventions. Sure, it stopped important people from ageing; it lengthened the lifespan of machinery; it helped create some really interesting archaeological tools; it offered peepholes into the past; it had brought the dinosaurs back from the dead . . . But somewhere along the line, the awesome Time Line of the world, it had caused such dreadful devastation that people wanted to escape from it in droves.

Nobody really knew much about that devastation—The Catastrophe, as it had been called. It had happened—would happen, from Danny's perspective—almost a million years in the future, or so the Time Techs believed. But Bryant was feeling its consequences now. Just as a stone sends ripples out over the water, so the effects of The Catastrophe came rippling back into the past, damaging the fabric of reality. When stray chronotron energy burst through into the present, its effects could be disastrous. Danny had seen a demonstration once where an airborne battletank was zapped with some C-particles. It had come apart like rotting fruit within seconds, reduced to dust inside a minute. The chronotron gun was the ultimate weapon, so terrible that no one dared to use it. At least not yet. But one day in the future, they probably had. And maybe that was what The Catastrophe was all about: the final war at the far end of time.

'Visual!' Kane yelled suddenly, startling Danny out of his dream. Sure enough, the craggy peak of West Hill was alive with electricity; or something like electricity, a spiderwork of red and white lightnings dancing over the rocks.

'Where do you suppose the zero point will be?'

Kane shrugged. They both slowed to a walk, each soldier's breathing coming fast over the other's intercom. Zero Point was a natural node in the time flow, the place where the refugees broke through—not necessarily at the centre of the lightning storm, but often set some distance from it. There would be a glow in the air, a quiet brightening, a flurry of twinklings, and a man would suddenly be standing there, some mother's son; or maybe a frightened family; or maybe a cadre of crack troops wanting to fight for their right to live in the past. But civs or sols, they were all refs that had to be stopped because, Rule One: you shouldn't tamper with the basic machinery of the universe.

'The rocks outcrop again on the south side,' Kane said. He had an instinct about such things. 'The energy usually follows the lie of the land.'

'Are you betting on it?' Danny quipped and this time Kane laughed, but said nothing.

They proceeded carefully, watching the head-up displays on their helmet visors with half an eye, but relying mainly on what they could see directly. The night was cloudy and marbled with moonlight; full of shadows and soft stirrings as the trees swayed in a warm southwesterly wind. High on the hill the lightnings flickered, and the ID lights of the field-soldiers winked as the teams continued their search pattern.

'I don't like it,' Kane said after some minutes of tautening silence.

'I'm getting odd sensor readings too—'

'Yeah, but it's more than that . . . Can't you *feel* it?'

Danny shook his head gently. Kane's gut instincts were often dead right, and rarely entirely wrong. Something was happening out there. Something different. Tomorrow's fingers tapping gently on the door of today.

Without warning the glows above the hill brightened and flared like fires fanned in a wind. There came a surge of pressure. Thunder rolled over. A vast auroral curtain of light swept out in all directions—

'Just there! Move—move!'

Kane had spotted it first, among the trees. He'd been right. The great energies, having ripped a hole into the here-and-now to let the refugees through, were soaking down through the granite bedrock, spraying free where outcrop stone lay bare. A hundred metres away the rock was on fire, and the night was suddenly awake, and a high keening note came screeching through Danny's carbon-fibre helmet.

Kane raced ahead in his excitement, disregarding rules. Danny called in their position as he ran to keep up, then yelled for Kane to slow down and wait.

He saw a movement in the undergrowth, a man-shaped afterglow. Danny lifted his weapon and fired.

The brilliant tracer rounds lit up the scene and caught the ref mid-leap into bracken. But the stun-pulse tagged him and he was out cold before he hit the ground. Just an ordinary man trying to put the future behind him.

'There'll be more,' Kane declared, though Danny didn't need telling. This was zero point, and the refs *had* to come through here, now, once they had started their journey from the future.

Two more popped into existence like a flash photograph, a young woman and man. Kane zapped them good and they flopped like dolls.

A child came into the world weeping. Danny stunned her and she folded, crumpling like empty clothes into the dust.

'We'll round 'em up shortly,' Kane said. He was in command. 'It's an almighty stampede!'

Danny realized, with some disgust, that his team buddy was enjoying himself. Maybe that was why he joined the Corps. Danny had signed up through sheer terror of the consequences if he didn't play his part.

'They might be hurt—' he started to say, but Kane was forging ahead again, aiming his gun at every small movement of leaf or branch.

They moved ahead thirty metres and picked off another four refs, a couple of them armed with conventional weaponry: guns, knives. These people were not from too far ahead—early twenty-second century, Danny estimated.

He and Kane drew closer to the glowing outcrop. There would be others around the hill, with other teams mopping up the incomers there. It looked like they had this zero point battened down tight tonight.

Through the trees, a crumbling jumble of big stones loomed in the dark. Kane had dropped some paces behind his friend. He was nosing through thick undergrowth, shooting off the occasional stun-pulse just to be sure.

'I guess maybe we got them all,' Kane began—his voice shutting off like a tap as someone leaped atop the rocks with a shriek and dived over Danny's head towards Kane.

Everything slowed to half-speed. The stranger's foot caught Danny's helmet, tumbling him backwards. As he fell, he saw the ref shine and then fly apart like a scarecrow in a hurricane. There was a second of red horror, and then just dust that blew away in the breeze.

'Kane!'

Far too late. Danny was on his back on the ground, and anyway the rocky outcrop protected him. But Kane was out in the open, catching the full freak blast of C-energy. His armour cracked, and in the fearsome dazzling light Danny saw, just for an instant, Kane turn into his father, his grandfather, and then into the shrivelled memory of his ancestors.

The chronotron surge was relentless. Kane had time only to realize his doom. His scream outlasted his bones.

Danny lay still, shuddering with fear and shock. Big surges like this were rare, but they were always a potential danger. It was like a sudden burst of seawater through a cleft in the rocks; a timelash that sent minutes and hours and years spinning wildly out of control. If you got caught in it, anything could happen. Kane's fate—time accelerated forward—was the most usual. At least it was quick.

The alert beacon in Danny's suit had been broadcasting its insistent helpcall since the accident. The rest of the team would be hurrying to the rescue . . . Not that they could do a thing . . . But now the beacon's note dropped half an octave and the helmet display said the danger was over.

Danny checked anyway. He pulled a small plant up out of the ground and tossed it high in the air. It dropped back unchanged. Time was back to normal here.

Far away now he could hear men shouting—and was about to shout back, until a movement in the bracken close by distracted him. Still frightened, washed with grief, Danny set his pulsegun to kill and held it shaking in front of him. And, as he'd been trained, he pumped the volume of his helmet speaker up to full and added some echo and feedback-roar and bellowed into the eerie aftermath darkness—

'Come out! Come out now or I'll fire!'

There was a moment's hesitation, then he slashed aside the ferns with his gun-barrel.

Echoes of forever quivered in front of his eyes. He saw a woman as old as the stones, a crone, an arch-witch. Then doubt. Then a young girl of Danny's own age curled up and cowering; pretty as a picture with startling blue eyes, and terrified of the monster who'd found her.

'Help me,' she whimpered, 'help me.' And reached out pathetically to touch him.

Her name was Guinette and she had come from far away, she said. From long long away. That's all Danny learned as he hauled her up and frog-marched her back to base accompanied by the other members of the team who'd joined him.

Twelve refs had been caught that night; none, it seemed, had escaped the field perimeter into the outside world. It was a clean sweep. They'd be processed, e-tagged, and housed in isolation for the rest of their lives. What the Time Techs couldn't do was send them back to the future—something about Temporal Potential: even though the future existed, it couldn't be accessed ahead of time. At least, not with today's technology. Also, the refs couldn't be allowed any contact with the rest of humanity, not now, not at any time in the past, because any small thing they did could cause massive unforeseen consequences tomorrow, or next week, or in ten thousand years' time. The TTs called it Chaos Theory. Danny called it an unholy mess.

Guessing their probable fate, and because they were desperate, most refs tried to bribe their way to freedom. They brought bits of technology back with them; astonishing, sometimes magical devices that today's scientists or politicians would give their eye-teeth to possess. The law came down hard in this matter, and all such devices were destroyed. Even the knowledge the refs had in their heads was forbidden. If a ref attempted to offer new information, he or she was placed in

solitary confinement. Words were loaded pistols. The wrong talk could kill, as it had in the past.

But they still tried. Danny listened as some of the refs tonight turned on the persuasion. There was a share dealer from 2063 who was willing to give advice on stocks if only they'd let him go free. There was a woman who carried a whole-world database on a slip of plastic the size of a credit card. She could tell you when you were scheduled to die, and how to avoid it if you did exactly as she said ... And there were other, simpler people who'd only wanted to escape from the horrors of the future. They'd sold everything to dodgy time-merchants to buy a short ride to nowhere. But didn't they ever realize that by their very act they were helping to create the future they so hated!

Danny shook his head sadly and gazed at Guinette. She hadn't played tactics, except to look back at him a few times with her beautiful childlike eyes. Danny'd blushed but his helmet spared his embarrassment. He wondered what her world had been like, and what she had hoped to gain by coming here to his.

They arrived at base campus a little after 1.00 a.m. The Tech teams took over. Refs were separated out to be searched, washed, and interrogated. Danny and the other soldiers went for debriefing. There was a general exchange of views, and then Keach—a senior tech—took Danny aside to another room, where he was surprised to find Dr Carlson himself waiting. The top man. The buck stopped at his door.

Carlson, fifty-something, stocky, with a full-lipped face, had overall control of the Ref Containment Project for the north-western quadrant, a quarter of the planet. He was also on the panel of the Directorate for Temporal Development worldwide. Danny could not possibly have done anything so wrong that warranted Carlson's involvement!

'Sit down. Watch this.'

Danny obeyed as Carlson touched a stud on his deskpad. A whole wall became a monitor screen filled with complicated readouts and displays.

'Do you understand this?'

'Some of it, sir,' Danny said. What he did understand made him shiver.

'The girl you caught—Guinette—is unique to us. She has come from further away in the future than any other ref so far.

We estimate half a million years. The technology of her age would look like sorcery to us. We think that perhaps her culture knows far more about the Catastrophe than we do. Perhaps they can even access the future. These people would be immensely powerful . . . And yet the girl came unequipped, unprepared to bargain for freedom. Or so it seems.'

Danny didn't even have time to ask the question. Carlson indicated other readings on the screen.

'But she must have brought something back with her. We don't know what, but it's big. Our instruments can detect its presence in this time stream, yet we simply can't see it. The girl is clever, and incredibly dangerous—' Carlson smiled thinly at Danny's expression. 'Yes, we thought of killing her, but it may be that we're safe only while she lives. Maybe she's arranged things so that her death would cause immense destruction.'

'I see that,' Danny said. 'But I don't understand—'

'Why you're here? Yours is the first face Guinette saw when she arrived. As far as she's concerned, you could have killed her then. But you spared her. Maybe she'll open up to you, I don't know. It's a long shot. We'd like you to try talking with her—if you're prepared to take the risk . . .'

The door opened and closed with a double sigh. Guinette was sitting on the edge of a bare bunk bed in an otherwise empty room. She was wearing drab grey prison overalls. A tray of uneaten food lay on the floor close to her feet.

'Um—' Danny said, feeling stupid.

'There's a storm coming.' She looked at him with astonishing frankness. Her gaze made his heart thump. 'I mean, a storm from the future.'

'You're not allowed to—'

'Dr Carlson sent you in here to talk with me.' She smiled sweetly. 'I heard every word. And I know he's listening now.'

She waved her hand and the air went dead.

'Now we can speak privately.'

Danny hit the red alarm stud close to the door. Nothing happened. He faced her again, feeling suddenly cold.

'There's not very much you need to know,' Guinette told him. 'Except that you and Carlson and everyone have got it all wrong. Oh yes, some of the refs are running because of future wars and hardships. But the Catastrophe—that's no war. It's a purification . . . What do I mean?'

Danny gasped. *She had reached inside his head and plucked out the thought.*

'Men couldn't help meddling in time. Oh, I know there are strict laws and punishments. But as the centuries wore on the technologists couldn't resist tampering with the basic machinery of the universe—until, a million years from now, it all came grinding to a halt. Yes,' she nodded, as Danny opened his mouth to ask. 'The clock of the cosmos stopped ticking. Mankind froze time; created an eternal Now, trapping the world in a temporal loop from which there could never be any escape.

'People saw it coming. Those living on the brink of it decided on radical action. They would sweep back through the millennia, erasing all knowledge of time travel—changing whatever needed to be changed to wipe the idea from our minds. Of course, that will cause some people to cease to exist, but it's a small price to pay. The cleansing will feel like a tidal wave washing back through history, sweeping everything aside. And afterwards, the sands will lie clean and innocent again, and we will play, innocent again, the Children of Eve . . .'

Guinette's gaze flicked to the door as the hammering began. There came a sharp crack and a hissing, and a second later an incandescent star burned through the metal and stretched into a line of white fire.

'Then why are you running?' Danny asked hurriedly. 'If you know there can be no escape?'

'Oh, I've found a way . . . Why here, why now, why you?' She got up from the bunk and came across and held his hand. And in a moment of utter horror Danny knew that Guinette's lovely blue eyes were not real. The Techs had searched her for devices, but they had never thought to look there.

She blinked, and the room was different. Something was appearing out of the air; a bulging lens of distortion; a shadow; a huge machine, vaguely humanoid, that stood jammed against ceiling and walls. It flexed its metals, and the room crumbled swiftly around them.

They were outside, running, while alarms shrilled and searchlights swept to and fro and guards yelled out warnings.

The machine followed behind at a slow lope. It turned once and spat a fist-sized plug of blue fire. Base campus bloomed like a flower and collapsed amidst a bed of hungry flames.

'You've killed them! You killed them all!' Danny couldn't believe it.

'Their time', Guinette said calmly, 'was up.'

Yet there was the greater threat: those from the future who were scouring all of time: the Makers of the Storm—

'They are more intelligent than I am, but not cleverer.' Guinette laughed and Danny thrilled at the sound. In another place, at another time . . .

They ran on through the night. The clouds had thinned and the moon was high and bright, the land washed silver.

'I can sense Them coming now.' Guinette slowed and then stood still. She was no longer holding Danny's hand, but his mind was hers and he stopped beside her helplessly.

'There.'

Beyond the hills a dark veil was rising up to blot out the stars. Outriders of some vast energy were already crawling like tendrils over the sky. Danny could feel time trembling in his blood; seconds and minutes and days running away helplessly like hourglass sand.

'They will snuff you out like an insect,' he said weakly.

'No.' Guinette laughed at the monstrous device standing a short distance away. 'This machine will open the door. I and my followers created it to give us this one chance . . . All the other refs ran backwards. We, Danny, you and I, are stepping *sideways.*'

She did nothing obvious; touched no device nor worked any magic. But in no time at all the world was fading like a dream and all the clocks were melting.

A colossal wave crashed over, disintegrating the towering machine into dust.

But by then, Guinette was standing on a hillside in another place and time, though just like the one she had left. It was open land, with no base campus or guards; and no one in the whole world except she knew how to walk into the future or the past.

'We'll have a lovely time together here, Danny,' she said. 'I'll still call you Danny, it's a nice name. We'll hide safe until the moment arrives, and then the door will open again by itself and we'll return and change the future again, forever. By then I will have taught you everything I know. You won't understand it, of course, but that won't matter. You'll pass it on to your son, and to his sons, and theirs, and theirs, until it reaches me, your distant, distant daughter.'

Guinette giggled impishly and gazed at the little baby in her arms. And he mimicked her smile and stared openly back at her with eyes empty of all doubt.

A Sound
of Thunder

RAY BRADBURY

T he sign on the wall seemed to quaver under a film of
sliding warm water. Eckels felt his eyelids blink over his
stare, and the sign burned in this momentary darkness:

> TIME SAFARI, INC.
> Safaris to any Year in the Past
> You name the animal
> We take you there
>
> You shoot it

A warm phlegm gathered in Eckels's throat; he swallowed
and pushed it down. The muscles around his mouth formed a
smile as he put his hand slowly out upon the air, and in that
hand waved a cheque for ten thousand dollars to the man behind
the desk.

'Does this safari guarantee I come back alive?'

'We guarantee nothing,' said the official, 'except the
dinosaurs.' He turned. 'This is Mr Travis, your Safari Guide in
the Past. He'll tell you what and where to shoot. If he says no
shooting, no shooting. If you disobey instructions, there's a
stiff penalty of another ten thousand dollars, plus possible
government action, on your return.'

Eckels glanced across the vast office at a mass and tangle, a
snaking and humming of wires and steel boxes, at an aurora
that flickered now orange, now silver, now blue. There was a

sound like a gigantic bonfire burning all of Time, all the years and all the parchment calendars, all the hours piled high and set aflame.

A touch of the hand and this burning would, on the instant, beautifully reverse itself. Eckels remembered the wording in the advertisements to the letter. Out of chars and ashes, out of dust and coals, like golden salamanders, the old years, the green years, might leap; roses sweeten the air, white hair turn Irish-black, wrinkles vanish; all, everything fly back to seed, flee death, rush down to their beginnings, suns rise in western skies and set in glorious easts, moons eat themselves opposite to the custom, all and everything cupping one in another like Chinese boxes, rabbits into hats, all and everything returning to the fresh death, the seed death, the green death, to the time before the beginning. A touch of a hand might do it, the merest touch of a hand.

'Hell and damn,' Eckels breathed, the light of the Machine on his thin face. 'A real Time Machine.' He shook his head. 'Makes you think. If the election had gone badly yesterday, I might be here now running away from the results. Thank God Keith won. He'll make a fine President of the United States.'

'Yes,' said the man behind the desk. 'We're lucky. If Deutscher had gotten in, we'd have the worst kind of dictatorship. There's an anti-everything man for you, a militarist, anti-Christ, anti-human, anti-intellectual. People called us up, you know, joking but not joking. Said if Deutscher became President they wanted to go live in 1492. Of course it's not our business to conduct Escapes, but to form Safaris. Anyway, Keith's President now. All you got to worry about is —'

'Shooting my dinosaur,' Eckels finished it for him.

'A *Tyrannosaurus rex*. The Thunder Lizard, the damnedest monster in history. Sign this release. Anything happens to you, we're not responsible. Those dinosaurs are hungry.'

Eckels flushed angrily. 'Trying to scare me!'

'Frankly, yes. We don't want anyone going who'll panic at the first shot. Six Safari leaders were killed last year, and a dozen hunters. We're here to give you the damnedest thrill a *real* hunter ever asked for. Travelling you back sixty million years to bag the biggest damned game in all Time. Your personal cheque's still there. Tear it up.'

Mr Eckels looked at the cheque for a long time. His fingers twitched.

'Good luck,' said the man behind the desk. 'Mr Travis, he's all yours.'

They moved silently across the room, taking their guns with them, towards the Machine, towards the silver metal and the roaring light.

First a day and then a night and then a day and then a night, then it was day-night-day-night-day. A week, a month, a year, a decade! AD 2055. AD 2019. 1999! 1957! Gone! The Machine roared.

They put on their oxygen helmets and tested the intercoms.

Eckels swayed on the padded seat, his face pale, his jaw stiff. He felt the trembling in his arms and he looked down and found his hands tight on the new rifle. There were four other men in the Machine. Travis, the Safari Leader, his assistant, Lesperance, and two other hunters, Billings and Kramer. They sat looking at each other, and the years blazed around them.

'Can these guns get a dinosaur cold?' Eckels felt his mouth saying.

'If you hit them right,' said Travis on the helmet radio. 'Some dinosaurs have two brains, one in the head, another far down the spinal column. We stay away from those. That's stretching luck. Put your first two shots into the eyes, if you can, blind them, and go back into the brain.'

The Machine howled. Time was a film run backwards. Suns fled and ten million moons fled after them. 'Good God,' said Eckels. 'Every hunter that ever lived would envy us today. This makes Africa seem like Illinois.'

The Machine slowed; its scream fell to a murmur. The Machine stopped.

The sun stopped in the sky.

The fog that had enveloped the Machine blew away and they were in an old time, a very old time indeed, three hunters and two Safari Heads with their blue metal guns across their knees.

'Christ isn't born yet,' said Travis. 'Moses has not gone to the mountain to talk with God. The Pyramids are still in the earth, waiting to be cut out and put up. *Remember* that. Alexander, Caesar, Napoleon, Hitler—none of them exists.'

The men nodded.

'That'—Mr Travis pointed—'is the jungle of sixty million two thousand and fifty-five years before President Keith.'

He indicated a metal path that struck off into green wilderness, over steaming swamp, among giant ferns and palms.

'And that,' he said, 'is the Path, laid by Time Safari for your use. It floats six inches above the earth. Doesn't touch so much as one grass blade, flower, or tree. It's an anti-gravity metal. Its purpose is to keep you from touching this world of the past in any way. Stay on the Path. Don't go off it. I repeat. *Don't go off*. For *any* reason! If you fall off, there's a penalty. And don't shoot any animal we don't OK.'

'Why?' asked Eckels.

They sat in the ancient wilderness. Far birds' cries blew on a wind, and the smell of tar and an old salt sea, moist grasses, and flowers the colour of blood.

'We don't want to change the Future. We don't belong here in the Past. The government doesn't *like* us here. We have to pay big graft to keep our franchise. A Time Machine is damn finicky business. Not knowing it, we might kill an important animal, a small bird, a roach, a flower even, thus destroying an important link in a growing species.'

'That's not clear,' said Eckels.

'All right,' Travis continued, 'say we accidentally kill one mouse here. That means all the future families of this one particular mouse are destroyed, right?'

'Right.'

'And all the families of the families of the families of that one mouse! With a stamp of your foot, you annihilate first one, then a dozen, then a thousand, a million, a *billion* possible mice!'

'So they're dead,' said Eckels. 'So what?'

'So what?' Travis snorted quietly. 'Well, what about the foxes that'll need those mice to survive? For want of ten mice, a fox dies. For want of ten foxes, a lion starves. For want of a lion, all manner of insects, vultures, infinite billions of life forms are thrown into chaos and destruction. Eventually it all boils down to this: fifty-nine million years later, a cave man, one of a dozen on the *entire world*, goes hunting wild boar or sabre-tooth tiger for food. But you, friend, have *stepped* on all the tigers in that region. By stepping on *one* single mouse. So the cave man starves. And the cave man, please note, is not just *any* expendable man, no! He is an *entire future nation*. From his loins would have sprung ten sons. From *their* loins one hundred sons, and thus onward to a civilization. Destroy this one man, and you destroy a race, a people, an entire history of life. It is comparable to slaying some of Adam's grandchildren. The stomp of your foot, on one mouse, could start an earthquake, the effects of which could shake our earth and destinies down through Time, to their very foundations. With the death of that one cave man, a billion others yet unborn are throttled in the womb. Perhaps Rome never rises on its seven hills. Perhaps Europe is forever a dark forest, and only Asia waxes healthy and teeming. Step on a mouse and you crush the Pyramids. Step on a mouse and you leave your print, like a Grand Canyon, across Eternity. Queen Elizabeth might never be born, Washington might not cross the Delaware, there might never be a United States at all. So be careful. Stay on the Path. *Never* step off!'

'I see,' said Eckels. 'Then it wouldn't pay for us even to touch the *grass*?'

'Correct. Crushing certain plants could add up infinitesimally. A little error here would multiply in sixty million years, all out of proportion. Of course maybe our theory is wrong. Maybe Time *can't* be changed by us. Or maybe it can be changed only in little subtle ways. A dead mouse here makes an insect imbalance there, a population disproportion later, a bad harvest further on, a depression, mass starvation, and, finally, a change in *social* temperament in far-flung countries. Something much more subtle, like that. Perhaps only a soft breath, a whisper, a hair, pollen on the air, such a slight, slight change that unless you looked close you wouldn't see it. Who knows? Who really can say he knows? We don't know. We're guessing. But until we do know for certain whether our messing around in Time *can* make a big roar or a little rustle in history, we're being damned careful. This Machine, this Path, your clothing and bodies, were sterilized, as you know, before the journey. We wear these oxygen helmets so we can't introduce our bacteria into an ancient atmosphere.'

'How do we know which animals to shoot?'

'They're marked with red paint,' said Travis. 'Today, before our journey, we sent Lesperance here back with the Machine. He came to this particular era and followed certain animals.'

'Studying them?'

'Right,' said Lesperance. 'I track them through their entire existence, noting which of them lives longest. Very few. How many times they mate. Not often. Life's short. When I find one that's going to die when a tree falls on him, or one that drowns in a tar pit, I note the exact hour, minute, and second. I shoot a paint bomb. It leaves a red patch on his hide. We can't miss it. Then I correlate our arrival in the Past so that we meet the Monster not more than two minutes before he would have died anyway. This way, we kill only animals with no future, that are never going to mate again. You see how *careful* we are?'

'But if you came back this morning in Time,' said Eckels eagerly, 'you must've bumped into *us*, our Safari! How did it turn out? Was it successful? Did all of us get through—alive?'

Travis and Lesperance gave each other a look.

'That'd be a paradox,' said the latter. 'Time doesn't permit that sort of mess—a man meeting himself. When such occasions threaten, Time steps aside. Like an airplane hitting an air pocket. You felt the Machine jump just before we stopped? That was us passing ourselves on the way back to the Future. We saw nothing. There's no way of telling *if* this expedition was a success, *if we* got our monster, or whether all of us—meaning *you*, Mr Eckels—got out alive.'

Eckels smiled palely.

'Cut that,' said Travis sharply. 'Everyone on his feet!'

They were ready to leave the Machine.

The jungle was high and the jungle was broad and the jungle was the entire world forever and forever. Sounds like music and sounds like flying tents filled the sky, and those were pterodactyls soaring with cavernous grey wings, gigantic bats out of delirium and a night fever. Eckels, balanced on the narrow Path, aimed his rifle playfully.

'Stop that!' said Travis. 'Don't even aim for fun, damn it! If your gun should go off—'

Eckels flushed. 'Where's our *Tyrannosaurus*?'

Lesperance checked his wrist watch. 'Up ahead. We'll bisect his trail in sixty seconds. Look for the red paint, for Christ's sake. Don't shoot till we give the word. Stay on the Path. *Stay on the Path!*'

They moved forward in the wind of morning.

'Strange,' murmured Eckels. 'Up ahead, sixty million years, Election Day over. Keith made President. Everyone celebrating. And here we are, a million years lost, and they don't exist. The things we worried about for months, a lifetime, not even born or thought about yet.'

'Safety catches off, everyone!' ordered Travis. 'You, first shot, Eckels. Second, Billings. Third, Kramer.'

'I've hunted tiger, wild boar, buffalo, elephant, but Jesus, this is *it*,' said Eckels. 'I'm shaking like a kid.'

'Ah,' said Travis.

Everyone stopped.

Travis raised his hand. 'Ahead,' he whispered. 'In the mist. There he is. There's His Royal Majesty now.'

The jungle was wide and full of twitterings, rustlings, murmurs, and sighs.

Suddenly it all ceased, as if someone had shut a door.

Silence.

A sound of thunder.

Out of the mist, one hundred yards away, came *Tyrannosaurus rex*.

'Jesus God,' whispered Eckels.

'Sh!'

It came on great oiled, resilient, striding legs. It towered thirty feet above half of the trees, a great evil god, folding its delicate watchmaker's claws close to its oily reptilian chest. Each lower leg was a piston, a thousand pounds of white bone, sunk in thick ropes of muscle, sheathed over in a gleam of pebbled skin like the mail of a terrible warrior. Each thigh was a ton of meat, ivory, and steel mesh. And from the great breathing cage of the upper body those two delicate arms dangled out front, arms with hands which might pick up and examine men like toys, while the snake neck coiled. And the head itself, a ton of sculptured stone, lifted easily upon the sky. Its mouth gaped, exposing a fence of teeth like daggers. Its eyes rolled, ostrich eggs, empty of all expression save hunger. It closed its mouth in a death grin. It ran, its pelvic bones crushing aside trees and bushes, its taloned feet clawing damp earth, leaving prints six inches deep wherever it settled its weight. It ran with a gliding ballet step, far too poised and balanced for its ten tons. It moved into a sunlit arena warily, its beautifully reptile hands feeling the air.

'My God!' Eckels twitched his mouth. 'It could reach up and grab the moon.'

'Sh!' Travis jerked angrily. 'He hasn't seen us yet.'

'It can't be killed.' Eckels pronounced this verdict quietly, as if there could be no argument. He had weighed the evidence and this was his considered opinion. The rifle in his hands seemed a cap gun. 'We were fools to come. This is impossible.'

'Shut up!' hissed Travis.

'Nightmare.'

'Turn around,' commanded Travis. 'Walk quietly to the Machine. We'll remit one half your fee.'

'I didn't realize it would be this *big*,' said Eckels. 'I miscalculated, that's all. And now I want out.'

'It *sees* us!'

'There's the red paint on its chest!'

The Thunder Lizard raised itself. Its armoured flesh glittered like a thousand green coins. The coins, crusted with slime, steamed. In the slime, tiny insects wriggled, so that the entire body seemed to twitch and undulate, even while the monster itself did not move. It exhaled. The stink of raw flesh blew down the wilderness.

'Get me out of here,' said Eckels. 'It was never like this before. I was always sure I'd come through alive. I had good guides, good safaris, and safety. This time, I figured wrong. I've met my match and admit it. This is too much for me to get hold of.'

'Don't run,' said Lesperance. 'Turn around. Hide in the Machine.'

'Yes.' Eckels seemed to be numb. He looked at his feet as if trying to make them move. He gave a grunt of helplessness.

'Eckels!'

He took a few steps, blinking, shuffling.

'Not *that* way!'

The Monster, at the first motion, lunged forward with a terrible scream. It covered one hundred yards in four seconds. The rifles jerked up and blazed fire. A windstorm from the beast's mouth engulfed them in the stench of slime and old blood. The Monster roared, teeth glittering with sun.

Eckels, not looking back, walked blindly to the edge of the Path, his gun limp in his arms, stepped off the Path, and walked, not knowing it, in the jungle. His feet sank into green moss. His legs moved him, and he felt alone and remote from the events behind.

The rifles cracked again. Their sound was lost in shriek and lizard thunder. The great lever of the reptile's tail swung up, lashed sideways. Trees exploded in clouds of leaf and branch. The Monster twitched its jeweller's hands down to fondle at the men, to twist them in half, to crush them like berries, to cram them into its teeth and its screaming throat. Its boulder-stone eyes levelled with the men. They saw themselves mirrored. They fired at the metallic eyelids and the blazing black iris.

Like a stone idol, like a mountain avalanche, *Tyrannosaurus* fell. Thundering, it clutched trees, pulled them with it. It wrenched and tore the metal Path. The men flung themselves back and away. The body hit, ten tons of cold flesh and stone. The guns fired. The Monster lashed its armoured tail, twitched its snake jaws, and lay still. A fount of blood spurted from its throat. Somewhere inside, a sac of fluids burst. Sickening gushes drenched the hunters. They stood, red and glistening.

The thunder faded.

The jungle was silent. After the avalanche, a green peace. After the nightmare, morning.

Billings and Kramer sat on the pathway and threw up. Travis and Lesperance stood with smoking rifles, cursing steadily.

In the Time Machine, on his face, Eckels lay shivering. He had found his way back to the Path, climbed into the Machine.

Travis came walking, glanced at Eckels, took cotton gauze from a metal box, and returned to the others, who were sitting on the Path.

'Clean up.'

They wiped the blood from their helmets. They began to curse too. The Monster lay, a hill of solid flesh. Within, you could hear the sighs and murmurs as the furthest chambers of it died, the organs malfunctioning, liquids running a final instant from pocket to sac to spleen, everything shutting off, closing up forever. It was like standing by a wrecked locomotive or a steam shovel at quitting time, all valves being released or levered tight. Bones cracked; the tonnage of its own flesh, off balance, dead weight, snapped the delicate forearms, caught underneath. The meat settled, quivering.

Another cracking sound. Overhead, a gigantic tree branch broke from its heavy mooring, fell. It crashed upon the dead beast with finality.

'There.' Lesperance checked his watch. 'Right on time. That's the giant tree that was scheduled to fall and kill this animal originally.' He glanced at the two hunters. 'You want the trophy picture?'

'What?'

'We can't take a trophy back to the Future. The body has to stay right here where it would have died originally, so the insects, birds, and bacteria can get at it, as they were intended to. Everything in balance. The body stays. But we *can* take a picture of you standing near it.'

The two men tried to think, but gave up, shaking their heads.

They let themselves be led along the metal Path. They sank wearily into the Machine cushions. They gazed back at the ruined Monster, the stagnating mound, where already strange reptilian birds and golden insects were busy at the steaming armour.

A sound on the floor of the Time Machine stiffened them. Eckels sat there, shivering.

'I'm sorry,' he said at last.

'Get up!' cried Travis.

Eckels got up.

'Go out on that Path alone,' said Travis. He had his rifle pointed. 'You're not coming back in the Machine. We're leaving you here!'

Lesperance seized Travis's arm. 'Wait—'

'Stay out of this!' Travis shook his hand away. 'This son of a bitch nearly killed us. But it isn't *that* so much. Hell, no. It's his *shoes*! Look at them! He ran off the Path. My God, that *ruins* us! Christ knows how much we'll forfeit! Tens of thousands of dollars of insurance! We guarantee no one leaves the Path. He left it. Oh, the damn fool! I'll have to report to the government. They might revoke our licence to travel. God knows *what* he's done to Time, to History!'

'Take it easy, all he did was kick up some dirt.'

'How do we *know*?' cried Travis. 'We don't know anything! It's all a damn mystery! Get out there, Eckels!'

Eckels fumbled his shirt. 'I'll pay anything. A hundred thousand dollars!'

Travis glared at Eckels's cheque book and spat. 'Go out there. The Monster's next to the Path. Stick your arms up to your elbows in his mouth. Then you can come back with us.'

'That's unreasonable!'

'The Monster's dead, you yellow bastard. The bullets! The bullets can't be left behind. They don't belong in the Past; they might change something. Here's my knife. Dig them out!'

The jungle was alive again, full of the old tremorings and bird cries. Eckels turned slowly to regard that primeval garbage dump, that hill of nightmares and terror. After a long time, like a sleepwalker, he shuffled out along the Path.

He returned, shuddering, five minutes later, his arms soaked and red to the elbows. He held out his hands. Each held a number of steel bullets. Then he fell. He lay where he fell, not moving.

'You didn't have to make him do that,' said Lesperance.

'Didn't I? It's too early to tell.' Travis nudged the still body. 'He'll live. Next time he won't go hunting game like this. OK.' He jerked his thumb wearily at Lesperance. 'Switch on. Let's go home.'

1492. 1776. 1812.

They cleaned their hands and faces. They changed their caking shirts and pants. Eckels was up and around again, not speaking. Travis glared at him for a full ten minutes.

'Don't look at me,' cried Eckels. 'I haven't done anything.'

'Who can tell?'

'Just ran off the Path, that's all, a little mud on my shoes— what do you want me to do—get down and pray?'

'We might need it. I'm warning you, Eckels, I might kill you yet. I've got my gun ready.'

'I'm innocent. I've done nothing!'

1999. 2000. 2055.

The Machine stopped.

'Get out,' said Travis.

The room was there as they had left it. But not the same as they had left it. The same man sat behind the same desk. But the same man did not quite sit behind the same desk.

Travis looked around swiftly. 'Everything OK here?' he snapped.

'Fine. Welcome home!'

Travis did not relax. He seemed to be looking at the very atoms of the air itself, at the way the sun poured through the one high window.

'OK, Eckels, get out. Don't ever come back.'

Eckels could not move.

'You heard me,' said Travis. 'What're you *staring* at?'

Eckels stood smelling of the air, and there was a thing to the air, a chemical taint so subtle, so slight, that only a faint cry of his subliminal senses warned him it was there. The colours, white, grey, blue, orange, in the wall, in the furniture, in the sky beyond the window, were . . . were . . . And there was a *feel*. His flesh twitched. His hands twitched. He stood drinking the oddness with the pores of his body. Somewhere, someone must have been screaming one of those whistles that only a dog can hear. His body screamed silence in return. Beyond this room, beyond this wall, beyond this man who was not quite the same man seated at this desk that was not quite the same desk . . . lay an entire world of streets and people. What sort of world it was now, there was no telling. He could feel them moving there, beyond the walls, almost, like so many chess pieces blown in a dry wind. . . .

But the immediate thing was the sign painted on the office wall, the same sign he had read earlier today on first entering. Somehow, the sign had changed:

> **TYME SEFARI, INC.**
> **Sefaris tu any Yeer en the Past**
> **<u>Yu</u> naim the animall**
> **<u>Wee</u> taek yu thair**
>
> **Yu shoot itt**

Eckels felt himself fall into a chair. He fumbled crazily at the thick slime on his boots. He held up a clod of dirt, trembling. 'No, it *can't* be. Not a *little* thing like that. No!'

Embedded in the mud, glistening green and gold and black, was a butterfly, very beautiful, and very dead.

'Not a little thing like *that*! Not a butterfly!' cried Eckels.

It fell to the floor, an exquisite thing, a small thing that could upset balances and knock down a line of small dominoes and then big dominoes and then gigantic dominoes, all down the years across Time. Eckels's mind whirled. It *couldn't* change things. Killing one butterfly couldn't be *that* important! Could it?

His face was cold. His mouth trembled, asking: 'Who—who won the presidential election yesterday?'

The man behind the desk laughed. 'You joking? You know damn well. Deutscher, of course! Who else? Not that damn weakling Keith. We got an iron man now, a man with guts, by God!' The official stopped. 'What's wrong?'

Eckels moaned. He dropped to his knees. He scrabbled at the golden butterfly with shaking fingers. 'Can't we,' he pleaded to the world, to himself, to the officials, to the Machine, 'can't we take it *back*, can't we *make* it alive again? Can't we start over? Can't we—'

He did not move. Eyes shut, he waited, shivering. He heard Travis breathe loud in the room; he heard Travis shift his rifle, click the safety catch, and raise the weapon.

There was a sound of thunder.

Vengeance Fleet

FREDRIC BROWN

They came from the blackness of space and from unthinkable distance. They converged on Venus—and blasted it. Every one of the two and a half million human beings on that planet, all the colonists from Earth, died within minutes, and all of the flora and fauna of Venus died with them.

Such was the power of their weapons that the very atmosphere of that suddenly doomed planet was burned and dissipated. Venus had been unprepared and unguarded, and so sudden and unexpected had been the attack and so quick and devastating had been its results that not a shot had been fired against them.

They turned towards the next planet outward from the sun, Earth.

But that was different. Earth was ready—not, of course, made ready in the few minutes since the invaders' arrival in the solar system, but ready because Earth was then—in 2820—at war with her Martian colony, which had grown half as populous as Earth itself and was even then battling for independence. At the moment of the attack on Venus, the fleets of Earth and Mars had been manoeuvring for combat near the moon.

But the battle ended more suddenly than any battle in history had ever ended. A joint fleet of Terrestrial and Martian ships, suddenly no longer at war with one another, headed to intercept the invaders, and met them between Earth and Venus. Our numbers were overwhelmingly superior and the invading ships were blasted out of space, completely annihilated.

Within twenty-four hours peace between Earth and Mars was signed at the Earth capital of Albuquerque, a solid and lasting peace based on recognition of the independence of Mars and a perpetual alliance between the two worlds—now the only two habitable planets of the solar system—against alien aggression. And already plans were being drawn for a vengeance fleet, to find the base of the aliens and destroy it before it could send another fleet against us.

Instruments on Earth and on patrol ships a few thousand miles above her surface had detected the arrival of the aliens—though not in time to save Venus—and the readings of those instruments showed the direction from which the aliens had come and indicated, although not showing exactly how far they had come, that they had come from an almost incredible distance.

A distance that would have been too great for us to span had not the C-plus drive—which enabled a ship to build up to a speed many times the speed of light—just been invented. It had not yet been used because the Earth–Mars war had taken all the resources of both planets, and the C-plus drive had no advantages within the solar system since vast distances were required for the purpose of building up to faster-than-light speeds.

Now, however, it had a very definite purpose; Earth and Mars combined their efforts and their technologies to build a fleet equipped with the C-plus drive for the purpose of sending it against the aliens' home planet to wipe it out. It took ten years, and it was estimated that the trip would take another ten.

The vengeance fleet—not large in numbers but incredibly powerful in armament—left Marsport in 2830.

Nothing was ever heard of it again.

Not until almost a century later did its fate become known, and then only by deductive reasoning on the part of Jon Spencer 4, the great historian and mathematician.

'We now know,' Spencer wrote, 'and have known for some time, that an object exceeding the speed of light travels backward in time. Therefore the vengeance fleet would have reached its destination, by our time, before it started.

'We have not known, until now, the dimensions of the universe in which we live. But from the experience of the vengeance fleet, we can now deduce them. In one direction, at least, the universe is C^C miles around—or across; they mean the same thing. In ten years, travelling forward in space and backward in time, the fleet would have traversed just that distance—$186,334^{186,334}$ miles. The fleet, travelling in a straight line, circled the universe, as it were, to its point of departure ten years before it left. It destroyed the first planet it saw and then, as it headed for the next, its admiral must have suddenly recognized the truth—and must have recognized, too, the fleet that came to meet it—and must have given a cease-fire order the instant the Earth–Mars fleet reached them.

'It is truly startling—and a seeming paradox—to realize that the vengeance fleet was headed by Admiral Barlo, who had also been admiral to the Earth fleet during the Earth–Mars conflict at the time the Earth and Mars fleets combined to destroy what they thought were alien invaders, and that many other men in both fleets on that day later became part of the personnel of the vengeance fleet.

'It is interesting to speculate just what would have happened had Admiral Barlo, at the end of his journey, recognized Venus in time to avoid destroying it. But such speculation is futile; he could not possibly have done so, for he had *already* destroyed it—else he would not have been there as admiral of the fleets sent out to avenge it. The past cannot be altered.'

All the Time in the World

ARTHUR C. CLARKE

When the quiet knock came on the door, Robert Ashton surveyed the room in one swift, automatic movement. Its dull respectability satisfied him and should reassure any visitor. Not that he had any reason to expect the police, but there was no point in taking chances.

'Come in,' he said, pausing only to grab Plato's *Dialogues* from the shelf beside him. Perhaps this gesture was a little too ostentatious, but it always impressed his clients.

The door opened slowly. At first, Ashton continued his intent reading, not bothering to glance up. There was the slightest acceleration of his heart, a mild and even exhilarating constriction of the chest. Of course, it couldn't possibly be a flatfoot: someone would have tipped him off. Still, any unheralded visitor was unusual and thus potentially dangerous.

Ashton laid down the book, glanced towards the door and remarked in a noncommittal voice: 'What can I do for you?' He did not get up; such courtesies belonged to a past he had buried long ago. Besides, it was a woman. In the circles he now frequented, women were accustomed to receive jewels and clothes and money—but never respect.

Yet there was something about this visitor that drew him slowly to his feet. It was not merely that she was beautiful, but she had a poised and effortless authority that moved her into a different world from the flamboyant doxies he met in the normal course of business. There was a brain and a purpose behind those calm, appraising eyes—a brain, Ashton suspected, the equal of his own.

He did not know how grossly he had underestimated her.

'Mr Ashton,' she began, 'let us not waste time. I know who you are and I have work for you. Here are my credentials.'

She opened a large, stylish handbag and extracted a thick bundle of notes.

'You may regard this', she said, 'as a sample.'

Ashton caught the bundle as she tossed it carelessly towards him. It was the largest sum of money he had ever held in his life—at least a hundred fivers, all new and serially numbered. He felt them between his fingers. If they were not genuine, they were so good that the difference was of no practical importance.

He ran his thumb to and fro along the edge of the wad as if feeling a pack for a marked card, and said thoughtfully, 'I'd like to know where you got these. If they aren't forgeries, they must be hot and will take some passing.'

'They are genuine. A very short time ago they were in the Bank of England. But if they are of no use to you throw them in the fire. I merely let you have them to show that I mean business.'

'Go on.' He gestured to the only seat and balanced himself on the edge of the table.

She drew a sheaf of papers from the capacious handbag and handed it across to him.

'I am prepared to pay you any sum you wish if you will secure these items and bring them to me, at a time and place to be arranged. What is more, I will guarantee that you can make the thefts with no personal danger.'

Ashton looked at the list, and sighed. The woman was mad. Still, she had better be humoured. There might be more money where this came from.

'I notice', he said mildly, 'that all these items are in the British Museum, and that most of them are, quite literally, priceless. By that I mean that you could neither buy nor sell them.'

'I do not wish to sell them. I am a collector.'

'So it seems. What are you prepared to pay for these acquisitions?'

'Name a figure.'

There was a short silence. Ashton weighed the possibilities. He took a certain professional pride in his work, but there were some things that no amount of money could accomplish. Still, it would be amusing to see how high the bidding would go.

He looked at the list again.

'I think a round million would be a very reasonable figure for this lot,' he said ironically.

'I fear you are not taking me very seriously. With your contacts, you should be able to dispose of these.'

There was a flash of light and something sparkled through the air. Ashton caught the necklace before it hit the ground, and despite himself was unable to suppress a gasp of amazement. A fortune glittered through his fingers. The central diamond was the largest he had ever seen—it must be one of the world's most famous jewels.

His visitor seemed completely indifferent as he slipped the necklace into his pocket. Ashton was badly shaken; he knew she was not acting. To her, that fabulous gem was of no more value than a lump of sugar. This was madness on an unimaginable scale.

'Assuming that you can deliver the money,' he said, 'how do you imagine that it's physically possible to do what you ask? One might steal a single item from this list, but within a few hours the Museum would be solid with police.'

With a fortune already in his pocket, he could afford to be frank. Besides, he was curious to learn more about his fantastic visitor.

She smiled, rather sadly, as if humouring a backward child.

'If I show you the way,' she said softly, 'will you do it?'

'Yes—for a million.'

'Have you noticed anything strange since I came in? Is it not—very quiet?'

Ashton listened. My God, she was right! This room was never completely silent, even at night. There had been a wind blowing over the roof tops; where had it gone now? The distant rumble of traffic had ceased; five minutes ago he had been cursing the engines shunting in the marshalling yard at the end of the road. What had happened to them?

'Go to the window.'

He obeyed the order and drew aside the grimy lace curtains with fingers that shook slightly despite all attempt at control. Then he relaxed. The street was quite empty, as it often was at this time in the midmorning. There was no traffic, and hence no reason for sound. Then he glanced down the row of dingy houses towards the shunting yard.

His visitor smiled as he stiffened with the shock.

'Tell me what you see, Mr Ashton.'

He turned slowly, face pale and throat muscles working.

'What are you?' he gasped. 'A witch?'

'Don't be foolish. There is a simple explanation. It is not the world that has changed—but you.'

Ashton stared again at that unbelievable shunting engine, the plume of steam frozen motionless above it as if made from cotton wool. He realized now that the clouds were equally immobile; they should have been scudding across the sky. All around him was the unnatural stillness of the high-speed photograph, the vivid unreality of a scene glimpsed in a flash of lightning.

'You are intelligent enough to realize what is happening, even if you cannot understand how it is done. Your time scale has been altered: a minute in the outer world would be a year in this room.'

Again she opened the handbag, and this time brought forth what appeared to be a bracelet of some silvery metal, with a series of dials and switches moulded into it.

'You can call this a personal generator,' she said. 'With it strapped about your arm, you are invincible. You can come and go without hindrance—you can steal everything on that list and bring it to me before one of the guards in the Museum has blinked an eyelid. When you have finished, you can be miles away before you switch off the field and step back into the normal world.

'Now listen carefully, and do exactly what I say. The field has a radius of about seven feet, so you must keep at least that distance from any other person. Secondly, you must not switch it off again until you have completed your task and I have given you your payment. *This is most important.* Now, the plan I have worked out is this . . .'

No criminal in the history of the world had ever possessed such power. It was intoxicating—yet Ashton wondered if he would ever get used to it. He had ceased to worry about explanations, at least until the job was done and he had collected his reward. Then, perhaps, he would get away from England and enjoy a well-earned retirement.

His visitor had left a few minutes ahead of him, but when he stepped out into the street the scene was completely unchanged. Though he had prepared for it, the sensation was still unnerving. Ashton felt an impulse to hurry, as if this condition couldn't possibly last and he had to get the job done before the gadget ran out of juice. But that, he had been assured, was impossible.

In the High Street he slowed down to look at the frozen traffic, the paralysed pedestrians. He was careful, as he had been warned, not to approach so close to anyone that they came within his field. How ridiculous people looked when one saw them like this, robbed of such grace as movement could give, their mouths half open in foolish grimaces!

Having to seek assistance went against the grain, but some parts of the job were too big for him to handle by himself. Besides, he could pay liberally and never notice it. The main difficulty, Ashton realized, would be to find someone who was intelligent enough not to be scared—or so stupid that he would take everything for granted. He decided to try the first possibility.

Tony Marchetti's place was down a side street so close to the police station that one felt it was really carrying camouflage too far. As he walked past the entrance, Ashton caught a glimpse of the duty sergeant at his desk and resisted a temptation to go inside to combine a little pleasure with business. But that sort of thing could wait until later.

The door of Tony's opened in his face as he approached. It was such a natural occurrence in a world where nothing was normal that it was a moment before Ashton realized its implications. Had his generator failed? He glanced hastily down the street and was reassured by the frozen tableau behind him.

'Well, if it isn't Bob Ashton!' said a familiar voice. 'Fancy meeting you as early in the morning as this. That's an odd bracelet you're wearing. I thought I had the only one.'

'Hello, Aram,' replied Ashton. 'It looks as if there's a lot going on that neither of us knows about. Have you signed up Tony, or is he still free?'

'Sorry. We've a little job which will keep him busy for a while.'

'Don't tell me. It's at the National Gallery or the Tate.'

Aram Albenkian fingered his neat goatee. 'Who told you that?' he asked.

'No one. But, after all, you *are* the crookedest art dealer in the trade, and I'm beginning to guess what's going on. Did a tall, very good-looking brunette give you that bracelet and a shopping list?'

'I don't see why I should tell you, but the answer's no. It was a man.'

Ashton felt a momentary surprise. Then he shrugged his shoulders. 'I might have guessed that there would be more than one of them. I'd like to know who's behind it.'

'Have you any theories?' said Albenkian guardedly.

Ashton decided that it would be worth risking some loss of information to test the other's reactions. 'It's obvious they're not interested in money—they have all they want and can get more with this gadget. The woman who saw me said she was a collector. I took it as a joke, but I see now that she meant it seriously.'

'Why do we come into the picture? What's to stop them doing the whole job themselves?' Albenkian asked.

'Maybe they're frightened. Or perhaps they want our—er—specialized knowledge. Some of the items on my list are rather well cased in. My theory is that they're agents for a mad millionaire.'

It didn't hold water, and Ashton knew it. But he wanted to see which leaks Albenkian would try to plug.

'My dear Ashton,' said the other impatiently, holding up his wrist. 'How do you explain this little thing? I know nothing about science, but even I can tell that it's beyond the wildest dreams of our technologies. There's only one conclusion to be drawn from that.'

'Go on.'

'These people are from—somewhere else. Our world is being systematically looted of its treasures. You know all this stuff you read about rockets and spaceships? Well, someone else has done it first.'

Ashton didn't laugh. The theory was no more fantastic than the facts.

'Whoever they are,' he said, 'they seem to know their way around pretty well. I wonder how many teams they've got? Perhaps the Louvre and the Prado are being reconnoitred at this very minute. The world is going to have a shock before the day's out.'

They parted amicably enough, neither confiding any details of real importance about his business. For a fleeting moment Ashton thought of trying to buy over Tony, but there was no point in antagonizing Albenkian. Steve Regan would have to do. That meant walking about a mile, since of course any form of transport was impossible. He would die of old age before a bus completed the journey. Ashton was not clear what would happen if he attempted to drive a car when the field was operating, and he had been warned not to try any experiments.

It astonished Ashton that even such a nearly certified moron as Steve could take the accelerator so calmly; there was something to be said, after all, for the comic strips which were probably his only reading. After a few words of grossly simplified explanation, Steve buckled on the spare wristlet which, rather to Ashton's surprise, his visitor had handed over without comment. Then they set out on their long walk to the Museum.

Ashton, or his client, had thought of everything. They stopped once at a park bench to rest and enjoy some sandwiches and regain their breath. When at last they reached the Museum, neither felt any the worse for the unaccustomed exercise.

They walked together through the gates of the Museum—

unable, despite logic, to avoid speaking in whispers—and up the wide stone steps into the entrance hall. Ashton knew his way perfectly. With whimsical humour he displayed his Reading Room ticket as they walked, at a respectful distance, past the statuesque attendants. It occurred to him that the occupants of the great chamber, for the most part, looked just the same as they normally did, even without the benefit of the accelerator.

It was a straightforward but tedious job collecting the books that had been listed. They had been chosen, it seemed, for their beauty as works of art as much as for their literary content. The selection had been done by someone who knew his job. Had *they* done it themselves, Ashton wondered, or had they bribed other experts as they were bribing him? He wondered if he would ever glimpse the full ramifications of their plot.

There was a considerable amount of panel-smashing to be done, but Ashton was careful not to damage any books, even the unwanted ones. Whenever he had collected enough volumes to make a comfortable load, Steve carried them out into the courtyard and dumped them on the paving stones until a small pyramid had accumulated.

It would not matter if they were left for short periods outside the field of the accelerator. No one would notice their momentary flicker of existence in the normal world.

They were in the library for two hours of their time, and paused for another snack before passing to the next job. On the way Ashton stopped for a little private business. There was a tinkle of glass as the tiny case, standing in solitary splendour, yielded up its treasure: then the manuscript of *Alice* was safely tucked into Ashton's pocket.

Among the antiquities, he was not quite so much at home. There were a few examples to be taken from every gallery, and sometimes it was hard to see the reasons for the choice. It was as if—and again he remembered Albenkian's words—these works of art had been selected by someone with totally alien standards. This time, with a few exceptions, *they* had obviously not been guided by the experts.

For the second time in history the case of the Portland Vase was shattered. In five seconds, thought Ashton, the alarms would be going all over the Museum and the whole building would be in an uproar. And in five seconds he could be miles away. It was an intoxicating thought, and as he worked swiftly to complete his contract he began to regret the price he had asked. Even now, it was not too late.

He felt the quiet satisfaction of the good workman as he watched Steve carry the great silver tray of the Mildenhall Treasure out into the courtyard and place it beside the now impressive pile. 'That's the lot,' he said. 'I'll settle up at my place this evening. Now let's get this gadget off you.'

They walked out into High Holborn and chose a secluded side street that had no pedestrians near it. Ashton unfastened the peculiar buckle and stepped back from his cohort, watching him freeze into immobility as he did so. Steve was vulnerable again, moving once more with all other men in the stream of time. But before the alarm had gone out he would have lost himself in the London crowds.

When he re-entered the Museum yard, the treasure had already gone. Standing where it had been was his visitor of—how long ago? She was still poised and graceful, but, Ashton thought, looking a little tired. He approached until their fields merged and they were no longer separated by an impassable gulf of silence. 'I hope you're satisfied,' he said. 'How did you move the stuff so quickly?'

She touched the bracelet around her own wrist and gave a wan smile. 'We have many other powers besides this.'

'Then why did you need my help?'

'There were technical reasons. It was necessary to remove the objects we required from the presence of other matter. In this way, we could gather only what we needed and not waste our limited—what shall I call them?—transporting facilities. Now may I have the bracelet back?'

Ashton slowly handed over the one he was carrying, but made no effort to unfasten his own. There might be danger in what he was doing, but he intended to retreat at the first sign of it.

'I'm prepared to reduce my fee,' he said. 'In fact I'll waive all payment—in exchange for this.' He touched his wrist, where the intricate metal band gleamed in the sunlight.

She was watching him with an expression as fathomless as the Giaconda smile. (Had *that*, Ashton wondered, gone to join the treasure he had gathered? How much had they taken from the Louvre?)

'I would not call that reducing your fee. All the money in the world could not purchase one of those bracelets.'

'Or the things I have given you.'

'You are greedy, Mr Ashton. You know that with an accelerator the entire world would be yours.'

'What of that? Do you have any further interest in our planet, now you have taken what you need?'

There was a pause. Then, unexpectedly, she smiled. 'So you have guessed I do not belong to your world.'

'Yes. And I know that you have other agents besides myself. Do you come from Mars, or won't you tell me?'

'I am quite willing to tell you. But you may not thank me if I do.'

Ashton looked at her warily. What did she mean by that? Unconscious of his action, he put his wrist behind his back, protecting the bracelet.

'No, I am not from Mars, or any planet of which you have ever heard. You would not understand *what* I am. Yet I will tell you this. I am from the Future.'

'The Future! That's ridiculous!'

'Indeed? I should be interested to know why.'

'If that sort of thing were possible, our past history would be full of time travellers. Besides, it would involve a *reductio ad absurdum*. Going into the past could change the present and produce all sorts of paradoxes.'

'Those are good points, though not perhaps as original as you suppose. But they only refute the possibility of time travel in general, not in the very special case which concerns us now.'

'What is peculiar about it?' he asked.

'On very rare occasions, and by the release of an enormous amount of energy, it is possible to produce a—*singularity*—in time. During the fraction of a second when that singularity occurs, the past becomes accessible to the future, though only in a restricted way. We can send our minds back to you, but not our bodies.'

'You mean,' said Ashton, 'that you are *borrowing* the body I see?'

'Oh, I have paid for it, as I am paying you. The owner has agreed to the terms. We are very conscientious in these matters.'

Ashton was thinking swiftly. If this story was true, it gave him a definite advantage.

'You mean,' he continued, 'that you have no direct control over matter, and must work through human agents?'

'Yes. Even those bracelets were made here, under our mental control.'

She was explaining too much too readily, revealing all her weaknesses. A warning signal was flashing in the back of Ashton's mind, but he had committed himself too deeply to retreat.

'Then it seems to me,' he said slowly, 'that you cannot force me to hand this bracelet back.'

'That is perfectly true.'

'That's all I want to know.'

She was smiling at him now, and there was something in that smile that chilled him to the marrow.

'We are not vindictive or unkind, Mr Ashton,' she said quietly. 'What I am going to do now appeals to my sense of justice. You have asked for that bracelet; you can keep it. Now I shall tell you just how useful it will be.'

For a moment Ashton had a wild impulse to hand back the accelerator. She must have guessed his thoughts.

'No, it's too late. I insist that you keep it. And I can reassure you on one point. It won't wear out. It will last you'—again that enigmatic smile—'the rest of your life.

'Do you mind if we go for a walk, Mr Ashton? I have done my work here, and would like to have a last glimpse of your world before I leave it for ever.'

She turned towards the iron gates, and did not wait for a reply. Consumed by curiosity, Ashton followed.

They walked in silence until they were standing among the frozen traffic of Tottenham Court Road. For a while she stood staring at the busy yet motionless crowds; then she sighed.

'I cannot help feeling sorry for them, and for you. I wonder what you would have made of yourselves.'

'What do you mean by that?'

'Just now, Mr Ashton, you implied that the future cannot reach back into the past, because that would alter history. A shrewd remark, but, I am afraid, irrelevant. You see, *your* world has no more history to alter.'

She pointed across the road, and Ashton turned swiftly on his heels. There was nothing there except a newsboy crouching over his pile of papers. A placard formed an impossible curve in the breeze that was blowing through this motionless world. Ashton read the crudely lettered words with difficulty:

SUPER-BOMB TEST TODAY

The voice in his ears seemed to come from a very long way off.

'I told you that time travel, even in this restricted form, requires an enormous release of energy—far more than a single bomb can liberate, Mr Ashton. But that bomb is only a trigger—'

She pointed to the solid ground beneath their feet. 'Do you know anything about your own planet? Probably not; your race has learned so little. But even your scientists have discovered that, two thousand miles down, the Earth has a dense, liquid core. That core is made of compressed matter, and it can exist in either of two stable states. Given a certain stimulus, it can change from one of those states to another, just as a seesaw can tip over at the touch of a finger. But that change, Mr Ashton, will liberate as much energy as all the earthquakes since the beginning of your world. The oceans and continents will fly into space; the sun will have a second asteroid belt.

'That cataclysm will send its echoes down the ages, and will open up to us a fraction of a second in your time. During that instant, we are trying to save what we can of your world's treasures. It is all that we can do; even if your motives were purely selfish and completely dishonest, you have done your race a service you never intended. And now I must return to our ship, where it waits by the ruins of Earth almost a hundred thousand years from now. You can keep the bracelet.'

The withdrawal was instantaneous. The woman suddenly froze and became one with the other statues in the silent street. He was alone.

Alone! Ashton held the gleaming bracelet before his eyes, hypnotized by its intricate workmanship and by the powers it concealed. He had made a bargain, and he must keep it. He could live out the full span of his life—at the cost of an isolation no other man had ever known. If he switched off the field, the last seconds of history would tick inexorably away.

Seconds? Indeed, there was less time than that. For he knew that the bomb must already have exploded.

He sat down on the edge of the pavement and began to think. There was no need to panic; he must take things calmly, without hysteria. After all, he had plenty of time.

All the time in the world.

...And Three to Go

Above Abergavenny the land fans out into a series of valleys and ridges which collectively make up the Black Mountains, so called not for any dark reputation they might have but for the peaty soil and dead or dying heather and bracken which cloak their winter flanks and capture whatever sunlight manages to struggle through the sullen, rain-swollen clouds of winter. A place to be avoided out of season except by the most masochistic of fell walkers and by hill farmers who have no choice but to remain, growing poorer by the year, trapped by the accident of birth.

But in the summer the whole aspect changes. Then the Black Mountains are overwhelmingly green, with an abundance of coniferous forest struggling up from deep valley to airy moorland where Welsh ponies and sheep graze, oblivious of the harsh months to come. There is a timelessness about the area which may in part explain what happened to Matthew on one of the last days of summer.

On this day, a Thursday in late September on the cusp of autumn, Matthew's destination was the Vale of Ewyas. He had recently taken early retirement on terms which had left him comfortable, at least financially, from his post as a BBC researcher, and since he had never been encumbered with wife or family, he was free to come and go as he pleased. Now that the second Severn River bridge crossing was in place the journey could be accomplished in little more than an hour from his home, a flat in the fashionable surburb of Clifton on the outskirts of Bristol. Because it was midweek he was looking forward to a day of the comparative solitude which he increasingly sought. The problems which led to his retirement were counter-balanced by a stubborn lifestyle based on the 'use it or lose it' principle which had, for the time being, left him with a body still capable of a brisk ten mile fell walk through wild, lonely country. The important thing was to enjoy every outing as if it were his last.

To reach the Black Mountains you leave Abergavenny on the A465(T) heading in the direction of Hereford but after a drive of only a few miles you fork left at the village of Llanfihangel Crucorney, where you take the turning up the Vale of Ewyas to the Llanthony Priory. Although the road is narrow and twisty it is nevertheless the only one which runs directly through the Black Mountains, exiting via the Gospel Pass, and you cannot in any case miss it because there, just before the turning, is the dark slate frontage of what is reputed to be the oldest inn in Wales, the Skirrid. The inn faces Skirrid Fawr, the Holy Mountain from which it takes its name, unmistakable because of the great gouge out of its western flank which, according to one local legend, was made by the Devil on a bad day, or, if you prefer an alternative explanation, was created by a landslip which occurred two thousand years ago when the outrage of the Crucifixion caused the very earth to shudder. Quaint though either story is, both are indicative of the excesses of faith which in the witch hunts of the late Middle Ages led to the death of so many unfortunate creatures.

Matthew was not planning a full day's expedition and so, attracted by the inn's appearance, he broke his journey for a morning glass of real ale in what he hoped would be the right setting. He was not disappointed. Inside were medieval windows and doorways, ships' beams, stone floors, oaken tables and the delicious smell of woodsmoke. Finding a place near enough to the first open fire of autumn to warm his aching bones without roasting him, he made good use of his short stay by reading the cheerfully grisly tourist information on leaflets scattered liberally about the place. He was, after all, a researcher, a gatherer of information which might be put together to form the basis of a radio or television programme or a freelance article in the Press, and the working habits of a lifetime die hard. What better way to enjoy oneself than by contemplating the miseries, the casual brutalities of an age long gone, from a vantage point of comfort and indulgence?

Apparently the inn, parts of which dated back nearly nine hundred years, once did double duty as a courthouse which, as was the custom of the time and country, provided facilities for trial, verdict and execution of sentence, all within the space of twenty-four hours. In fact, if one looked very carefully one might even find the beam from which the condemned performed their last involuntary little dance. The worst part, reflected Matthew as he made entries in his old-fashioned shorthand in the dog-eared notebook he was never without, the cruellest part was that the poor devils were confined above stairs throughout the night, sheepstealers cheek by jowl with alleged practitioners of the black arts, anticipation of their elevation on the morrow being rendered all the more poignant by the sounds of revelry filtering up from below.

When he made his way to the toilet, idle curiosity drew Matthew to look for the actual makeshift gibbet which, he persuaded himself, could well be the age-blackened beam above the foot of the stair. The area was too gloomy for close examination, but surely there should be rope marks? In those days the victims of justice did not die easily and it could be many minutes before the rope stopped jerking and twisting and became mercifully still. Standing on tiptoe he felt along the edge, receiving only a slight shock for his pains which he attributed to static electricity from the near-fossilized and therefore possibly conductive beam. He pulled his hand away, fingers still tingling from the contact, and vaguely wished that he hadn't passed under the blasted thing, hadn't touched it. Although slight, the sensation had been unpleasant, a most unwelcome contact. Anyway, it was too late now.

The barman looked up as Matthew passed and smiled at him in a conspiratorial fashion, as if he had caught him out in a minor misdemeanour. Although his lips did not appear to move, and the words seemed to come from a distance, Matthew could swear that the man behind the counter, or someone further back in the depths of the inn, whispered in a hoarse voice:

'One to be ready, sir, one to be ready!'

Although the words made little sense they echoed in Matthew's head, words tinged with malice. He thought of challenging the barman but the whole thing was too trivial to pursue.

Retrieving his battered but still serviceable Volvo Estate from the rear of the inn, Matthew headed left up the valley, past another hostelry, the Queen's Head, and so into a small walkers' car park which he was pleased to observe was otherwise unoccupied. Then into his boots and on with his rucksack, which he repacked to add waterproofs from the boot of his car to the sandwiches and vacuum flask it already held, being careful to ensure that the material provided a cushion between the unyielding container and his tender spine. Although the day had started out fine, some of the warmth of the late September sunshine had departed and he had felt chilled ever since leaving the inn. A mischievous wind had sprung into being, the kind which promises to push rain in front of it before nightfall, and protective clothing might well be needed on the high ground ahead.

A steady climb took him up Hatterrall Hill, where he joined the Offa's Dyke long distance footpath and the ascent gradually levelled out, leaving the walker free to take his eyes off the immediate path ahead and drink in a landscape which has changed little if at all in a thousand years. Matthew's bones and joints were troubling him more than usual today and when, just above the fifteen hundred foot contour, he reached the concrete trig point, he was glad to pause, lean against it, and look back the way he had come. Clouds were beginning to pile up, partially obscuring the sun and leaching much of the colour out of the prospect. He frowned, for there about a mile behind was a lone figure threatening his solitude, an odd figure dressed all in black which, as he spied it, seemed to stoop over as if examining the ground, and then straighten up and wave in his direction as it increased its pace. In all that wide expanse there was no other living soul in sight so Matthew deduced that the unwelcome wave was meant for him. Although the figure was too far away for him to make out details there was something odd about its gait and bearing which left Matthew reluctant to make its closer acquaintance.

He tried to pin down his train of thought. The scenario seemed vaguely familiar. At last he had it. 'Pure M. R. James,' he ruminated, 'and here I am, alone and unprotected on the bleak hillside, the archetypal, inquisitive academic, about to be punished for no apparent reason, unless curiosity itself is a crime.' He laughed out loud at this fancy, but the laugh sounded harsh, and the echoes from it were flung back at him from the opposite ridge. He turned and hurried on, comforting himself with the thought that he would shortly be leaving the ridge and descending to his halfway point and lunchtime venue, the picnic site at Llanthony Priory. He noted that there were a few cars in the car park, so he would not be alone. He looked back up the slanting path, but whoever had been following him had disappeared, doubtless continuing along the ridge above and so on down into the Oichon Valley on the other side. In spite of himself a feeling of relief swept over him. Even though there were good reasons for his morbidity, he did not like to surrender to them.

Coffee and sandwiches disposed of, he did not linger in the increasingly chill grounds of the ruined Priory but wandered into the adjacent parish church of St David where, for the second time that day, he felt the dead weight of history settling upon him like a dusty cloak. Nevertheless, after the splendid ammunition obtained at the Skirrid Inn, he had virtually decided to do a feature for the local paper on the superstitions and legends of the area, and the church proved fruitful. Amidst the antiquities was a relatively new stained glass memorial window, its colours fresh as paint, depicting St David visiting this very place, and the light from it illuminated many slate tablets from which it was possible to piece together something of the story of the people of the valley. One in particular caught his eye, in memory of Master John & Mistress Mary Trumper, which read: '*My debts are paid, my grave you see, therefore prepare to follow me.*' Despite the banality of the sentiment there was a resonance to the doggerel which struck close to home, and Matthew shivered. In his over-imaginative state he seemed to hear a mocking whisper in the gloom, the second line of a child's rhyme.

'*And two to be steady, sir, and two to be steady!*'

There was a threatening quality to the voice, the kind of voice he imagined his follower of the morning might have possessed. An absurd thought, but he did seem to have laid himself open to some very odd influences in the past few hours. Berating himself all the time for a fanciful fool he still could not leave the church without peering along each shadowed pew, but of course there was no crouching white-faced figure, head wagging, nothing but himself and his imaginings. Even so, when he left the church he could not disabuse himself of the feeling that he was not alone.

The way back was less arduous, now beside the busy waters of the Afon Honddu, now climbing above the stream through pleasant woods and farmland, and for the time being he managed to shake off the sense of something uninvited poking its misshapen head through the curtains. The spring returned to his step and he ignored the odd twinges which reminded him of his mortality. However the clouds were massing higher and higher above him, the sun dimmed and he could feel the differential charge growing between earth and sky. The storm was still holding its breath but when it came it would be a spectacular one, with bolts of lightning marching across the tops on fiery feet.

He consulted his large-scale ordnance survey leisure map, cursing the rule which says that on a two-sided map the area one wants is always on the other side. The map seemed to develop a will of its own in the rising wind. However, after a struggle with the contrary folds, yes, here it was, the hamlet of Cwmyoy, with its famous crooked church, the last point on his itinerary and just half a mile from his waiting car. Matthew decided to risk the weather and headed down between solid stone walls to the graveyard. The church tower leant at an odd angle above him, but was buttressed safely against the demolition which once threatened when the great landslip rent the hill behind it. The interior of the church was still bright enough to read by, with cream-washed walls making the most of the dying light. There was a simple wooden altar and, Matthew was pleased to observe, many inscriptions which would add to the story already partly told by his earlier investigations. One, dating from the year 1781 saddened him with its all too familiar tale of infant mortality. Another, from the previous century, defeated him for a while because its sentiments, carved in a florid script, were crammed into an area too small to accommodate them adequately.

As he squinted at it in the growing darkness, the surface blurred then sharpened and the words sprang out: '*Matthew he takes his nap, in our common mother's lap, waiting to hear the bridegroom say, away my dear, come away.*' Matthew spoke the words aloud before realizing the trick his mind had played upon him, and the dying echoes repeated the last phrase—'*come away . . . come away.*' He shook himself, rubbed his eyes and looked again. The inscription was still there but this time the name was of course no longer Matthew's but that of one Thomas Price, a local worthy called home more than three hundred years before. This was his day for seeing and hearing things, he reflected, wondering whether it had anything to do with his condition.

As he stood in the porch struggling to don his waterproofs, it became increasingly obvious that he was not going to escape the rain. One leg inside his overtrousers and the other still without, Matthew whirled and nearly fell as the great door of the church, impelled by a trick of the wind (surely it was the wind?), crashed shut behind him. The first angry spatters of rain were blowing into the porch and his priorities became simple. He could either stay here, very much alone with his fears and fancies in the growing darkness, or he could make a dash for the car park. A dry chuckle in his ear decided him.

'*And three to go, sir, and three to go!*'

Matthew arrived at his car somewhat out of breath but not as drenched as he had expected to be. The fury of the storm still held off, as if waiting for a signal. He drove back the way he had come but had hardly reached the main road when a bolt of lightning crackled directly overhead, a clap of thunder like the last trump detonated almost simultaneously and the heavens opened up. He drove on a little way but even with the help of the blower the heater was not yet producing air warm enough to cope with the inevitable fogging inside the windscreen, and the wipers had no chance against the torrent outside. Nose hard up against the glass, Matthew heaved a sigh of relief as that most welcoming of all sights, the lighted windows of an inn, emerged from utter blackness, and he paid his last visit to the Skirrid.

Parking as near as he could to the door, he made a dash for it and erupted inside. It was still early in the evening and thanks to the weather the place was empty, except for the barman who took his order—a large helping of home-made shepherd's pie with all the trimmings and a glass of the house red—and, remembering him, enquired about the quality of his day. The damp had entered into Matthew's bones with a vengeance and, cutting the amenities as short as he politely could, he retired to a table in the far corner near the fire where he sat quietly, awaiting his meal and jotting down a few further details of the inn's history.

Later, he sat back replete, no longer in any hurry now that his evening meal had been taken care of, nursing his wine and enjoying the warmth from the fire which was hissing and spitting as a few errant raindrops found their way down the broad chimney from the storm lashing outside. He closed his eyes contentedly, just for a moment.

Matthew woke up with a start. There was a great stillness outside, but not within. Where there had been emptiness, the long, low room now seemed to be crowded with people, all staring at him, and although their shapes and faces shifted in and out of focus, he sensed extreme hostility. He was disorientated still but one sensation outweighed all others, a great sense of fear. His surroundings became clearer. The furnishings had changed little but the bar itself was primitive, with little more than a riven counter, barrels, jugs and tankards, wine glasses, and oddly shaped bottles. The cold light was supplemented by oil lamps, the floor was covered with sawdust and the bare stone walls were free of all decoration. But it was

the people who disturbed him the most. The majority were coarse and oafish, dressed simply in shirts that had once been white and fusty, shapeless trousers. Standing apart were a few smarter, cloaked figures in embroidered waistcoats, frilled shirts, cutaway coats, knee breeches, and fine shiny boots—the local gentry, no doubt, come to see the show. Directly in front of him was a very severe looking gentleman garbed all in black who was reading from a scroll of paper so stiff that it required some effort to keep it from rolling up in his hands.

Matthew was looking down on the crowd from a slightly raised position, standing on a surface which was none too steady and rocked every time he shifted his position. Behind him was the one he feared the most, a hooded man who was laying rough hands upon him, pinioning his arms.

Whilst he was very, very afraid, Matthew was professional enough after a lifetime of research, much of it into the past, to date the proceedings. Judging from the clothing and surroundings, the date must be the late seventeenth or early eighteenth century, and the occasion a rough and ready execution. Which still left the question of who and why. The why was easily answered; the mob were jeering at him, calling him witch or warlock, challenging him to use his spells to save himself, little realizing that the guilty party had fled the scene by some three hundred years. No doubt the other 'he' was just awakening, looking round in wonder at all the paraphernalia of a twentieth century inn. Matthew felt that the link which had been growing all day was still there, but becoming very tenuous.

They were asking him if he had anything to say, but what would be the use? Prayers were being said. He felt something abrasive being adjusted about his throat and knew he had very little time left. He wished his unknown benefactor could have made the exchange sooner so that he could have seen a little more of the long-gone world he could only previously imagine. However, he reasoned, the proximity of the killing beam must be necessary for the spell to work. He must contact the usurper, warn him of the kind of body he had inhabited. But then he would find out soon enough for himself when the day's ration of drugs wore off and the pain resumed gnawing at him. From an infinite distance, he heard very distinctly the words: '*Thankyou, good sir, thankyou, and goodbye.*' He had heard that voice three times already today. He wished he had time to reply, to thank the bygone warlock for relieving him of the cancer-ridden body which had become so painful a burden and would soon become intolerable as metastasis advanced. This had been his last walk. What was being done to him now was no worse than what he had planned to do to himself when the drugs were no longer effective, when the pain became too much.

The shadowy figure behind him kicked away the stool and Matthew's last rational thought was that a fair exchange is no robbery.

Room 409

NANCE DONKIN

About four o'clock, I jacked up. Well, wouldn't you?
We'd started rather early that morning with a quick
whisk around a cathedral, then at ten thirty it was a
ruined castle—a pretty small castle, not much left of it but the
walls; and from there it was straight on to an Abbey, walls again
and roof open to the sky, piles of fallen stones everywhere and
an underground room supposed to have been the Abbot's
kitchen. Then there was a village church, not much bigger than
our back verandah, and close enough to a Roman fort for us to
get there before the end of the morning session.

That wasn't bad and we had a jolly good lunch at the café
next door. But it still wasn't enough for Mum, who's a dedicated
history teacher, still misty-eyed and thrilled to the back teeth
about England's Past and what it means to the rest of the world.

Even after touring England by car for six solid weeks. Dad goes along all the way with her pokings about in history because he left England as a boy of twelve to go with his parents to live in Australia and he's trying to catch up on all the things he thinks he missed. But I'd had almost enough.

At two o'clock that afternoon we were waiting on the steps for a museum to open. It was a good one and I reckon I learned a lot there, but after two hours I was ready to stop. Then Dad suggested rounding off the afternoon by visiting an old cousin and that's when I said NO THANKS! We'd seen at least six of England's Ancient Monuments in the last three days and the thought of visiting another one, even if it was human, just wasn't my scene. We'd met some of Dad's relatives already, not one of them under seventy. I knew just how this one would behave; she'd rave on and on about how Dad had grown and how much he'd changed—scarcely surprising, is it, after twenty-seven years?

We'd arrived in this latest cathedral town on our itinerary very early that same morning, and had immediately checked into a hotel. That is, Dad made sure we were booked in for the night, left two suitcases at the desk and we drove off. By four o'clock, the parents were still fresh-footed and chirpy but I was half-dead. I begged off the visit to Cousin Eleanor and said to Dad that if he would drop me off at the hotel, I'd get our key from the desk and go up to my room to have a read. He nodded, then thought perhaps he had better come in with me, to prove that I was his son and not some young toughie trying to get a free bed or put over some crooked deal.

So we did it that way. I mean, I'm thirteen and tall and fairly good at looking after myself, but I haven't had much experience of walking into hotels on my own and asking for the room key. Dad vouched for who I was and the man on the reception desk nodded and smiled and said to excuse him, just for a few seconds. All the keys were in the manager's office for some special inspection and he would bring them back immediately.

I walked to the door with Dad and watched him get into the car with my mother and drive off. Through the big, glass doors I could see the car until it turned the next corner. Then I went across to the desk for the room key. The first man wasn't there but there was someone else on duty, a funny old boy who looked half-asleep and certainly in need of a good brush-up. He didn't seem to fit in at all well with the modern decor of the place, but I got the key from him and went towards the lift.

The foyer was very bright, with red carpets and great bowls of flowers and electric lights blazing from tables and walls and ceiling. It felt rather good to be parading around there on my own; I sort of felt like a world traveller, an important one, not just a boy having a marvellous three-months-off-school-because-it-will-be-so-wonderfully-stimulating-and educational-for-him. I wondered if I looked any different. I *felt* two metres tall . . . I'd just left the Jag outside for the parking attendant to put away, and before the night was over, I might well have clinched a couple of Big International Contracts. I thought about High Finance as I walked about the foyer (by the way, dollars into pounds didn't seem to go far in England and maybe Dad would advance me a bit more); I waved my fingers around as though I were knocking the ash off the end of a fat, expensive cigar. I had a quick peek into the Smoking Room but there was nobody there who looked like a Big Time Financier waiting to meet another of the same kind, so I pressed the lift button with a casual air. There was nobody else waiting for it; I had the lift to myself. The light was just as strong in there as in the foyer— which made it all the more shocking when the lift stopped, the door opened and I walked out into complete darkness. I took a couple of steps forward before the darkness registered properly, and then I turned to get back into the lift, but it had already gone. My fingers couldn't find the press button. They couldn't even find the door.

It really was scary. It was crazy, too. I mean, three seconds ago I was in a lighted lift, thinking about important things like what I would do for the World; then suddenly there was nothing of the world left but this darkness, and me alone in it. I knew the lift must be there. It had to be there because I'd just got out of it. I knew roughly just where it was, too, but I had a feeling that I'd sensed space just beside it, maybe a staircase, and I didn't want to go crashing down a flight of stairs in the dark. I put my hand out, found a wall and groped my way along it, fingers feeling for a switch. But there didn't seem to be a switch; no lift, then no switch.

That was when the James Bond type with the Jag, the Big-Time Financier and wheeler-dealer, melted away and left a thirteen-year-old boy whose insides began to swish about like a milkshake. I fingered my way along the wall until I felt the shape of a corner and knew I must be turning into the corridor where all the bedroom doors were. But I still couldn't find a light switch and I began to feel panicky and *very* peculiar. A word which my mother used rather a lot came into my mind. *Utterly*. Until then I hadn't had any reason to think about the true meaning of the word. Now it became part of me because I was utterly alone and around me was utter darkness. Downstairs were lights and people and flowers and a bright carpet; downstairs was the memory of the Marvellous-Me game I'd been having with myself; upstairs there was just Little-Me, alone in the utterly utter blackness.

I turned and stumbled down the other side of the corridor but couldn't find a light switch there either and the thought of that open staircase I was sure was there stopped me from searching too hard for the lift. I couldn't understand why it was all dark until I realized that this floor might have been empty until we booked in, so they'd turned off the lights to save money. So here I was, groping around in the dark, scared as hell, because some stingy hotel manager wanted to save on the electricity bills. It made me really mad, but I felt sick too. How I wished I'd gone with Dad! A dreary old lady chatting away about my father's nice nature and his lovely yellow curls was a bore but it wasn't frightening. Being alone in this black, black, long, long hall was frightening. The dark was closing in on me, I could smell it; it was moving about me in waves, brushing against me, not soft like fur, but clammy.

Then came the bright idea. The room number was 409; I felt my way across to a door, and, hoping that the figures would not be just painted on, put my fingers out to find them. It took a while because my hands had started to shake, but soon I could feel hard metal shapes of numbers on the door and I stroked them carefully. The pads on the end of my fingers throbbed as though they were electrified. Perhaps they were, because I was *seeing* through them, as I suppose blind people must. Four . . . one . . . eight . . . my fingers told me, so that meant our room would be on the opposite side and probably at the other end of the corridor as well. I smoothed my way along with my hands until I was sure the numbers were increasing, then turned and went back the other way until I had found four-nought-one.

The hall was as dark as ever, but now I wasn't quite so scared. It was more like a game, though I was still absolutely spitting mad with the hotel people for leaving a whole floor unlit. For the sake of saving that tiny bit of money on light bills they were willing to risk people breaking their necks or being scared silly! We'd been in a lot of hotels while we were travelling about and I never remembered before experiencing such silence. There had always been somebody moving around, at whatever time we were going to or from our room, a maid checking linen, maybe, a man fetching his briefcase, or children running matchbox-cars about the hall.

There had always been light; I guessed Dad would have a few strong words to say to the management about this. I said a few strong words myself, because it took much longer than I thought it would to find room 409, and when I had, I couldn't fit the confounded key into the keyhole.

There was something very wrong with that keyhole. I pushed the key in harder and tried to turn it and nothing happened. I tried again and the key slipped round and round in the hole. By that time I wasn't scared any more. I was simply foaming-at-the-mouth mad! After all that stumbling around in the dark there I was, still on one side of the door crouching in pitch blackness over a keyhole that wouldn't work; knowing perfectly well that the second I got that door open, I could put a hand up to a wall switch and flood the place with light, or else just stand and look gratefully towards light coming through a window—because I knew that the room must face the street.

Suddenly the key seemed to fit properly. I must have been jamming it into the keyhole too fiercely at first. I pulled it right out and put it in very gently, and it turned quite easily.

Slowly the door began to open. The gloom was slightly less; dark cobweb-grey instead of pitch black, but all the heat I'd felt inside me a few moments ago had turned to cold. I didn't even try to step inside. I took a step back instead. The wind which came through that slightly opened doorway was icy. I knew that if I took one step forward I would fall. It was pointless to look for light coming through windows that faced the street, no use at all to put up a hand to turn on a switch. The chilled wind and a kind of damp sighing silence told me that. There was nothing there, I knew, nothing except shattered walls and broken floor beams.

The cold began to settle down over me, spreading through feet and hands and face and through to my bones. It was like an iron coat, weighing me down. I was so terrified that for a while I did not even try to move. The years of doing things on my own to prove that I could fell away. I was three, not thirteen. I was three years old and I wanted my history-mad mother; I was crying for my big father. I couldn't understand why nobody came, because I thought I was screaming like a hurt dog. But in fact my mouth was just opening and shutting with no sound coming out. The cold spread and spread and I knew that if I didn't move soon, I might just have to stay there, frozen. I pulled my feet away from the floor, forced them to turn about, and staggered down the hall until I felt there was space around me which must be the area near the lift and the stairs.

In the dark I put out both hands, grabbed a staircase railing and began to inch my way down, carefully, carefully. My breathing sounded like bronchitis and my heartbeats like a kitchen clock. There was a bend in the staircase and I felt my way around it, still in complete darkness. Then I fell. I bumped down and down most painfully, because now there was no carpet to cushion the way. The steps were solid uncovered concrete and I seemed to be falling for ever, down and down and down into a cold black night.

Dad and Mother found me lying in the lighted hall by the lift on the third floor and they couldn't understand what I was talking about. Nor could the manager, who came to find out what all the noise was about, because I had started to yell and to throw myself around.

Mother looked twice as tall and was demanding a doctor, a solicitor, a policeman, while she crouched on the floor with me. Dad was telling her to calm down and wait until the boy could explain the situation. The manager was alarmed but dictatorial. He said that obviously, the boy had fallen and given himself a very nasty bump, must have even lost consciousness for a while and had a kind of nightmare.

'Because, Mr Jenkins,' he said to my father, 'he is talking a lot of rubbish. There *is* no fourth floor in this hotel. We are now on the top floor, which is the third, and your room number is not 409 but 309. Check with your key.'

Dad looked down at the key in his hand and nodded. 'That's right. Now, what's this all about, Rob? Surely you're a bit too old for this kind of caper!'

Mother said indignantly, patting me on the cheek and the head, 'Of course it's not a caper. He's a very truthful boy.'

Like a conjuror producing a nice fat rabbit from his hat, I opened my own hand and showed them the key I'd grabbed back out of the lock. 'Then what's this?'

Quite clearly it was numbered 409.

Dad and Mother looked puzzled but relieved. The manager, a tall, bulky chap, looked like an outraged emu.

'I—I don't understand it,' he said. 'I just don't understand it. Who gave you that key?'

'The old man at the desk, a funny old boy with a lot of white hair and a dusty green coat. He seemed a bit shaky.'

'Ridiculous!' The manager was quite snappy. 'Not one member of my staff fits that strange description. They are all well-trained, alert, and moderately young, which means they are certainly *not* shaky and *never* dusty! Will you please come downstairs. If somebody has been playing practical jokes, then I intend to find out who it was.'

There was nobody like that old man at the desk. There was just a real dishy girl at the switchboard, a pimply baggage boy not much older than me, and a toffee-nosed desk clerk who said that he had never given me a key. He remembered my coming in that afternoon with my father, certainly he did. Then he had gone to the manager's office to collect the keys and when he came back, I'd gone. He thought I must have decided to go with my father, after all. Or perhaps—well, *Australians*, he said with a smile, were well-known as practical jokers. There could be more in this than met the eye!

Dad snorted but the desk clerk hadn't finished. 'Furthermore,' he said, looking at me as though I was just a smear of boot-polish on the carpet, 'furthermore, that is an old key. It looks like one from that boxful we found in the basement—spares from the old place.'

'The old place?' my father asked sharply.

The manager said smoothly, 'The first Royal Hotel was badly bombed during the war. It was such a complete wreck that it was left as it was, made safe, of course, with hoardings around it, until money was found for rebuilding. Then it was rebuilt, years later, in courtyard style, with only three floors but with greater width. I assure you, Mr Jenkins, that we never have had a fourth floor.'

'Then where in hell did this key come from?' my father demanded. 'And who the hell gave it to my son? Describe him again, Rob.'

Again I told my tale. 'He was old, quite old, and sort of shaky. He had a terrific lot of white hair and a dark-green coat with braid on it, and the coat looked kind of dusty.'

The manager was exasperated. 'And I repeat there is nobody on the staff who even *begins* to fit that description.' The look he gave me suggested that the most desirable place for me would be the mincing-machine and next appearance, meat balls for breakfast!

I was thinking hard. 'And one of his eyes kind of drooped— like this. His left eye, it was.'

I let the lid on my left eye fall halfway down so that it quivered and I didn't try to let it look pretty. Between them, the manager and the snooty clerk had really put my back up, so that eye-droop was quite a performance. Just to make sure they knew what I meant I screwed my chin up too, tried to give a good old twitch effect with the right eye and waggled my hands about loosely. The desk clerk turned a pale-yellow and flopped against the counter like a fish flapping in a boat.

'My Gawd! My Gawd! Uncle Jack!'

The manager's face was not yellow, but scarlet. He shouted: 'This has gone far enough. If you're in on this, this *stunt*, then you can take your notice straight away. What can your Uncle Jack, if there is such a person, have to do with this?'

'*Was*, not *is*!' the clerk said. 'Gave me the creeps to see the boy do that. My Uncle Jack's left eye was exactly like it, used to give me the horrors. I never liked to look at him.'

'So?' the manager asked.

'So, I thought you knew. Old Jack Trehaire was my uncle. He was the night porter at the old Royal.'

The manager looked suddenly interested, and quite pale; his cheeks seemed to melt and run down towards his chin. He whispered: '*That one?*'

The desk clerk whispered back.

'Yes. You remember what happened—a couple of minutes before the bomb hit he took a case up to the fourth floor. They only found his boots and a key.'

He looked at the key which was on the desk. We all looked and the clerk gulped, nodded, and said in a thread of a voice, '409.'

The Love Letter

JACK FINNEY

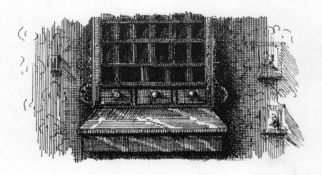

I've heard of secret drawers in old desks, of course; who hasn't? But the day I bought my desk I wasn't thinking of secret drawers and I know very well I didn't have any premonition or feeling of mystery about it. I spotted it in the window of a secondhand store near my apartment, went in to look it over, and the proprietor told me where he got it. It came from one of the last of the big old mid-Victorian houses in Brooklyn; they were tearing it down over on Brock Place a few blocks away, and he'd bought the desk along with some other furniture, dishes, glassware, light fixtures, and so on. But it didn't stir my imagination particularly; I never wondered or cared who might have used it long ago. I bought it and lugged it home because it was cheap and because it was small; a legless little wall desk that I fastened to my living-room wall with heavy screws directly into the studding.

I'm twenty-four years old, tall and thin, and live in Brooklyn to save money and work in Manhattan to make it. When you're twenty-four and a bachelor, you usually figure you'll be married before much longer and since they tell me that takes money I'm reasonably ambitious and bring work home from the office every once in a while. And maybe every couple weeks or so I write a letter to my folks in Florida. So I'd been needing a desk; there's no table in my phone-booth kitchenette, and I'd been trying to work at a wobbly end table I couldn't get my knees under.

I bought the desk one Saturday afternoon and spent an hour or more fastening it to the wall. It was after six when I finished. I had a date that night, so I had time to stand and admire it for only a minute or so. It was made of heavy wood with a slant top like a kid's school desk and with the same sort of space underneath to put things into. But the back of it rose a good two feet above the desk top and was full of pigeonholes like an old-style roll-top desk. Underneath the pigeonholes was a row of three brass-knobbed little drawers. It was all pretty ornate; the drawer ends carved, some fancy scrollwork extending up over the back and out from the sides to help brace it against the wall. I dragged a chair up, sat down at the desk to try it for height, then got showered, shaved, and dressed, and went over to Manhattan to pick up my date.

I'm trying to be honest about what happened and I'm convinced that includes the way I felt when I got home around two or two thirty that morning; I'm certain that what happened wouldn't have happened at all if I'd felt any other way. I'd had a good enough time that evening; we'd gone to an early movie that wasn't too bad, then had dinner, a drink or so and some dancing afterwards. And the girl, Roberta Haig, is pretty nice—bright, pleasant, good-looking. But walking home from the subway, the Brooklyn streets quiet and deserted, it occurred to me that while I'd probably see her again I didn't really care whether I did or not. And I wondered, as I often had lately, whether there was something wrong with me, whether I'd ever meet a girl I desperately wanted to be with—the only way a man can get married, it seems to me.

So when I stepped into my apartment I knew I wasn't going to feel like sleep for a while. I was restless, half-irritated for no good reason, and I took off my coat and yanked down my tie, wondering whether I wanted a drink or some coffee. Then— I'd half forgotten about it—I saw the desk I'd bought that afternoon and I walked over and sat down at it, thoroughly examining it for the first time.

I lifted the top and stared down into the empty space underneath it. Lowering the top, I reached into one of the pigeonholes and my hand and shirt cuff came out streaked with old dust; the holes were a good foot deep. I pulled open one of the little brass-knobbed drawers and there was a shred of paper in one of its corners, nothing else. I pulled the drawer all the way out and studied its construction, turning it in my hands; it was a solidly made, beautifully mortised little thing. Then I pushed my hand into the drawer opening; it went in to about the middle of my hand before my fingertips touched the back; there was nothing in there.

For a few moments I just sat at the desk, thinking vaguely that I could write a letter to my folks. Then it suddenly occurred to me that the little drawer in my hand was only half a foot long while the pigeonholes just above the drawer extended a good foot back.

Shoving my hand into the opening again, exploring with my finger tips, I found a tiny grooved indentation and pulled out the secret drawer which lay in the back of the first. For an instant I was excited at the glimpse of papers inside it. Then I felt a stab of disappointment as I saw what they were. There was a little sheaf of folded writing paper, plain white but yellowed with age at the edges, and the sheets were all blank. There were three or four blank envelopes to match, and underneath them a small, round, glass bottle of ink; and because it had been upside down, the cork remaining moist and tight in the bottle mouth, a good third of the ink had remained unevaporated still. Beside the bottle lay a plain, black wooden pen holder, the pen point reddish-black with old ink. There was nothing else in the drawer.

And then, putting the things back into the drawer, I felt the slight extra thickness of one blank envelope, saw that it was sealed, and I ripped it open to find the letter inside. The folded paper opened stiffly, the crease permanent with age, and even before I saw the date I knew this letter was old. The handwriting was obviously feminine, and beautifully clear—it's called Spencerian, isn't it?—the letters perfectly formed and very ornate, the capitals especially being a whirl of dainty curlicues. The ink was rust-black, the date at the top of the page was May 14, 1882, and reading it I saw that it was a love letter. It began:

Dearest! Papa, Mamma, Willy, and Cook are long retired and to sleep. Now, the night far advanced, the house silent, I alone remain awake, at last free to speak to you as I choose. Yes, I am willing to say it! Heart of mine, I crave your bold glance, I long for the tender warmth of your look; I welcome your ardency, and prize it; for what else should these be taken but sweet tribute to me?

I smiled a little; it was hard to believe that people had once expressed themselves in elaborate phrasings of this kind, but they had. The letter continued, and I wondered why it had never been sent:

Dear one, do not change your ways. Never address me other than with what consideration my utterances should deserve. If I be foolish and whimsical, deride me sweetly if you will. But if I speak with seriousness, respond always with what care you deem my thoughts worthy. For, oh my beloved, I am sick to death of the indulgent smile and tolerant glance with which a woman's fancies are met. As I am repelled by the false gentleness and nicety of manner which too often ill conceal the wantonness they attempt to mask. I speak of the man I am to marry; if you could but save me from that!

But you cannot. You are everything I prize; warmly and honestly ardent, respectful in heart as well as in manner, true and loving. You are as I wish you to be—for you exist only in my mind. But figment though you are, and though I shall never see your like, you are more dear to me than he to whom I am betrothed.

I think of you constantly. I dream of you. I speak with you in my mind and heart; would you existed outside them! Sweetheart, good night; dream of me, too.

With all my love, I am,
your Helen

At the bottom of the page, as I'm sure she'd been taught in school, was written, 'Miss Helen Elizabeth Worley, Brooklyn,

New York', and as I stared down at it now I was no longer smiling at this cry from the heart in the middle of a long-ago night.

The night is a strange time when you're alone in it, the rest of your world asleep. If I'd found that letter in the daytime I'd have smiled and shown it to a few friends, then forgotten it. But alone here now, a window partly open, a cool late-at-night freshness stirring the quiet air, it was impossible to think of the girl who had written this letter as a very old lady or maybe long since dead. As I read her words, she seemed real and alive to me, sitting, or so I pictured her, pen in hand at this desk in a long, white old-fashioned dress, her young hair piled on top of her head, in the dead of a night like this, here in Brooklyn almost in sight of where I now sat. And my heart went out to her as I stared down at her secret hopeless appeal against the world and time she lived in.

I am trying to explain why I answered that letter. There in the silence of a timeless spring night it seemed natural enough to uncork that old bottle, pick up the pen beside it, and then, spreading a sheet of yellowing old notepaper on the desk top, to begin to write. I felt that I was communicating with a still-living young woman when I wrote:

> *Helen: I have just read the letter in the secret drawer of your desk and I wish I knew how I could possibly help you. I can't tell what you might think of me if there were a way I could reach you. But you are someone I am certain I would like to know. I hope you are beautiful but you needn't be; you're a girl I could like, and maybe ardently, and if I did, I promise you I'd be true and loving. Do the best you can, Helen Elizabeth Worley, in the time and place you are; I can't reach you or help you. But I'll think of you. And maybe I'll dream of you, too.*
>
> > *Yours,*
> > *Jake Belknap*

I was grinning a little sheepishly as I signed my name, knowing I'd read through what I'd written, then crumple the old sheet and throw it away. But I was glad I'd written it and I didn't throw it away. Still caught in the feeling of the warm, silent night, it suddenly seemed to me that throwing my letter away would turn the writing of it into a meaningless and foolish thing, though maybe what I did seems more foolish still. I folded the paper, put it into one of the envelopes and sealed it. Then I dipped the pen into the old ink, and wrote 'Miss Helen Worley' on the face of the envelope.

I suppose this can't be explained. You'd have to have been where I was and felt as I did to understand it, but I wanted to mail that letter. I simply quit examining my feelings and quit trying to be rational; I was suddenly determined to complete what I'd begun, just as far as I was able to go.

My parents sold their old home in New Jersey when my father retired two years ago, and now they live in Florida and enjoy it. And when my mother cleared out the old house I grew up in, she packed and mailed me a huge package of useless things I was glad to have. There were class photographs dating from grammar school through college, old books I'd read as a kid, Boy Scout pins—a mass of junk of that sort, including a stamp collection I'd had in grade school. Now I found these things on my hall-closet shelf in the box they'd come in, and I found my old stamp album.

It's funny how things can stick in your mind over the years; standing at the open closet door I turned the pages of that beat-up old album directly to the stamps I remembered buying from another kid with seventy-five cents I'd earned cutting grass. There they lay, lightly fastened to the page with a little gummed-paper hinge—a pair of two, mint condition two-cent United States stamps, issued in 1869. Standing in the hallway looking down at them I once again got something of the thrill I'd had as a kid when I acquired them. It's a handsome stamp, square in shape, with an ornate border and a tiny engraving in the centre, a rider on a galloping post horse. For all I knew they might have been worth a fair amount of money by now, especially an unseparated pair of two stamps. But back at the desk I pulled one of them loose, tearing carefully through the perforation, licked the back and fastened it to the faintly yellowing old envelope.

I'd thought no further than that; by now, I suppose, I was in a kind of trance. I shoved the old ink bottle and pen into a hip pocket, picked up my letter, and walked out of my apartment.

Brock Place, three blocks away, was deserted when I reached it; the parked cars motionless at the kerbs, the high, late moonlight softening the lines of the big concrete supermarket at the corner. Then, as I walked on, my letter in my hand, there stood the old house just past a little shoe-repair shop. It stood far back from the broken cast-iron fence in the centre of its weed-grown lot, black-etched in the moonlight, and I stopped on the walk and stood staring up at it.

The high-windowed old roof was gone, the interior nearly gutted, the yard strewn with splintered boards and great chunks of torn plaster. The windows and doors were all removed, the openings hollow in the clear wash of light. But the high old walls, last of all to go, still stood tall and dignified in their old-fashioned strength and outmoded charm.

I walked through the opening where a gate had once hung, up the cracked and weed-grown brick pavement toward the wide old porch. And there on one of the ornate fluted posts I saw the house number deeply and elaborately carved into the old wood. At the wide, flat porch rail leading down to the walk I brought out my ink and pen and copied the number carefully on to my envelope; 972 I printed under the name of the girl who had once lived here, Brock Place, Brooklyn, New York. Then I turned towards the street again, my envelope in my hand.

There was a mailbox at the next corner and I stopped beside it. But to drop this letter into the box, knowing in advance that it could go only to the dead-letter office, would again, I couldn't help feeling, turn the writing of it into an empty meaningless act; and after a moment I walked on past the box, crossed the street and turned right, knowing exactly where I was going.

I walked four blocks through the night passing a hack stand with a single cab, its driver asleep with his arms and head cradled on the wheel; passing a night watchman sitting on a standpipe protruding from the building wall smoking a pipe—he nodded as I passed and I nodded in response. I turned left at the next corner, walked half a block more, then turned up on to the worn stone steps of the Wister postal substation.

It must easily be one of the oldest postal substations in the borough, built, I suppose, not much later than during the decade following the Civil War. And I can't imagine that the inside has changed much. The floor is marble, the ceiling high, the woodwork dark and carved. The outer lobby is open at all times as are post office lobbies everywhere, and as I pushed through the old swinging doors I saw that it was deserted. Somewhere behind the opaque windows a light burned dimly far in the rear of the post office and I had an impression of subdued activity back there. But the lobby was dim and silent and, as I walked across the worn stone of its floor, I knew I was seeing all around me precisely what Brooklynites had seen for no telling how many generations long dead.

The post office has always seemed an institution of mystery to me, an ancient, worn, but still functioning mechanism that is not operated but only tended by each succeeding generation of men to come along. It is a place where occasionally plainly addressed letters with clearly written return addresses go astray and are lost, to end up no one knows where and for reasons impossible to discover, as the postal employee from whom you enquire will tell you. Its air of mystery, for me, is made up of stories—well, you've read them, too, from time to time, the odd little stories in your newspaper. A letter bearing a postmark of 1906, written over half a century ago, is delivered today— simply because inexplicably it arrived at some post office along with the other mail with no explanation from anyone now alive. Sometimes it's a postcard of greeting—from the Chicago World's Fair of 1893, maybe. And once, tragically, as I remember reading, it was an acceptance of a proposal of marriage offered in 1901 and received today, a lifetime too late, by the man who made it and who married someone else and is now a grandfather.

I pushed the worn brass plate open, dropped my letter into the silent blackness of the slot, and it disappeared forever with no sound. Then I turned and left to walk home with a feeling of fulfilment of having done, at least, everything I possibly could in response to the silent cry for help I'd found in the secrecy of the old desk.

Next morning I felt the way almost anyone might. Standing at the bathroom mirror shaving, remembering what I'd done the night before, I grinned, feeling foolish but at the same time secretly pleased with myself. I was glad I'd written and solemnly mailed that letter and now I realized why I'd put no return address on the envelope. I didn't want it to come forlornly back to me with no such person, or whatever the phrase is, stamped on the envelope. There'd once been such a girl and last night she still existed for me. And I didn't want to see my letter to her—rubber-stamped, scribbled on, and unopened—to prove that there no longer was.

I was busy all the next week. I work for a wholesale grocery company; we got a big new account, a chain of supermarkets, and that meant extra work for everyone. More often than not I had my lunch at my desk in the office and worked several evenings besides. I had dates the two evenings I was free. On Friday afternoon I was at the main public library in Manhattan at Fifth Avenue and Forty-second copying statistics from half a dozen trade publications for a memorandum I'd been assigned to write over the weekend on the new account.

Late in the afternoon the man sitting beside me at the big reading-room table closed his book, stowed away his glasses, picked up his hat from the table and left. I sat back in my chair glancing at my watch. Then I looked over at the book he'd left on the table. It was a big one-volume pictorial history of New York put out by Columbia University, and I dragged it over, and began leafing through it.

I skimmed over the first section on colonial and pre-colonial New York pretty quickly, but, when the old sketches and drawings began giving way to actual photographs, I turned the pages more slowly. I leafed past the first photos, taken around the mid-century, and then past those of the Civil War period. But when I reached the first photograph of the 1870s—it was a view of Fifth Avenue in 1871—I began reading the captions under each one.

I knew it would be too much to hope to find a photograph of Brock Place, in Helen Worley's time especially, and of course I didn't. But I knew there'd surely be photographs taken in Brooklyn during the 1880s, and a few pages further on I found what I'd hoped I might. In clear, sharp detail and beautifully reproduced lay a big half-page photograph of a street less than a quarter mile from Brock Place; and staring down at it, there in the library, I knew that Helen Worley must often have walked along this very sidewalk. VARNEY STREET, 1881, the caption said. A TYPICAL BROOKLYN RESIDENTIAL STREET OF THE PERIOD.

Varney Street today—I walk two blocks of it every night coming home from work—is a wasteland. I pass four cinder-packed used-car lots; a shabby concrete garage, the dead earth in front of it littered with rusting car parts and old tyres; and a half dozen or so nearly paintless boarding houses, one with a solid card in its window reading MASSAGE. It's a nondescript joyless street and it's impossible to believe that there has ever been a tree on its entire length.

But there has been. There in sharp black-and-white in the book on the table before me lay Varney Street, 1881, and from the wide grass-covered parkways between the cut-stone kerb and sidewalks, the thick old long-gone trees rose high on both sides to meet, intertwine and roof the wide street with green. The photograph had been taken, apparently, from the street—it had been possible to do that in a day of occasional slow-trotting horses and buggies—and the camera was aimed at an angle to one side towards the sidewalk and the big houses beyond it, looking down the walk for several hundred feet.

The old walk, there in the foreground under the great trees, appeared to be at least six feet wide—spacious enough easily for a family to walk down it four or five abreast, as families did in those times walk together down the sidewalks under the trees. Beyond the walk, widely separated and set far back across the fine old lawns, rose the great houses, the ten-, twelve-, and fourteen-room family houses two or more storeys high and with attics above them for children to play in and discover the relics of childhoods before theirs. Their windows were tall and they were framed on the outside with ornamented wood. And in the solid construction of every one of those lost houses in that ancient photograph there had been left over the time, skill, money, and inclination to decorate their eaves with scrollwork; to finish a job with craftsmanship and pride. And time, too, to build huge, wide porches on which families sat on summer evenings with palmleaf fans.

Far down that lovely tree-sheltered street—out of focus and indistinct—walked the retreating figure of a long-skirted puff-sleeved woman, her summer parasol open at her back. Of the thousands of long-dead girls it might have been I knew this could not be Helen Worley. Yet it wasn't completely impossible, I told myself; this was a street, precisely as I saw it now down which she must often have walked; and I let myself think that, yes, this was she. Maybe I live in what is for me the wrong time and I was filled now with the most desperate yearning to be there on that peaceful street—to walk off past the edges of the scene on the printed page before me into the old and beautiful Brooklyn of long ago. And to draw near and overtake that bobbing parasol in the distance, and then turn and look into the face of the girl who held it.

I worked that evening at home, sitting at my desk, with a can of beer on the floor beside me, but once more Helen Elizabeth Worley was in my mind. I worked steadily all evening and it was around twelve thirty when I finished—eleven handwritten pages which I'd get typed at the office on Monday. Then I opened the little centre desk drawer into which I'd put a supply of rubber bands and paper clips, took out a clip and fastened the pages together, and sat back in my chair, taking a swallow of beer. The little centre desk drawer stood half open as I'd left it and as my eye fell on it I realized that of course it, too, must have another secret drawer behind it.

I hadn't thought of that. It simply hadn't occurred to me the week before, in my interest and excitement over the letter I'd found behind the first drawer of the row; and I'd been too busy all week to think of it since. But now I set down my beer, pulled the centre drawer all the way out, reached behind it, and found the little groove in the smooth wood I touched. Then I brought out the second secret little drawer.

I'll tell you what I think, what I'm certain of, though I don't claim to be speaking scientifically; I don't think science has a thing to do with it. The night *is* a strange time; things *are* different then, as every human being knows. And I think this: Brooklyn has changed over seven decades; it is no longer the same place at all. But here and there, still, are little islands—isolated remnants of the way things once were. And the Wister postal substation is one of them; it hasn't really changed at all. And I think that at night—late at night, the world asleep, when the sounds of things as they are now are nearly silent and the sight of things as they are now is vague in the darkness—the boundary between here and then wavers. At certain moments and places it fades. I think in the dimness of the old Wister post office in the dead of night lifting my letter to Helen Worley towards the old brass door of the letter drop—I think that I stood on one side of that slot in the year 1962 and that I dropped my letter, properly stamped, written and addressed in ink and on the very paper of Helen Worley's youth, into the Brooklyn of 1882 on the other side of that worn old slot.

I believe that—I'm not interested in proving it—but I believe it. Because now from that second secret little drawer I brought out the paper I found in it, opened it, and in rust-black ink on yellowing old paper I read:

> *Please, oh, please—who are you? Where can I reach you? Your letter arrived today in the second morning post, and I have wandered the house and garden ever since in an agony of excitement. I cannot conceive how you saw my letter in its secret place, but since you did, perhaps you will see this one too. Oh, tell me your letter is no hoax or cruel joke! Willy, if it is you; if you have discovered my letter and think to deceive your sister with a prank, I pray you to tell me! But if it is not—if I now address someone who has truly responded to my most secret hopes— do not longer keep me ignorant of who and where you are. For I, too— and I confess it willingly—long to see you! And I, too, feel and am most certain of it, that if I could know you I would love you. It is impossible for me to think otherwise.*
>
> *I must hear from you again; I shall not rest until I do.*
>
> > *I remain, most sincerely,*
> > *Helen Elizabeth Worley*

After a long time I opened the first drawer of the old desk and took out the pen and ink I'd found there, and a sheet of the note paper.

For minutes then, the pen in my hand, I sat there in the night staring down at the empty paper on the desk top; finally I dipped the pen into the old ink and wrote:

> *Helen, my dear: I don't know how to say this so it will seem even comprehensible to you. But I do exist, here in Brooklyn, less than three blocks from where you now read this—in the year 1962. We are separated not by space but by the years which lie between us. Now I own the desk which you once had and at which you wrote the note I found in it. Helen, all I can tell you is that I answered that note, mailed it late at night at the old Wister station, and that somehow it reached you as I hope this will too. This is no hoax! Can you imagine anyone playing a joke that cruel?*

I live in a Brooklyn within sight of your house that you cannot imagine. It is a city whose streets are now crowded with wheeled vehicles propelled by engines. And it is a city extending far beyond the limits you know, with a population of millions, so crowded there is hardly room any longer for trees. From my window as I write I can see—across Brooklyn Bridge, which is hardly changed from the way you, too, can see it now—Manhattan Island, and rising from it are the lighted silhouettes of stone-and-steel buildings more than one thousand feet high.

You must believe me. I live, I exist eighty years after you read this, and with the feeling that I have fallen in love with you.

I sat for some moments staring at the wall, trying to figure out how to explain something I was certain was true. Then I wrote:

Helen, there are three secret drawers in our desk. Into the first you put only the letter I found. You cannot now add something to that drawer and hope that it will reach me. For I have already opened that drawer and found only the letter you put there. Nothing else can now come down through the years to me in that drawer for you cannot alter what you have already done.

Into the second drawer you put the note which lies before me, which I found when I opened that drawer a few minutes ago. You put nothing else into it, and now that, too, cannot be changed.

But I haven't opened the third drawer, Helen. Not yet! It is the last way you can still reach me and the last time. I will mail this as I did before, then wait. In a week I will open the last drawer.

Jake Belknap

It was a long week. I worked. I kept busy daytimes, but at night I thought of hardly anything but the third secret drawer in my desk. I was terribly tempted to open it earlier, telling myself whatever might lie in it had been put there decades before and must be there now, but I wasn't sure and I waited.

Then, late at night, a week to the hour I'd mailed my second letter at the old Wister post office, I pulled out the third drawer, reached in and brought out the last little secret drawer which lay behind it. My hand was actually shaking and for a moment I couldn't bear to look directly—something lay in the drawer—

and I turned my head away. Then I looked.

I'd expected a long letter, very long, of many pages, her last communication with me, and full of everything she wanted to say. But there was no letter at all. It was a photograph, about three inches square, a faded sepia in colour, mounted on heavy stiff cardboard, and with the photographer's name in tiny gold script down in the corner. *Brunner & Holland, Parisian Photography, Brooklyn, NY.*

The photograph showed the head and shoulders of a girl in a high-necked dark dress with a cameo brooch at the collar. Her dark hair was swept tightly back, covering the ears, in a style which no longer suits our ideas of beauty. But the stark severity of that dress and hair style couldn't spoil the beauty of the face that smiled out at me from the old photograph. It wasn't beautiful in any classic sense, I suppose. The brows were unplucked and somewhat heavier than we are used to. But it is the soft warm smile of her lips and her eyes—large and serene as she looks out at me over the years—that made Helen Elizabeth Worley a beautiful woman. Across the bottom of her photograph she had written, 'I will never forget'. And as I sat there at the old desk staring at what she had written, I understood that of course that was all there was to say—what else?—on this, the last time, as she knew, that she'd ever be able to reach me.

It wasn't the last time, though. There was one final way for Helen Worley to communicate with me over the years and it took me a long time, as it must have taken her, to realize it. Only a week ago, on my fourth day of searching, I finally found it. It was late in the evening and the sun was almost gone, when I found the old headstone among all the others stretching off in rows under the quiet trees. Then I read the inscription etched in the weathered old stone:

HELEN ELIZABETH WORLEY
1861–1934

I NEVER FORGOT

And neither will I.

If

HARRY HARRISON

W e are there; we are correct. The computations were perfect. That is the place below.'

'You are a worm,' 17 said to her companion 35, who resembled her every way other than in number. 'That is the place. But nine years too early. Look at the meter.'

'I am a worm. I shall free you of the burden of my useless presence.' 35 removed her knife from the scabbard and tested the edge, which proved to be exceedingly sharp. She placed it against the white wattled width of her neck and prepared to cut her throat.

'Not now,' 17 hissed. 'We are shorthanded already, and your corpse would be valueless to this expedition. Get us to the correct time at once. Our power is limited, you may remember.'

'It shall be done as you command,' 35 said as she slithered to the bank of controls. 44 ignored the talk, keeping her multicell eyes focused on the power control bank, with her spatulate fingers in response to the manifold dials.

'That is it,' 17 announced, rasping her hands together with pleasure. 'The correct time, the correct place. We must descend and make our destiny. Give praise to the Saur of All who rules the destinies of all.'

'Praise Saur,' her two companions muttered, all of their attention on the controls.

Straight down from the blue sky the globular vehicle fell. It was round and featureless, save for the large rectangular port, on the bottom now, and made of some sort of blue metal, perhaps anodized aluminium, though it looked harder. It had no visible means of flight or support, yet it fell at a steady and controlled rate. Slower and slower it moved until it dropped from sight behind the ridge at the northern end of Johnson's Lake, just at the edge of the tall pine grove. There were fields nearby, with cows, who did not appear at all disturbed by the visitor. No human being was in sight to view the landing. A path cut in from the lake here, a scuffed dirt trail that went to the highway.

An oriole sat on a bush and warbled sweetly: a small rabbit hopped from the field to nibble a stem of grass. This bucolic and peaceful scene was interrupted by the scuff of feet down the trail and monotone whistling. The bird flew away, a touch of soundless colour, while the rabbit disappeared into the hedge. A boy came over the shore. He wore ordinary boy clothes and carried a school bag in one hand, a small and homemade cage of wire screen in the other. In the cage was a small lizard which clung to the screen, its eyes rolling in what presumably was fear. The boy, whistling shrilly, trudged along the path and into the shade of the pine grove.

'Boy,' a high pitched and tremulous voice called out. 'Can you hear me, boy?'

'I certainly can,' the boy said, stopping and looking around for the unseen speaker. 'Where are you?'

'I am by your side, but I am invisible. I am your fairy godmother—'

The boy made a rude sound by sticking out his tongue and blowing across it while it vibrated. 'I don't believe in invisibility or fairy godmothers. Come out of those woods, whoever you are.'

'All boys believe in fairy godmothers,' the voice said, but a worried tone edged the words now. 'I know all kinds of secrets. I know your name is Don and—'

'Everyone knows my name is Don, and no one believes any more in fairies. Boys now believe in rockets, submarines, and atomic energy.'

'Would you believe space travel?'

'I would.'

Slightly relieved, the voice came on stronger and deeper. 'I did not wish to frighten you, but I am really from Mars and have just landed.'

Don made the rude noise again. 'Mars has no atmosphere and no observable forms of life. Now come out of there and stop playing games.'

After a long silence the voice said, 'Would you consider time travel?'

'I could. Are you going to tell me that you are from the future?'

With relief: 'Yes I am.'

'Then come out where I can see you.'

'There are some things that the human eye should not look upon.'

'Horseapples! The human eye is OK for looking at anything you want to name. You come out of there so I can see who you are—or I'm leaving.'

'It is not advisable.' The voice was exasperated. 'I can prove I am a temporal traveller by telling you the answers to tomorrow's mathematics test. Wouldn't that be nice? Number one, 1.76. Number two—'

'I don't like to cheat, and even if I did you can't cheat on the new maths. Either you know it or you fail it. I'm going to count to ten, then go.'

'No, you cannot! I must ask you a favour. Release that common lizard you have trapped and I will give you three wishes—I mean answer three questions.'

'Why should I let it go?'

'Is that the first of your questions?'

'No. I want to know what's going on before I do anything. This lizard is special. I never saw another one like it around here.'

'You are right. It is an Old World acrodont lizard of the order Rhiptoglossa, commonly called a chameleon.'

'It *is*!' Don was really interested now. He squatted in the path and took a red-covered book from the school bag and laid it on the ground. He turned the cage until the lizard was on the bottom and placed it carefully on the book. 'Will it really turn colour?'

'To an observable amount, yes. Now if you release her . . .'

'How do you know it's a her? The time traveller bit again?'

'If you must know, yes. The creature was purchased from a pet store by one Jim Benan and is one of a pair. They were both released two days ago when Benan, deranged by the voluntary drinking of a liquid containing quantities of ethyl alcohol, sat on the cage. The other, unfortunately, died of his wounds, and this one alone survives. The release—'

'I think this whole thing is a joke and I'm going home now. Unless you come out of there so I can see who you are.'

'I warn you . . .'

'Goodbye.' Don picked up the cage. 'Hey, she turned sort of brick red!'

'Do not leave. I will come forth.'

Don looked on, with a great deal of interest, while the creature walked out from between the trees. It was purple in colour, had large goggling eyes, was slightly scaly, wore a neatly cut brown jumpsuit and had a pack slung on its back. It was also only about seven inches tall.

'You don't much look like a man from the future,' Don said. 'In fact you don't look like a man at all. You're too small.'

'I might say that you are too big. Size is a matter of relevance, and I am from the future, though I am not a man.'

'That's for sure. In fact you look a lot like a lizard.' In sudden inspiration, Don looked back and forth at the traveller and at the cage. 'In fact you look a good deal like this chameleon here. What's the connection?'

'That is not to be revealed. You will now do as I command or I will injure you gravely.' 17 turned and waved towards the woods. '35, this is an order. Appear and destroy that growth over there.'

Don looked on with increasing interest as the blue basketball of metal drifted into sight from under the trees. A circular disc slipped away on one side and a gleaming nozzle, not unlike the hose nozzle on a toy firetruck, appeared through the opening. It pointed towards a hedge a good thirty feet away. A shrill whining began from the depths of the sphere, rising in pitch until it was almost inaudible. Then, suddenly, a thin line of light spat out towards the shrub which crackled and instantly burst into flame. Within a second it was a blackened skeleton.

'The device is called a roxidizer and is deadly,' 17 said. 'Release the chameleon at once.'

Don scowled. 'All right. Who wants the old lizard anyway?' He put the cage on the ground and started to open the cover. Then he stopped—and sniffed. Picking up the cage again he started across the grass towards the blackened bush.

'Come back,' 17 screeched. 'We will fire if you go another step.'

Don ignored the lizardoid, which was now dancing up and down in an agony of frustration, and ran to the bush. He put his hand out—and apparently right through the charred stems.

'I thought something was fishy,' he said. 'All that burning and everything just upwind of me—and I couldn't smell a thing.' He turned to look at the time traveller who was slumped in gloomy silence. 'It's just a projected image of some kind, isn't it? Some kind of three-dimensional movie.' He stopped in sudden thought, then walked over to the still hovering temporal transporter. When he poked at it with his finger he apparently pushed his hand right into it.

'And this thing isn't here either. Are you?'

'There is no need to experiment. I, and our ship, are present only as what might be called temporal echoes. Matter cannot be moved through time, that is an impossibility, but the concept of matter can be temporally projected. I am sure that this is too technical for you . . .'

'You're doing great so far. Carry on.'

'Our projections are here in a real sense to us, though we can only be an image or a sound wave to any observers in the time we visit. Immense amounts of energy are required and almost the total resources of our civilization are involved in this time transfer.'

'Why? And the truth for a change. No more fairy godmother and that kind of malarky.'

'I regret the necessity to use subterfuge, but the secret is too important to reveal casually without attempting other means of persuasion.'

'Now we get to the real story.' Don sat down and crossed his legs comfortably. 'Give.'

'We need your aid, or our very society is threatened. Very recently—on our time scale—strange disturbances were detected by our instruments. Ours is a simple saurian existence, some million or so years in the future, and our race is dominant. Yours has long since vanished in a manner too horrible to mention to your young ears. Something is threatening our entire race. Research quickly uncovered the fact that we are about to be overwhelmed by a probability wave and wiped out, a great wave of negation sweeping towards us from our remote past.'

'You wouldn't mind tipping me off to what a probability wave is, would you?'

'I will take an example from your own literature. If your grandfather had died without marrying, you would not have been born and would not now exist.'

'But I do.'

'The matter is debatable in the greater plan of the universe, but we shall not discuss that now. Our power is limited. To put the affair simply, we traced our ancestral lines back through all the various mutations and changes until we found the individual proto-lizard from which our line sprung.'

'Let me guess.' Don pointed at the cage. 'This is the one?'

'She is.' 17 spoke in solemn tones as befitted the moment.

'Just as somewhen, somewhere there is a proto-tarsier from which your race sprung, so is there this temporal mother of ours. She will bear young soon, and they will breed and grow in this pleasant valley. The rocks near the lake have an appreciable amount of radioactivity which will cause mutations. The centuries will roll by and, one day, our race will reach its heights of glory.

'But not if you don't open that cage.'

Don rested his chin on fist and thought. 'You're not putting me on any more? This is the truth?'

17 drew herself up and waved both arms—or front legs—over her head. 'By the Saur of All, I promise,' she intoned. 'By the stars eternal, the seasons vernal, the clouds, the sky, the matriarchal I . . .'

'Just cross your heart and hope to die, that will be good enough for me.'

The lizardoid moved its eyes in concentric circles and performed this ritual.

'OK then, I'm as soft-hearted as the next guy when it comes to wiping out whole races.'

Don unbent the piece of wire that sealed the cage and opened the top. The chameleon rolled one eye up at him and looked at the opening with the other. 17 watched in awed silence and the time vehicle bobbed closer.

'Get going,' Don said, and shook the lizard out into the grass.

This time the chameleon took the hint and scuttled away among the bushes, vanishing from sight.

'That takes care of the future,' Don said. 'Or the past, from your point of view.'

17 and the time machine vanished silently. Don was alone again on the path.

'Well, you could have at least said thanks before taking off like that! People have more manners than lizards any day, I'll tell you that.'

He picked up the now empty cage and his school bag and started for home.

He had not heard the quick rustle in the bushes, nor did he see the prowling tomcat with the limp chameleon in its jaws.

Time Shift

KENNETH IRELAND

The car drove slowly along the narrow road on the outskirts of the town, and finally stopped at a gate. The occupants, Mr and Mrs Nicholson, peered out to find if they had arrived at the right house.

Take the first turning on the right after the second traffic island, the letter had said. We live in the last house on the left. There had even been a little sketch map with the letter to show exactly where they meant, but it hadn't been very clear.

But this was the right house, sure enough. Almost as soon as they had parked in front of it, Mrs Shipley came out of a door somewhere round the side.

'So there you are!' she exclaimed, smiling a welcome.

'Sylvia!' said Mrs Nicholson as she got out.

'Betty!' said Mrs Shipley.

They kissed.

'Hello, John,' said Sylvia as Mr Nicholson got out of the car. Just a quick peck on the cheek.

John Nicholson unloaded the two suitcases from the boot, locked the car and they went inside. They had met the Shipleys on holiday, had spent a lot of time with them, and had promptly been urged to stay with them for a few days whenever it was convenient.

Now it was. After several exchanges of letters, here they were, just a little doubtful because of course people are often rather different on holiday from how they are at home.

Sylvia Shipley led them along a passage and into a large kitchen where Mr Shipley was waiting to greet them.

'Hello, Betty, hello, John.' A kiss for one, a handshake for the other.

'Hello, Richard,' said Mr Nicholson.

'You'll want a cup of coffee, I expect,' said Sylvia Shipley. Cups and saucers were ready on the table, and there were chairs set round it. 'You both take sugar, don't you?'

She poured.

'Did you have much trouble finding us?'

'Well, we did take one wrong turn, so we looked at the map you sent us, and after that there was no problem.' That was John Nicholson.

It was all just chat so far, as the visitors got used to their new surroundings.

Sylvia glanced at the large clock on the kitchen wall. 'Ben and Liz will be home from school any time now,' she announced. 'You haven't met them yet, of course.'

The visitors hadn't met them because they had not been on holiday with their parents. They had been off together on a school trip of some sort at the same time instead. But of course their holiday friends had mentioned them every now and then.

'Bring your coffees into the other room, where we'll all be more comfortable,' suggested Sylvia.

It was a large house, Betty Nicholson noted enviously. Victorian, she wouldn't wonder. This room was large, too, and furnished with heavy old-fashioned furniture. Over the fireplace hung a large, framed photograph of a boy and a girl smiling at the camera.

'There are Ben and Liz,' said Sylvia. 'Really Benedict and Elizabeth, but they both prefer their shorter names. The photograph was taken last year.'

There was a loud bang as the door leading into the kitchen opened and closed violently.

'Here they are now,' said Sylvia, smiling indulgently.

Some sort of argument was going on out there.

'Well, I'm not going to,' they heard a boy's voice say. There was the sound of water running from a tap.

'If I say you are—' they heard a girl's voice.

'You can shut up about it.'

'Is Liz older than Ben?' Betty asked into the temporary silence, looking up at the photograph.

'Yes, but only by eighteen months,' replied Richard Shipley.

'That's probably why they're always quarrelling,' explained Sylvia, 'being so close in age. We just get used to it.'

'Ben, I'm sick to death of you!' Liz yelled. Then she gave a little scream of anger. She appeared at the door with her face and hair dripping. 'Mummy, Ben's just thrown his glass of water all over me!'

The Nicholsons looked at her with interest coupled with a little embarrassment.

'It's not all over you, it's only wet your face,' soothed Sylvia.

'I'll go and see what's what,' muttered Richard, and left to go into the kitchen.

'I wish he wasn't here!' stormed Liz. 'I wish he'd never been born!'

'That sounds exactly the same as my brother and I used to go on,' said Betty. 'Later on, you'll wonder why you argued so much.'

'These are Betty and John Nicholson,' Liz's mother introduced. 'You know, we told you they were coming for the weekend, after we met them on holiday.'

Liz nodded to them. 'I'm going upstairs to get dry.'

Richard returned. 'Just some stupid argument about nothing, as usual,' he said.

Another door slammed, probably Liz storming into the bathroom. Then a boy poked his head round the door of the sitting room. 'Hello,' he said to the visitors.

'Hello, Ben,' said Betty.

He grinned, then he was gone again. His father called him back.

'Could you carry Mr and Mrs Nicholson's suitcases from the kitchen up to their room?' he asked.

'Of course.'

'If they're too heavy, carry them one at a time,' called his father.

'No trouble,' they heard a few seconds later.

Then they heard him lumping them up the stairs, then his footsteps in the room directly above where they sat, then two bumps as he put them down.

'He seems a pleasant lad,' remarked John.

Much more pleasant than his sister, he considered, rather gloomily. He was beginning to wonder what sort of weekend they were going to have in this house if this was how it was going to be all the time.

'The main problem is they're alike in so many ways,' commented Sylvia.

'They'd probably get on a lot better if they weren't,' agreed her husband. 'A pity we couldn't have rolled them both into one, but there you are . . .'

After finishing their coffee, the Nicholsons went to their room to unpack. Upstairs they found a long carpeted landing with a heavy wooden balustrade. Their room, at the front of the house, was at the far end. Next to that was another bedroom, then beyond the stairs on the opposite side of the landing another, next to that the bathroom, then along a short corridor the door to another bedroom.

'It's very nice, isn't it?' whispered Betty, still envious.

'I still wonder if we've done the right thing,' John whispered back. 'Still, it can only get better, I suppose.'

When they came out they found Ben coming towards them from the little corridor. Obviously it was his room along there.

'Did you find everything all right?' he asked solicitously.

'You've got a very nice house,' said Betty.

'We like it,' said Ben, 'most of the time. But you just wait till you see what Mum's done to the dining room.'

As they sat down for dinner that evening they saw at once what he meant. Amazing, thought John Nicholson as he looked around. It really was like living in Victorian times in there. It was exactly as he imagined a Victorian dining room must have looked more than a century ago.

'The house was built in 1894,' said Sylvia, noticing the admiring glances. 'So we decided to decorate and furnish this room exactly as it might have looked when it was new. Apart from the gas lamps, of course. It's astonishing what you can find in antique shops.'

'She means junk shops,' interrupted Liz.

'I mean, look at those old photographs in their ornate frames we've hung on the wall. We got them very cheaply,' said Sylvia.

'But they're not our family,' Liz interrupted again. 'Waste of time, really.'

Her father glanced at her sharply. Mr and Mrs Nicholson looked at each other. Liz was certainly nothing like as pleasant as her brother, they both decided.

'But they suit the room, don't you think?' continued her mother.

'You'd almost expect to find a ghost in the house,' remarked Betty, for want of anything better to say.

'I don't believe in ghosts,' said Richard.

'I think I do,' said Ben.

'You would!' jeered his sister.

'I know a theory about ghosts,' remarked John Nicholson slowly. 'The idea is they might not come from the past at all— if they exist, that is. They might come from some sort of parallel time to our own instead. I suppose it's possible, especially since we still don't know what time really is.'

'Go on,' said Ben, interested.

'You can tell the time by looking at a clock,' snorted Liz.

'But we still aren't sure what time is.'

'You mean like in America,' remembered Ben. 'On the east coast when it's twelve o'clock, on the west coast it's still only nine o'clock, because of the difference in time from one side of the country to the other.'

'That's the sort of thing I mean,' said Mr Nicholson approvingly.

'What's that got to do with ghosts?' demanded Liz.

'It's obvious,' said Ben.

'Is it?' asked Liz ominously.

John Nicholson carried on quickly before another argument could break out. 'Well, we fix time to suit what we want it to be. For instance, up in space time means a different thing entirely from what it does down here.

'Do you know,' he said to Liz, 'that before the whole of Britain set their clocks to what the time was in London, all over the country people kept their clocks at different times, depending on where they lived? And that's only a few centuries ago.'

Richard nodded. 'I've heard of that,' he said.

'So what if time is shifting all the while, only we don't know that it's happening? Then ghosts could simply be in a different dimension of time we don't normally come into contact with, and only appear when theirs and ours come together. Sort of two lots of time, running side by side. And probably always moving. See?'

'Not really,' said Liz.

'Everyone ready for dessert?' asked Sylvia Shipley brightly. She hadn't really understood what he was talking about anyway.

After he had gone to bed, Ben lay awake thinking. He was not sure that he had really understood either. But if time really was shifting all the while, and we didn't realize . . . a ghost really could be someone in a different time zone which had somehow drifted into ours. He supposed.

Then if you somehow accidentally slipped across at the same time as that was happening—then you'd no longer be here at all! Rubbish, he thought.

In her room Liz was thinking very similar thoughts, because she was like her brother in so many ways. But with a slight difference. If that man hadn't been talking utter rubbish, what a pity she couldn't somehow push her brother into another zone of time—like to before he'd ever been born. And then come back just by herself.

That would certainly be an improvement. Everything else would be the same—but with no Ben.

She concentrated for a moment, trying to imagine how it might happen.

She felt the bedroom suddenly shudder, as if everything in it had flickered for a moment then returned to where it had been.

Strange. Perhaps she'd eaten too much at dinner. Her mother had laid on a really splendid meal for those boring guests; just to impress, she supposed.

She turned out the light, since nothing else seemed to be happening now, and went to sleep.

Ben felt the same sensation at exactly the same moment. His light was already out, but he noticed as he looked towards the curtains that the entire window gave the impression of having shifted, just for a brief moment, then back again.

He turned over, then felt for the little pimple he'd noticed on his face that morning. He couldn't find it. He felt more carefully.

His face just wasn't there. It had gone! In horror he quickly rolled over on to his back and felt again. Nothing. Just space. He opened his mouth to scream, but found that he couldn't, for he had no voice. And very quickly no mouth to open, either . . . nothing.

He was relieved to find in the morning that he was awake. That had been the most frightening dream ever. He didn't remember even going to sleep. He didn't know what the time was, because his alarm clock had stopped. Not that it mattered, because today was Saturday.

Ben got out of bed at once, and shortly afterwards went downstairs. They always had breakfast in the kitchen, and that was where he found his mother making the coffee and his father finishing laying the table.

Then Betty and John came in.

'Did you sleep all right?' he asked, since there seemed to be a strange silence from everyone. His parents had simply ignored him.

Now Betty and John ignored him as well.

'Make a start on the cereals if you want,' his mother told the Nicholsons.

They sat down. Ben noticed the places which his father had laid at the table. Five? But there were six of them in the house!

Then Liz strolled in. Ben stayed where he was. She glanced towards him, and a tiny smile appeared on her face, but she didn't speak to him either.

'What's wrong with me this morning?' he asked generally.

His father and mother, and Liz, also sat at the table and began their breakfast now.

'Have you any older brothers or sisters, Liz?' Betty asked her—'married and left home, I mean?'

'No, she's the only one,' Sylvia answered for her. 'It does mean we spoil her, of course.'

'I thought I saw—I seem to remember a photograph, in the sitting room—' began John Nicholson, then broke off. 'No, it must have been somewhere else.'

'You're thinking of Harry and Christine's,' Betty told him. 'You remember, last year.'

In a panic, Ben dashed out through the open door of the kitchen towards the sitting room. Of course there was a photograph of the two of them. He remembered the argument they'd had just before it was taken. He flung open the sitting room door.

There it was on the wall, him and Liz. But as he watched, somehow his image began to fade, until finally only Liz remained, smiling sweetly. He no longer existed, not even on the photograph.

He hurtled back into the kitchen.

'You know what you were saying last night,' his father was saying to John, 'about how time might sometimes shift without our knowing it was happening . . .?'

'Oh, forget it,' said John. 'I think I might have been talking rubbish, really. I got a bit carried away.'

'So where are the *five* of us going today?' Liz was asking. 'We ought to take John and Betty somewhere interesting in the car, since they haven't been here before.'

Then she looked towards where Ben was standing. And he was almost sure that now her smile was directed straight at him.

The Brighton Monster

GERALD KERSH

I found one of the most remarkable stories of the century—a story related to the most terrible event in the history of mankind—in a heap of rubbish in the corridor outside the office of Mr Harry Ainsworth, editor of the *People*, in 1943.

Every house in London, in those dark, exciting days, was being combed for salvage, particularly scrap metal and waste paper. Out of Mr Ainsworth's office alone came more than three hundred pounds of paper that, on consideration, was condemned to pulp as not worth keeping.

The pamphlet I found must have been lying at the bottom of a bottom drawer—it was on top of the salvage basket. If the lady, or gentleman, who sent it to the *People* will communicate with me I will gladly pay her (or him) two hundred and fifty English pounds.

As literature it is nothing but a piece of pretentious nonsense written by one of those idle dabblers in 'Natural Philosophy' who rushed into print on the slightest provocation in the eighteenth century. But the significance of it is formidable.

It makes me afraid.

The author of my pamphlet had attempted to tickle his way into public notice with the feather of his pen by writing an account of a Monster captured by a boatman fishing several miles out of Brighthelmstone in the county of Sussex in the summer of the year 1745.

The name of the author was the Reverend Arthur Titty. I see him as one of those pushing self-assertive vicars of the period, a rider to hounds, a purple-faced consumer of prodigious quantities of old port; a man of independent fortune, trying to persuade the world and himself that he was a deep thinker and a penetrating observer of the mysterious works of God.

I should never have taken the trouble to pocket his *Account of a Strange Monster Captured Near Brighthelmstone in the County of Sussex on August 6th in the Year of Our Lord 1745* if it had not been for the coincidence of the date: I was born on August 6th. So I pushed the yellowed, damp-freckled pages into the breast pocket of my battledress, and thought no more about them until April 1947, when a casual remark sent me running, yelling like a maniac, to the cupboard in which my old uniforms were hanging.

The pamphlet was still in its pocket.

I shall not waste your time or strain your patience with the Reverend Arthur Titty's turgid, high-falutin' prose or his references to *De rerum*—this, that, and the other. I propose to give you the unadorned facts in the very queer case of the Brighthelmstone Monster.

Brighthelmstone is now known as Brighton—a large, popular, prosperous holiday resort delightfully situated on the coast of Sussex by the Downs. But in the Reverend Titty's day it was an obscure fishing village.

If a fisherman named Hodge had not had an unlucky night on August 5th, 1745, on the glass-smooth sea off Brighthelmstone, this story would never have been told. He had gone out with his brother-in-law, George Rodgers, and they had caught nothing but a few small and valueless fishes.

Hodge was desperate. He was notorious in the village as a spendthrift and a drunkard, and it was suspected that he had a certain connection with a barmaid at the Smack Inn—it was alleged that she had a child by Hodge in the spring of the following year. He had scored up fifteen shillings for beer and needed a new net. It is probable, therefore, that Hodge stayed out in his boat until after the dawn of August 6th because he feared to face his wife—who also, incidentally, was with child.

At last, glum, sullen, and thoroughly out of sorts, he prepared to go home.

And then, he said, there was something like a splash—only it was not a splash: it was rather like the bursting of a colossal bubble: and there, in the sea, less than ten yards from his boat, was the Monster, floating.

George Rodgers said: 'By gogs, Jack Hodge, yon's a man!'

'Man? How can 'a be a man? Where could a man come from?'

The creature that had appeared with the sound of a bursting bubble drifted closer, and Hodge, reaching out with a boat-hook, caught it under the chin and pulled it to the side of the boat.

'That be a Mer-man,' he said, 'and no Christian man. Look at 'un, all covered wi' snakes and firedrakes, and yellow like a slug's belly. By the Lord, George Rodgers, this might be the best night's fishing I ever did if it's alive, please the Lord! For if it is I can sell that for better money than ever I got for my best catch this last twenty years, or any other fisherman either. Lend a hand, Georgie-boy, and let's have a feel of it.'

George Rodgers said: 'That's alive, by hell—look now, and see the way the blood runs down where the gaff went home.'

'Haul it in, then, and don't stand there gaping like a puddock.'

They dragged the Monster into the boat. It was shaped like a man and covered from throat to ankle with brilliantly coloured images of strange monsters. A green, red, yellow, and blue thing like a lizard sprawled between breast-bone and navel. Great serpents were coiled about its legs. A smaller snake, red and blue, was pricked out on the Monster's right arm: the snake's tail covered the forefinger and its head was hidden in the armpit. On the left-hand side of its chest there was a big heart-shaped design in flaming scarlet. A great bird like an eagle in red and green spread its wings from shoulderblade to shoulderblade, and a red fox chased six blue rabbits from the middle of his spine into some unknown hiding place between his legs. There were lobsters, fishes, and insects on his left arm and on his right buttock a devil-fish sprawled, encircling the lower part of his body with its tentacles. The back of his right hand was decorated with a butterfly in yellow, red, indigo, and green. Low down, in the centre of the throat, where the bone begins, there was a strange, incomprehensible, evil-looking symbol.

The Monster was naked. In spite of its fantastic appearance it was so unmistakably a male human being that George Rodgers—a weak-minded but respectable man—covered it with a sack. Hodge prised open the Monster's mouth to look at its teeth, having warned his brother-in-law to stand by with an axe in case of emergency. The man-shaped creature out of the sea had red gums, a red tongue, and teeth as white as sugar.

They forced it to swallow a little gin—Hodge always had a flask of gin in the boat—and it came to life with a great shudder, and cried out in a strange voice, opening wild black eyes and looking crazily left and right.

'Tie that up. You tie that's hands while I tie that's feet,' said Hodge.

The Monster offered no resistance.

'Throw 'un back,' said George Rodgers, suddenly overtaken by a nameless dread. 'Throw 'un back, Jack, I say!'

But Hodge said: 'You be mazed, George Rodgers, you born fool. I can sell 'e for twenty-five golden guineas. Throw 'un back? I'll throw *ee* back for a brass farthing, tha' witless fool!'

There was no wind. The two fishermen pulled for the shore. The Monster lay in the bilge, rolling its eyes. The silly, good-natured Rodgers offered it a crust of bread, which it snapped up so avidly that it bit his finger to the bone. Then Hodge tried to cram a wriggling live fish into its mouth, but 'the Monster spat it out *pop*, like a cork out of a bottle, saving your Honour's presence.'

Brighthelmstone boiled over with excitement when they landed. Even the Reverend Arthur Titty left his book and his breakfast, clapped on his three-cornered hat, picked up his cane, and went down to the fish-market to see what was happening. They told him that Hodge had caught a monster, a fish that looked like a man, a mer-man, a hypogriff, a sphinx—heaven knows what. The crowd parted, and Titty came face to face with the Monster.

Although the Monster understood neither Hebrew, Greek, Latin, Italian, nor French, it was obvious that it was a human being, or something remarkably like one. This was evident in its manner of wrinkling its forehead, narrowing its eyes, and demonstrating that it was capable of understanding— or of wanting to understand, which is the same thing. But it could not speak; it could only cry out incoherently and it was obviously greatly distressed. The Reverend Arthur Titty said: 'Oafs, ignorant louts! This is no sea monster, you fools, no *lusus naturæ*, but an unfortunate shipwrecked mariner.'

According to the pamphlet, Hodge said: 'Your Reverence, begging your Reverence's pardon, how can that be, since for the past fortnight there has been no breath of wind and no foreign vessel in these parts? If this be an unfortunate shipwrecked mariner, where is the wreck of his ship, and where was it wrecked? I humbly ask your Reverence how he appeared as you might say out of a bubble without warning on the face of the water, floating. And if your Honour will take the trouble to observe this unhappy creature's skin your Reverence will see that it shows no signs of having been immersed for any considerable period in the ocean.'

I do not imagine for a moment that this is what Hodge really said: he probably muttered the substance of the argument in the form of an angry protest emphasized by a bitten-off oath or two. However, the Reverend Arthur Titty perceived that what the fisherman said was 'not without some show of reason' and said that he proposed to take the Monster to his house for examination.

Hodge protested vigorously. It was his Monster, he said, because he had caught it in the open sea with his own hands, in his own boat, and parson or no parson, if Titty were the Archbishop himself, an Englishman had his rights. After some altercation, in the course of which the Monster fainted, the Reverend Arthur Titty gave Hodge a silver crown piece for the loan of the Monster for philosophical observation. They poured a few buckets of sea water over the Monster which came back to consciousness with a tremulous sigh. This was regarded as positive proof of its watery origin. Then it was carried to Titty's house on a hurdle.

It rejected salt water as a drink, preferring fresh water or wine, and ate cooked food, expressing, with unmistakable grimaces, a distaste for raw fish and meat. It was put to bed on a heap of clean straw and covered with a blanket which was kept moistened with sea water. Soon the Monster of Brighthelmstone revived and appeared desirous of walking. It could even make sounds reminiscent of human speech.

The Reverend Arthur Titty covered its nakedness under a pair of his old breeches and one of his old shirts . . . as if it had not been grotesque-looking enough before.

He weighed it, measured it, and bled it to discover whether it was thick or thin-blooded, cold or hot-blooded. According to Titty's fussy little account the Monster was about five feet one and three-quarter inches tall. It weighed exactly one hundred and nineteen pounds, and walked upright. It possessed unbelievable strength and superhuman agility. On one occasion the Reverend Arthur Titty took it out for a walk on the end of a leather leash. The local blacksmith, one of Hodge's boon companions, who was notorious for his gigantic muscular power and bad temper—he was later to achieve nation-wide fame as Clifford, who broke the arm of the champion wrestler of Yorkshire—accosted the Reverend Arthur Titty outside his smithy and said: 'Ah, so that's Hodge's catch as you stole from him. Let me feel of it to see if it be real,' and he pinched the Monster's shoulders very cruelly with one of his great hands—hands that could snap horse-shoes and twist iron bars into spirals. The inevitable crowd of children and gaping villagers witnessed the event. The Monster picked up the two-hundred-pound blacksmith and threw him into a heap of scrap iron three yards away. For an anxious second or two Titty thought that the Monster was going to run amok, for its entire countenance changed; the nostrils quivered, the eyes shone with fierce intelligence, and from its open mouth there came a weird cry. Then the creature relapsed into heavy dejection and let itself be led home quietly, while the astonished blacksmith, bruised and bleeding, limped back to his anvil with the shocked air of a man who has seen the impossible come to pass.

Yet, the Monster was an extremely sick Monster. It ate little, sometimes listlessly chewing the same mouthful for fifteen minutes. It liked to squat on its haunches and stare unblinkingly at the sea. It was assumed that it was homesick for its native element, and so it was soused at intervals with buckets of brine and given a large tub of sea water to sleep in if it so desired. A learned doctor of medicine came all the way from Dover to examine it and pronounced it human; unquestionably an air-breathing mammal. But so were whales and crocodiles breathers of air that lived in the water.

Hodge, alternately threatening and whimpering, claimed his property. The Reverend Arthur Titty called in his lawyer, who so bewildered the unfortunate fisherman with Latin quotations, legal jargon, dark hints, and long words that, cursing and growling, he scrawled a cross in lieu of a signature at the foot of a document in which he agreed to relinquish all claim on the Monster in consideration of the sum of seven guineas, payable on the spot. Seven guineas was a great deal of money for a fisherman in those days. Hodge had never seen so many gold pieces in a heap, and had never owned one. Then a travelling showman visited the Reverend Arthur Titty and offered him twenty-five guineas for the Monster, which Titty refused. The showman spoke of the matter in the Smack, and Hodge, who had been drunk for a week, behaved 'like one demented,' as Titty wrote in a contemptuous footnote. He made a thorough nuisance of himself, demanding the balance of the twenty-five guineas which were his by rights, was arrested and fined for riotous conduct. Then he was put in the stocks as an incorrigible drunkard, and the wicked little urchins of Brighthelmstone threw fish-guts at him.

Let out of the stocks with a severe reprimand, smelling horribly of dead fish, Hodge went to the Smack and ordered a quart of strong ale, which came in a heavy can. Rodgers, to whom Hodge had given only twelve shillings, came in for his modest morning draught, and told Hodge that he was nothing better than a damned rogue. He claimed half of the seven golden guineas. Hodge, having drunk his quart, struck Rodgers with the can, and broke his skull; for which he was hanged not long afterwards.

The Brighthelmstone Monster was an unlucky Monster.

The Reverend Arthur Titty also suffered. After the killing of

Rodgers and the hanging of Hodge the fishermen began to hate him. Heavy stones were thrown against his shutters at night. Someone set fire to one of his haystacks. This must have given Titty something to think about, for rick-burning was a hanging matter, and one may as well hang for a parson as for a haystack. He made up his mind to go to London and live in politer society. So he was uprooted by the Monster. The fishermen hated the Monster too. They regarded it as a sort of devil. But the Monster did not care. It was languishing, dying of a mysterious sickness. Curious sores had appeared at various points on the Monster's body—they began as little white bumps such as one gets from stinging-nettles, and slowly opened and would not close. The looseness of the skin, now, lent the dragons and snakes and fishes a disgustingly lifelike look: as the Monster breathed, they writhed. A veterinary surgeon poured melted pitch on the sores. The Reverend Titty kept it well soaked in sea water and locked it in a room, because it had shown signs of wanting to escape.

At last, nearly three months after its first appearance in Brighthelmstone, the Monster escaped. An old man-servant, Alan English, unlocked the door, in the presence of the Reverend Arthur Titty, to give the Monster its daily mess of vegetables and boiled meat. As the key turned the door was flung open with such violence that English fell forward into the room—his hand was still on the door-knob—and the Monster ran out, crying aloud in a high, screaming voice. The Reverend Arthur Titty caught it by the shoulder, whereupon he was whisked away like a leaf in the wind and lay stunned at the end of the passage. The Monster ran out of the house. Three responsible witnesses—Rebecca North, Herbert George, and Abraham Herris (or Harris)—saw it running towards the sea, stark naked, although a north-east wind was blowing. The two

men ran after it, and Rebecca North followed as fast as she could. The Monster ran straight into the bitter water and began to swim, its arms and legs vibrating like the wings of an insect. Herbert George saw it plunge into the green heart of a great wave, and then the heavy rain fell like a curtain and the Brighthelmstone Monster was never seen again.

It had never spoken. In the later stages of its disease its teeth had fallen out. With one of these teeth—probably a canine—it had scratched marks on the dark oak panels of the door of the room in which it was confined. These marks the Reverend Arthur Titty faithfully copied and reproduced in his pamphlet.

The Brighthelmstone fishermen said that the sea devil had gone back where it belonged, down to the bottom of the sea to its palace built of the bones of lost Christian sailors. Sure enough, half an hour after the Monster disappeared there was a terrible storm, and many seamen lost their lives. In a month or so Titty left Brighthelmstone for London. The city swallowed him. He published his pamphlet in 1746—a bad year for natural philosophy, because the ears of England were still full of the Jacobite Rebellion of '45.

Poor Titty! If he could have foreseen the real significance of the appearance of the Monster of Brighthelmstone he would have died happy . . . in a lunatic asylum.

Nobody would have believed him.

Now in April 1947 I had the good fortune to meet one of my oldest and dearest friends, a colonel in Intelligence who, for obvious reasons, must remain anonymous, although he is supposed to be in retirement now and wears civilian clothes, elegantly cut in the narrow-sleeved style of the late nineteen-twenties, and rather the worse for wear. The Colonel is in many ways a romantic character, something like Rudyard Kipling's Strickland Sahib. He has played many strange parts in his time, that formidable old warrior; and his quick black eyes, disturbingly Asiatic-looking under the slackly-drooping eyelids, have seen more than you and I will ever see.

He never talks about his work. An Intelligence officer who talks ceases automatically to be an Intelligence officer. A good deal of his conversation is of sport, manly sport—polo, pig-sticking, cricket, rugby football, hunting, and, above all, boxing and wrestling. I imagine that the Colonel, who has lived underground in disguise for so many years of his life, finds relief in the big wide-open games in which a man must meet his opponent face to face yet may, without breaking the rules, play quick tricks.

We were drinking coffee and smoking cigarettes after dinner in my flat and he was talking about oriental wrestling. He touched on wrestling technique among the Afghans and in the Deccan, and spoke with admiration of Gama, the Western Indian wrestler, still a rock-crusher at an age when most men are shivering in slippers by the fire, who beat Zybszko; remarked on a South-Eastern Indian named Patil who could knock a strong man senseless with the knuckle of his left thumb; and went on to Chinese wrestlers, especially Mongolians, who are tremendously heavy and powerful, and use their feet. A good French-Canadian lumberjack (the Colonel said), accustomed to dancing on rolling logs in a rushing river, could do dreadful things with his legs and feet, like the Tiger of Quebec, who, in a scissors-hold, killed Big Ted Glass of Detroit. In certain kinds of wrestling size and weight were essential, said the Colonel. The Japanese wrestlers of the heavy sort—the ones that weighed three or four hundred pounds and looked like pigs—those big ones that started on all fours and went through a series of ritual movements; they had to be enormously heavy. In fact the heavier they were the better.

'No, Gerald my lad, give me ju-jitsu,' he said. 'There is no one on earth who can defeat a master of ju-jitsu—except someone who takes him by surprise. Of course, a scientific boxer, getting a well placed punch in first, would put him out for the count. But the real adept develops such wonderful co-ordination of hand and eye that if he happens to be expecting it he can turn to his own advantage even the lightning punch of a wizard like Jimmy Wilde. He could give away eight stone to Joe Louis and make him look silly. Georges Hackenschmidt, for instance, is one of the greatest catch-as-catch-can wrestlers that ever lived, and one of the strongest men of his day. But I question whether he, wrestling Catch, might have stood up against Yukio Tani. Oh, by the way, speaking of Yukio Tani, did you ever hear of a wrestler called Sato?'

'I can't say that I have. Why? Should I have heard of him?'

'Why, he is, or was, a phenomenon. I think he was a better wrestler than Tani. My idea was to take him all round the world and challenge all comers—boxers, wrestlers, even fencers, to stand up against him for ten minutes. He was unbelievable. Furthermore, he *looked* so frightful. I won a hundred and fifty quid on him at Singapore in 1938. He took on four of the biggest and best boxers and wrestlers we could lay our hands on and floored the whole lot in seven minutes by the clock. Just a minute, I've got a picture in my wallet. I keep it because it looks so damn funny. Look.'

The Colonel handed me a dog-eared photograph of an oddly assorted group. There was a hairy mammoth of a man, obviously a wrestler, standing with his arms folded so that his biceps looked like coconuts, beside another man, almost as big, but with the scrambled features of a rough-and-tumble bruiser. There was one blond grinning man who looked like a light heavyweight, and a beetle-browed middleweight with a bulldog jaw. The Colonel was standing in the background, smiling in a fatherly way. In the foreground, smiling into the camera, stood a tiny Japanese. The top of his head was on a level with the big wrestler's breast-bone, but he was more than half as broad as he was tall. He was all chest and arms. The knuckles of his closed hands touched his knees. I took the picture to the light and looked more closely. The photographer's flashbulb had illuminated every detail. Sato had made himself even more hideous with tattooing. He was covered with things that creep and crawl, real and fabulous. A dragon snarled on his stomach. Snakes were coiled about his legs. Another snake wound itself about his right arm from forefinger to armpit. The other arm was covered with angry-looking lobsters and goggle-eyed fishes, and on the left breast there was the conventionalized shape of a heart.

It was then that I uttered an astonished oath and went running to look for my old uniform, which I found, with the Reverend Arthur Titty's pamphlet still in the inside breast pocket. The Colonel asked me what the devil was the matter with me. I smoothed out the pamphlet and gave it to him without a word.

He looked at it, and said: 'How very extraordinary!' Then he put away his eye-glass and put on a pair of spectacles; peered intently at the smudged and ragged drawing of the

Brighthelmstone Monster, compared it with the photograph of Sato and said to me: 'I have come across some pretty queer things in my time, but I'm damned if I know what to make of this.'

'Tell me,' I said, 'was your Sato tattooed behind? And if so, in what way?'

Without hesitation the Colonel said: 'A red-and-green hawk stooping between the shoulderblades, a red fox chasing six blue-grey rabbits down his spine, and an octopus on the right buttock throwing out tentacles that went round to the belly. Why?'

Then I opened Titty's pamphlet and put my finger on the relevant passage. The Colonel read it and changed colour. But he said nothing. I said: 'This is the damnedest coincidence. There's another thing. This so-called Monster of Brighton scratched something on the door of the room where he was locked up, and the old parson took a pencil rubbing of it. Turn over four or five pages and you'll see a copy of it.'

The Colonel found the page. The spongy old paper was worn into holes, blurred by time and the dampness of lumber-rooms and the moisture of my body. He said: 'It looks like Japanese. But no Japanese would write like that surely . . .'

'Remember,' I said, 'that the Brighton Monster scratched its message with one of its own teeth on the panel of an oak door. Allow for that; allow for the fact that it was weak and sick; take into consideration the grain of the wood; and then see what you make of it.'

The Colonel looked at the inscription for ten long minutes, copying it several times from several different angles. At last he said: 'This says: *I was asleep. I thought that it was all a bad dream from which I should awake and find myself by the side of my wife. Now I know that it is not a dream. I am sick in the head. Pity me, poor Sato, who went to sleep in one place and awoke in another. I cannot live any more. I must die. Hiroshima 1945.*'

'What do you make of that?' I asked.

The Colonel said: 'I don't know. I only know the bare facts about Sato because, as I have already told you, I was trying to find him. (a) He had a wife, and a home somewhere in Hiroshima. (b) He was in the Japanese Navy, and he went on leave in August 1945. (c) Sato disappeared off the face of the earth when they dropped that damned atom bomb. (d) This is unquestionably a picture of Sato—the greatest little wrestler the world has ever

known. (e) The description of the tattooing on the back of this Monster tallies exactly with Sato's . . . I don't know quite what to make of it. Sato, you know, was a Christian. He counted the years the Christian way. *Hiroshima 1945*. I wonder!'

'What do you wonder?'

'Why,' said the Colonel, 'there can't be the faintest shadow of a doubt that Sato got the middle part of the blast of that frightful atom bomb when we dropped it on Hiroshima. You may or may not have heard of Dr Sant's crazy theories concerning Time in relation to Speed. Now imagine that you happen to be caught up—without disintegrating—in a species of air-pocket on the fringe of an atomic blast and are flung away a thousand times faster than if you had been fired out of a cannon. Imagine it. According to the direction in which you happen to be thrown you may find yourself in the middle of Tomorrow or on the other side of Yesterday. Don't laugh at me. I may have been frying my brains in the tropics most of my life, and I may be crazy; but I've learned to believe all kinds of strange things. My opinion is that my poor little Sato was *literally blown back* two hundred years in time.'

I said: 'But why blown backwards only in time? How do you account for his being struck by the blast in Hiroshima and ending in Brighton?'

'I'm no mathematician,' said the Colonel, 'but as I understand, the earth is perpetually spinning and Space is therefore shifting all the time. If you, for example, could stand absolutely still, here, now, where you are, while the earth moved—if you stood still only for one hour, you'd find yourself in Budapest. Do you understand what I mean? That atomic blast picked little Sato up and threw him back in Time. When you come to think of that, and remember all the curious Monsters they used to exhibit in Bartholomew's Fair during the eighteenth century—when you think of all the Mermaids, Monsters, and Mermen that they picked out of the sea and showed on fairgrounds until they died . . . it makes you think.'

'It makes you think.'

'Do you observe, by the way,' said the Colonel, pointing to the Reverend Titty's pamphlet, 'that poor little Sato was sick with running sores, and that his teeth were falling out? Radioactivity poisoning: these are the symptoms. Poor Sato! Can you wonder why he got desperate and simply chucked himself back into the sea to sink or swim? Put yourself in his position. You go to sleep in Hiroshima, in August 1945 and then—*Whoof!*—you find yourself in Brighton, in 1745. No wonder the poor wretch couldn't speak. That shock would be enough to paralyse anyone's tongue. It scares me, Kersh, my boy—it puts a match to trains of thought of the most disturbing nature. It makes me remember that Past and Future are all one. I shall really worry, in future, when I have a nightmare . . . one of those nightmares in which you find yourself lost, struck dumb, completely bewildered in a place you've never seen before—a place out of this world. God have mercy on us, I wish they'd never thought of that disgusting Secret Weapon!'

You are free to argue the point, to speculate and to draw your own conclusions. But this is the end (or, God forbid, the beginning) of the story of the Brighton Monster.

Let's go to Golgotha!

GARRY KILWORTH

The Time-Travel Agency was the third room along one of the branches of a Banyan building. It was a long way up, and it took Simon Falk a considerable time to reach the pink glass doors. A notice outside read,

---

PAN PACKAGE TOURS
OFFER YOU THE REMARKABLE!

This is your chance to see

**THE BATTLE OF MARATHON
THE WARS OF THE ROSES
THE FIRST MANNED SPACE FLIGHT**

ABSOLUTELY **NO** PERSONAL RISK

Simon stared into the interior and then went, reluctantly, it seemed, inside. An assistant slid silently to his side the moment he was in the room, with hands clasped before him in deference to his customer. Perhaps he was requesting aid from above, thought Simon, to get him through his potential sale?

'Can I help you, sir?'

Simon knotted his own fingers behind his back to even the balance and to hint gently that he was not yet ready to buy.

'Just some brochures, please. Can I take some away with me to, er, study at leisure?'

'Certainly, sir.' The fingers unravelled themselves and began deftly plucking multi-coloured sheets of paper from the display shelves with the expertise of a seasoned fruit-picker.

'When you and your . . .?'

'Family,' Simon finished for him.

'Precisely!' The words were neat and well cared-for. Trimmed to the correct length and each separated by a time pause fitting for the intended effect. 'When you have made your minds up,' he continued, 'perhaps you will give us a call and we will see what can be arranged. There is no need to come personally for the booking . . .'

Simon wriggled uncomfortably. 'I was just on my way home—I know I could have ordered them by mail but my wife is impatient.'

'Yes,' the salesman smiled silkily. 'Um, the Coronation of Elizabeth the First is fully booked, I'm afraid, and the Revolution of Mars has only a limited number of seats available.'

'I don't believe we are too interested in those events,' said Simon.

'Your first time, sir?'

'Yes, as a matter of fact it is.'

'Then may I recommend the Sacking of Carthage? We mingle with the camp followers on a neighbouring slope. However, I must add that it's not for the squeamish.'

Simon asked, 'Isn't that a little dangerous?'

'Er, no, not as long as you follow our little instructions.' The agent wagged a finger playfully. 'We've never lost a customer yet.'

Simon murmured his thanks and almost ran out of the room. He hated these pre-holiday forays, but he owed his family a vacation and they were going to get it. It had to be one of these time-tours: he could not afford space travel. There was nothing else to do. Earth was a solid block of brick and concrete flourishing with Banyan buildings, and ocean cruises made his children ill. He stepped out of the building and hailed a floater, avoiding the blast of the air purifiers as he crossed the tiled roof to meet it.

Mandy was waiting at the door of their flat in the same mantis-like attitude employed by travel agents.

'Did you get the brochures?'

He sighed a resigned sigh. 'Yes, I got them.'

She grabbed at the wad. 'Wonderful, let me see them. Oh, don't look so depressed, you know you always enjoy it once we get away. A trip through time!' She clutched the brochures to her breast. 'I'm going to love every minute of it.'

'Well, I hope it'll be up to your expectations,' Simon said drily. 'It's going to cost us enough, and my business is not doing as well as it should.' He trailed his sentence over to the cocktail cabinet, and made himself a drink.

'Oh, tish,' she replied. 'A holiday will do you good. You'll come back full of fresh ideas and thoroughly relaxed.' She turned over some of the brochures in her hands. 'We don't want anything too violent—it might upset the children.'

Simon gave a snort. 'The children would wallow in it. James likes nothing better than the sight of blood, and Julie would rather see a space war picture than a live ballet performance.'

'Don't be cynical, dear. Anyway, that's all the more reason to get them away,' protested Mandy. 'They have nothing else to do but play on the rooftops these days.'

'Nothing else to do,' he cried, overdoing the incredulous tone. 'Did I have underground free-play fairgrounds when I was a boy? Did you have . . .?'

'Oh, don't start that again. When will you understand that children cannot appreciate what they have always had? Let them see how children lived in other ages, other countries.' Mandy paused. Then she continued, 'We should have shown them before. Perhaps we should take them to Sparta. Did you know that the children of Sparta were placed in military academies at the age of eight and told to steal their food or starve? The crime was getting caught. I wonder what our children would think of the boy that let a fox gnaw on his abdomen rather than let his elders discover he had stolen it, and had hidden it up his smock?' Her blue eyes searched his face for signs of agreement.

'They would probably think he was a damn fool, and so do I,' Simon replied.

She tried again. 'Perhaps we should take them to Rome . . .?'

'Or Pompeii the day before it erupted—and leave them there.'

'Don't be nasty. What about the Holy Land . . .'

'. . . at the time of the Crusades,' finished twelve-year-old James, who had entered the kitchen eating.

'Not before your dinner, James,' complained his mother. 'Your father and I will decide where we are going—go and wash your hands. Where's Julie?'

'She's coming.'

That evening Simon and Mandy Falk sat at the table poring over brochures and fighting over places, prices, and dates until the front door sang softly, telling them that their closest friends were waiting to enter the house. Simon pressed a switch and shortly afterwards Harry and Sarah Tolbutt entered the room.

'Hello, hello, holiday time again?' chirped Harry, unzipping his outwear suit.

Simon smiled and scratched the bridge of his nose.

'Yep. We can't decide where to go. Or should I say *when* to go? It's a bit confusing.'

'If you are talking about time-tours, why don't you come with us? We're going to see the Crucifixion,' said Sarah, with a little flick of her head.

'The what!' cried the Falks together.

'The Crucifixion of Christ,' said Harry nonchalantly. He became earnest. 'You see, we thought the children needed to see exactly what happened so that they had a real understanding of religion and what it means. You know what children are like.'

'We know,' said Simon in a hollow tone.

Sarah continued. 'If they could see exactly how Jesus died to save us—or our souls or whatever it was that he saved—it might have a profound effect on them. At least, we hope it will.'

Simon began mixing the drinks. 'Isn't it a bit sacrilegious?' he said quietly. 'I mean, after all . . .'

Harry spoke again. 'Well, I suppose on the surface it does seem a bit ghoulish and bloodthirsty, but as long as one goes with the right attitude I think it is all right. As long as one bears in mind what one is there for.'

Mandy said, 'Do you know, that is exactly what I was thinking before you came over? Wasn't I, Simon?'

'Yes, I'm a mind-reader,' he winked at Harry. Mandy ignored him. 'We are drawing too far away from the things that matter in life, like religion.'

'You've not mentioned going to church in ten years,' scoffed Simon.

Mandy dismissed this remark with a flick of her hand. 'That's not important,' she retorted. 'A pack of old men droning out of the scriptures is not religion. I want to see the real thing— I think we should go, Simon.'

Thus it was decided by Mandy and Sarah. Simon, his family and their friends were going to see the Crucifixion, at modest package tour prices, of course.

Pan Time-Tours Limited had its offices in Southend High Square. The Falks and the Tolbutts shared a floater to the pre-tour lecture to economize on the fare. The day was unusually bright for the season and in the floater, protected from the fresh sea breeze, they were warm and excited. Simon always felt good on a day when the sun managed to cut its way through the layers of cloud and he could see it twinkling on the giant floating platform that launched the starships high above the sky. He had never been into space. Simon Falk was secretly a confirmed homebody.

They reached the small lecture hall and took seats inside. Simon looked around him.

'There's quite a few people here,' he whispered to Harry. 'Do you think they are all on our tour?'

'Must be,' said Harry. 'There's no other lecture booked for today.'

'Can I have your attention, please?' A young, serious-looking clergyman stood on the small rostrum before them. The murmuring died down. The vicar was a short man with old-fashioned glass spectacles. It was an affectation of the clergy. His glasses flashed like metal discs in the sunlight that fell in stripes down the east side of the hall.

'First of all, welcome to Pan Time-Tours. I am one of your Preparation Officers and I am here to give you advice on what to expect and how you must conduct yourselves.' He smiled. 'We do not lay down any rules, but it is important you should know how to act because on this tour, as on many others, you will be mixing with the locals. You must be inconspicuous— this is the primary rule.'

One or two hands shot up, but the clergyman waved them

down. 'Now, I know a lot of you will have questions, but I must ask you to be patient. We will give you time at the termination of the lecture to get your queries answered. Many of them will probably be dealt with as the lecture continues. We have done all this before.'

He looked up and smiled again. The sunlight from the window struck his left cheek, smearing it with holy gold, and the audience settled comfortably in their soft chairs.

'You will all be issued with the appropriate clothing before you embark, and everyone will go through our treatment room to ensure that their outward appearance does not clash with that of the natives. This is a perfectly harmless process and is easily reversible on return from your holiday. We can't have any giant Nordic blondes standing out like poorly disguised Vikings at a Ramadan feast.

'A few days before the trip you will all be invited to visit our language laboratory, where you will be taught Hebrew by the knowledge-injection principle during one afternoon. As you probably know, the knowledge will only last about a month before it disappears completely from your brains. We can't stuff it in in two or three hours and expect it to remain there, otherwise we would all be brilliant.'

He gave a soft snigger.

'Can't I be a Roman soldier?' a spotty-faced youth shouted from behind Simon.

The clergyman reproved the caller with a stern finger and said gravely, 'Sir, I did warn you not to ask questions until the end. You will be given ample opportunity then. However, I will give you a reply because I was shortly coming to the importance of being Hebrews. The tour needs to stay together. A Roman soldier or two tagging along behind civilians will not look right, and besides, occupation troops have commitments—they might be recalled to barracks at short notice. You might be stopped for dirty buttons or something—a soldier is too vulnerable. Apart from all this, soldiers act in a particular fashion and have gestures and phrases peculiar to their profession—we would be sure to give ourselves away. Take it from me that we need to go as civilians.'

'I don't want to be a Jew,' muttered James. Simon nudged him to be quiet.

The speaker continued. 'Now, this last part is most important—

and I shall understand if any of you wish to drop out. If you do—only at this juncture, mind you—your deposit money will be refunded. If any of you are thrown in prison for any reason, we might not be able to get you out in time—that is, before you disappear into the bowels of a slave galley or end up at the bottom of the stoning pit.'

There was a loud shuffling of feet and muttering of voices from his audience, and he waited with bowed head until it had ceased.

'There is no risk,' he continued, 'providing you do exactly as you are told. I cannot stress the importance of this too much. You know what happened and how it happened. We will arrive on the day that Pilate asks the inhabitants of Jerusalem whom he should set free, as the citizens are permitted to grant amnesty to one prisoner over the Feast of the Passover. When the crowd begins to shout "Barabbas", as we know it must, then you must shout it too. You must not appear to be different in any way from the rest of the citizens. This is vitally important. You have to appear to be in agreement with the rest of the crowd. You must jeer at Christ and shake your fists as he drags the cross through the streets. You must remember that communities in those times were not very large, and if a small section of people is silent the others will begin to wonder why and will question you. You will be sure to give yourselves away under stress—not because you are idiots but because you are clever. People in those times were simple. They followed the ringleaders, and they will regard anyone who does not with great suspicion. It is far more difficult to think and speak with simplicity under pressure than it is the reverse, so do as I say and everyone will be perfectly safe. It may be distasteful and even repugnant to your nature, but it is a necessity. When they nail up the sign "Jesus of Nazareth, King of the Jews", you must laugh. Those that remain awestruck while the rest of the crowd are dancing and prancing, screaming and shouting, will only draw attention to themselves by their silence. I repeat, it is for your own safety. Now, are there any questions?'

The sermon was at an end. Only two childless couples asked for a refund of their deposit.

'How could they do that?' asked Julie for about the fifth time, just before they left for Jerusalem. 'How could they crucify him? His own people. The same people that cheered and threw palm leaves before his feet such a short time before. It's like giving someone a ticker-tape parade and then hanging him.'

'I don't suppose that is unknown either,' replied Simon.

The children, after their initial reluctance to enjoy the pre-holiday plans, had settled down to the idea and had been studying their Bibles.

'Don't forget what the man said, they were a very simple people.'

Simon was pleased with Julie. She was going with the right objectives in mind: to study the people who had executed Christ and to attempt to analyse their motives.

Julie went on, 'I can't believe they *had* to do it. I know Christ had to die to save us all from sin but . . .'

'It was mankind that was to blame. You must think in general terms. You can't blame individual nations like the Romans or the Jews.'

'Well, I still think it is terrible, the way they treated him.'

Yes, Simon was well pleased with Julie. He was not too sure about James yet. James was a deeper one than Julie and had to be plumbed over a longer period of time than had been available.

The treatment room, as promised, was painless, and the journey itself was almost a delight. It left you with a slightly dizzy feeling but if you kept your eyes closed the sensation was that of sliding down a seemingly endless helter-skelter. There really was nothing to it. When Simon opened his eyes he found himself sitting on warm sand beside a narrow goat track. The others were in the positions they had held inside the time room. They all climbed to their feet and made their way along the goat track towards the town that shimmered in the heat in the distance. The sun pressed hot on the backs of their necks and Simon put an arm round James to stop him from stumbling. None of them were used to walking on uneven ground covered in sharp stones. Simon felt sorry for some of the older members of the party.

The courier entered the town first. He was recognizable by his matted hair, rags, and the ancient staff he carried, but no one was to speak to him except in dire emergency. The walk was a long one and the rough smocks were uncomfortable. Several children were beginning to complain of the heat and that their skins were sore where the cloth was rubbing, but there was a general atmosphere of excitement pervading the adults. At least we look authentic enough, thought Simon. The smocks and sandals were genuine, bought on a previous trip by a Tour Preparation Officer. Some of the members had elected to go barefoot at the request of the firm. Their feet had been hardened during the process in the treatment room. Nevertheless, thought Simon, they will be raw by the time we go back. Presumably Pan Time-Tours relied on the suffering of Christ to overawe the visitors and make them ashamed of their own trivial problems. A dog ran in and out of their legs, barking, as they trailed down a narrow dusty street. Their first meeting with one of the locals. Simon glanced at Mandy. Her new brown eyes flashed at him, and she looked very beautiful in a gypsyish sort of way.

'Glad you came?' she whispered in Hebrew.

'I don't know yet,' he said in all seriousness.

Finally they passed between some hard mud dwellings and out into a square in the middle of the town.

'Just in time,' said the courier. 'Spread out, everyone.'

The mob was dense, but Harry procured a clear place just inside the periphery of the crowd. A tall, thin man with an intelligent face was addressing the people from the steps of a stone building. He looked harassed and a little ill. He was speaking in Latin.

'What is he saying?' whispered Simon to Harry, who had studied the classics in his youth.

'He is asking us to choose the one to go free,' answered Harry. 'You know, you've read the book.'

'Oh,' said Simon.

The crowd shuffled but remained silent. A fly settled on the end of Simon's perspiring nose and he flicked it away impatiently. God, it was hot, he thought. The Roman repeated his previous sentence. Suddenly, as if he had just comprehended the question, James cried out 'Barabbas!' in a high voice. He had been daydreaming, and the question, as did many questions in Latin in the classroom at school, had taken him off his guard. The sound echoed over the hard, baked square, and James looked a little frightened at his outburst.

Then the mutterings in the crowd began, and soon everyone was yelling.

'Barabbas! Barabbas!'

Simon felt relieved that the shouting had started. He had been startled by his son's yell and was afraid that attention had been drawn to them. No one was looking at them, however.

'What did you do that for?' he hissed under the uproar.

James was nervous and tense.

'I'm sorry. I thought we were supposed to. He asked us and the man said . . . I don't know.'

'Never mind,' intervened Harry. 'It would have happened anyway. You just jumped the gun, that's all. Don't do it again, though, or we may be in trouble.'

James looked miserable, but Simon let it go at that. There was no sense in causing a scene, and what was done was done. They stood for about an hour in the square, with none of them quite sure what was happening, and then Julie said she felt sick. Simon and Mandy took her behind one of the strawbrick houses, leaving James with Harry and Sarah and their children.

'It must be the heat,' said Mandy after a while. 'It's getting at me a bit too. Couldn't we sit down somewhere in the shade?'

She looked down the narrow street for somewhere to rest but there was nothing in view. Then, having an idea, she walked over to one of the houses and looked in from the open doorway. A Hebrew family was sitting on stools in the middle of the room with their hands clasped in front of them. The old man of the group raised his eyes enquiringly. It was cool in the doorway, but it was obvious that she was intruding on something very private.

'Sorry,' said Mandy, and stepped back into the street. The heat from the ground came up through the soles of her sandals again and she walked on to the next house. It was also occupied: so was the next, and the next. She returned to where Simon and Julie stood.

'There's something funny here,' she whispered to Simon when she reached him. 'The houses have people in them.'

'So?' said Simon in an irritated tone.

'Well, one would think they would be out on a day like today. Why aren't they watching Christ pull his cross through the streets? All the other inhabitants are.'

'Perhaps they are . . . Well, I don't know. What's the point?' Then he looked thoughtful. 'You know, you have something there. Let's check a few more of the houses.'

They went from house to house, through dozens of streets, peering into doorways, looking through curtains until they knew they had covered a large portion of the town. Enough to know that there was something terribly wrong. The realization of what that wrong was began to sink in very rapidly, and no matter how hard Simon's mind tried to reject it or concoct excuses to cover it, the awful thought remained. Julie followed her agitated parents, not understanding and obviously unwell.

'I want a drink,' she finally complained.

'Well, you can't have one,' snapped Mandy. 'The water isn't fit to drink. It's got all sorts of germs in it.'

'These people are all right,' Julie sniffed to deaf ears.

Simon felt a hot wave of air pass over his face. His eyes were sore, his mouth felt dry, and the dust was mixing with the sweat on his feet to form a slimy grime between his toes. His physical discomfort, however, was nothing compared to his mental stress. He felt very afraid.

'Doesn't it strike you as peculiar that the crowd was so large?' he asked, wiping his brow with his sleeve at the same time.

Mandy's voice was taut. 'Well, it has been boosted by time-tours from the future. There's more than one agency, don't forget.'

Simon was visibly trembling now. 'There are dozens of agencies,' he cried. 'And all the inhabitants of this town are in their houses, praying. Quickly, we've got to find Harry and the others.'

Simon grabbed Julie and swung her on to his back. They ran through the streets with the perspiration dripping from their eyebrows and their eyes stinging with the salt and dust. In the distance they could hear the crowd chanting and jeering; they could hear the shrieks of laughter and high-pitched catcalls. It was an ugly, frightening sound, like the screaming of monkeys as a lion pads beneath their trees. It was the forced laughter of hyenas that circle the lion's den at a safe distance as the lord lies, unconcerned, in the warm sun. Then, suddenly, there was silence.

Simon slowed, gasping for breath. He could see the rut made

by the corner of the cross snaking along the street and disappearing into the distance. A shudder went through him.

'My God,' he sobbed to his wife, 'we've killed him.'

A sandal slipped from his foot as he ran but he disregarded it. He felt none of the sharp stones that cut the soles and heels of his feet.

The pair of them stumbled on, following the tell-tale mark in the dust, until they reached the crowd. The faces were all turned in one direction and wore expressions of shocked sympathy. Simon did not dare look towards the crosses. He knew he would faint if he did, and he had seen the shadows out of the corner of his eye. It was enough. They found Harry and Sarah and the children on the edge of the crowd, as silent and watchful as the others. Sarah's cheeks were blotched with white and Harry's mouth was half-open.

'Harry,' choked Simon, as quickly as his emotion would allow. 'Harry, we've got to get him down.'

Harry's stunned mind took time to register the fact that Simon was with them once more. He did not take his eyes from the man on the centre cross.

Licking his lips, he replied helplessly, 'Can't do it, Simon. It's got to happen, you know. This is the way it is, but, my God, I wish we had never come. He looked at me, you know. I'll never forget his eyes as long as I live. They were so . . .' he paused to find a word, '. . . so deep.'

Simon was frantic. 'Harry, Harry. Look at the crowd! Look around you! There are no Jews here. No natives. The only ones here are us. The holiday-makers. Do you realize the enormity of what we've done? The whole guilt of mankind rests on our shoulders.'

He was sobbing violently now. 'We've crucified the Son of God, and we're going to do it next tour, and the next and the next . . .'

'For ever and ever, time without end, amen,' finished Harry, humbly.

What Time Is It?

RITA LAMB

This is my father's time travel story. It doesn't involve machines. It involves his belief that 'the only real place and time is inside your own head'.

It happened in August 1980, in a room off the geriatric ward of a large hospital. My father was fifteen, and he was there to visit his grandmother Ellen Bates, who was eighty-six, and dying. She'd always been a strong-minded woman, little but sharp, but now she was a frail, light wisp drifting in and out of dreams, only tethered to the world by the saline drip in her arm. The nurses called her 'love' and when she didn't answer them would smile indulgently, thinking she was senile. 'She wasn't,' my father said. 'She just hated to be called "love". By anyone.' My father was her most frequent visitor, coming two or three times a week. He liked his Nana Bates. He was always her favourite grandchild. (He said this was because he was her only male grandchild; she disapproved of modern girls.)

'Nana was fairly lucid until the last two months before she died,' he said. 'Or I suppose you could say she was lucid to the end, but she wasn't always living in the present. Sometimes she was a lucid fourteen-year-old Nell Godrich, trying not to be frightened because she was in a house full of strangers instead of back with her mother and brothers in the cottage where she'd been born. Sometimes she was Nell Bates in her forties, very reasonably worrying about rations and air-raids. When she was confused, it wasn't because she wasn't making sense but because the world wasn't.

'Once I got the hang of guessing from her voice which Nell she was, we got rid of all the confusion. If she was Nell of 1908 and not sure where we were, I'd say she was in the maid's bedroom at Lord Ampner's, because she'd come over to visit her brother Jem at the stables and got a blow on the head from being kicked by a horse. (This had actually happened. She'd told me about it.) And I said the nurse who came in and out was the parlourmaid, and that Jem had gone over to their cottage in the trap to fetch their mother. I knew all about Nell's early life on the Ampner estate, you see. Or I thought I did.

'I learned a lot about her family over those last weeks, things she'd forgotten herself long ago. I mean, whenever she'd mentioned her brothers to me they'd been "my poor elder brother, William" or "your great-uncle James, who died in the war". Very respectful. But now they were just Billy and Jem, and I learned who they were courting and what tricks they'd got up to as schoolboys and what Mother really thought of Billy's intended, Flo Mayhew, who was "a gadding wench". Poor Flo and Billy never did wed, because they were still saving for a place of their own when the war broke out and Billy volunteered. I knew what had happened to both brothers: Jem died at Ypres and Billy was gassed but survived and came back home, only to die the winter after the war, of flu. I had to be careful what I said. Fourteen-year-old Nell didn't know any of this, and wouldn't have thanked me for telling her.

'The evening before the day she died I was sitting by the bed, chatting about my friends—and I actually *was* telling her about my friends, alive in 1980. But since she was in 1908 and hadn't got a son let alone a grandson, she thought I was a boy called Arthur Bell who worked in the stables with Jem, and had permission to sit with her till her mother came; and that it was Arthur telling her about *his* friends in 1908. Well, it was a running joke with her that I'd not got my dog with me, because apparently I was never known to go anywhere without my dog, Bobs. "Arthur Bell and Bobs, always a pair." The room was warm—overheated actually, hospital wards always are—and I felt pleasantly tired. I'd talked, she'd drowsed, I'd fallen quiet. A clock in the distance chimed and she murmured, "What time is it?" "Eleven o'clock," I yawned. I had my eyes closed against the sunshine pouring through the window. I heard a kind of gruff, impatient whine.

' "Oh, you've never brought that dog of yours into the house, have you? Housekeeper'll skin you, Arthur."

'And drowsily I put my hand down to where I felt the warm, heavy head shifting restlessly on my knee, and I stroked the silky crown, and I looked into the puzzled brown eyes of a young dog.

'And was wide awake at once! It wasn't sunny at all. It was evening. It was half-past seven by the electric clock on the wall, and there was no dog anywhere near me.'

Sometimes I contradict my father at this point and insist he'd just dozed off for a moment and dreamed it all.

'Could be,' he'll say. 'Could easily be. But I tell you what. When my mother and my auntie went through Nana's things after she died, they found a photo in an old tarnished frame. It was taken in a stable yard. You can see a clock over the archway in the distance. There's a man standing by a stable door, with a shotgun under his arm, and two youngsters near him, one standing, one sitting down. There's a glossy young mongrel dog at the knee of the seated boy.

' "That one with the gun is her brother William," my auntie said. "We've got a photo of him in uniform. He was a gamekeeper at the Ampners. Wonder if one of the others might be James?"

' "It's the one standing next to William," I said, "because the one sitting down is Arthur Bell."

'Well, I wasn't believed, of course, because how could I know something like that? But when they took the photo out of the frame, there on the back it said *Billy and Jem, with Arthur B.*' '

And at this point my father will describe—rather smugly— how puzzled and vexed his auntie had been.

'Well, how *could* you know him?' she'd asked crossly. 'How the devil d'you know this Arthur Bell?'

'I don't,' my father had answered truthfully. 'I only recognize him because he's with Bobs.'

The Silver Box

LOUISE LAWRENCE

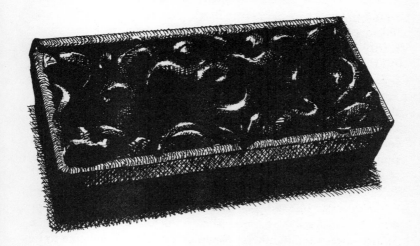

There was nothing special about number Forty Seven. It was indistinguishable from all the other houses in Gossington Square, part of a Victorian terrace divided into flats, its stone façade showing signs of decay. Rooms were big and gloomy and full of draughts, and during the day most of the residents were out.

Carole took a throat lozenge from the silver box, sat on the window seat and watched the snow. Lime trees at the centre of the Square looked black against the whirling whiteness and the street was empty of traffic and people. Except for Carole the house was empty too . . . everyone away at work . . . her mother teaching at the comprehensive school . . . Mrs Dawkins from downstairs helping in the Oxfam shop . . . and the man from the basement gone to his office.

And overhead the attic flat was once more unoccupied. Someone had died there, Mrs Dawkins claimed. A housemaid whose sweetheart had been killed in the First World War had committed suicide, and no one stayed for very long. Carole did not believe in ghosts, but the house creaked with stillness and the silence oppressed her. She was sick of being alone.

She had glandular fever, the doctor said. It was caused by a virus and was slightly contagious so she should not return to school until after Easter. Now it was January and Carole had nothing to look forward to for the next three months but paracetamols and a pain in the neck, headaches and fatigue and feelings of grottiness, and a fluctuating temperature that made reality look strange. Perspectives were unstable. Walls seemed either too near, or too far away. The floor had a slope to it and the wind rattling the window got on her nerves.

Carole shivered and returned to bed. A sensible move, except that most of it was occupied by a fat black and white cat. Officially Splodge belonged to Mrs Dawkins and was there on loan to keep Carole company until Mrs Dawkins returned at one o'clock to prepare the lunch. But all he ever did was sleep, warm and heavy in the place where her legs ought to be.

'Shove over, you great dozy beast!' Carole said irritably.

Green eyes opened, glared at her in annoyance, before he curled and settled again in the crook of her knees. When Splodge was sleeping, Mrs Dawkins said, he did not like to be disturbed. And in consideration Carole was trapped there for the rest of the morning.

Lonely and boring, the hours stretched endlessly ahead. She might have switched on the radio or studied her school books, but listening to music made her headache worse and she could not concentrate. Curled with the cat she tried to sleep but then she grew hot and sweaty and small sounds distracted her . . . the whine of the wind down the boarded-up chimney, the flutter of snow against the window pane, and the creak of a floorboard. It was as if someone were there, quietly moving at the far end of her room. Carole raised her head. She saw nothing unusual . . . just a shimmer of heated air above the electric convector heater and the walls receding into distances, the effects of her fever. But the sounds went on, movements and footsteps, soft and disturbing. And did she imagine the room was growing dark?

There was a humming noise too, like high frequency static almost beyond the range of her hearing. Once more Carole raised her head and for one panic-stricken moment she thought she was going blind. There was light around her bed but the rest of the room had vanished, dissolved in a curtain of shimmering air and darkness beyond it. Or maybe something was wrong with the convector heater? The electronic hum was clearer now, increasing in pitch. Even the cat could hear it. And they moved together, Carole and Splodge, propelled by the same fear. He rose from the bed with green eyes blazing, arched and spat and bolted for the door, his tail bushed as a fox's brush . . . and she switched off the convector heater and made to follow.

But the humming noise ceased and the shimmering grew steady, hung as a veil of sheer air from ceiling to floor, and beyond it the room was still there. Carole paused to stare, her curiosity conquering her fear. It was as if she were seeing into another world. It was morning where she stood but there it was night. A full moon shone through a broken window and trees in leaf made flickering shadows on the floor. She could smell warmth and flowers and sweet summer air, and in the room a smell of musty decay. She sensed, rather than saw, that time had changed. The house was old. Paper peeled from the walls, the ceiling sagged and the floorboards rotted. It was long ago, thought Carole, or maybe not. She noticed wires and cables, arc lights and cameras and video-recorders, computer terminals and electronic equipment. It was as if her room had been turned into a television studio or the set for a horror film.

Unless she was dreaming?

'Hold it!' said a voice.

'What now?' asked another.

'There's a definite energy reading here.'

'It's probably a rat.'

'Just let me check.'

Suddenly someone appeared beyond the wall of wavering air. For all it was dark at that end of the room Carole could see him quite clearly . . . a boy in a black catsuit, his fair curls blowing in the wind. She saw the silver shine of his wristwatch, slim limbs, and the flash of his smile. And through him she saw the window frame, the moon through his face, the stars behind his eyes. He was there and yet not there. Beautiful, she thought, and as transparent as a ghost.

'Hey, Zak!' he said excitedly. 'Come and take a look!'

'No way, screwball!' the other replied. 'I'm not falling for that.'

'This is for real, Zak. We've actually got one!'

'A grey rat or black?'

'A girl standing by an antique bed. She has long brown hair and is wearing a floral nightdress buttoned to the neck. It's pink and old-fashioned and she's very pale. We've done it, Zak!'

'Bullshit!' Zak replied.

He too came suddenly into view . . . another ghost, big and bearded and bespectacled, scruffy as a student, with some unreadable slogan printed on the whiteness of his T-shirt. By his accent Carole guessed he was American and although he stared directly at her she had the peculiar feeling he was unable to see her, that in some way she was invisible. His words confirmed it.

'You're imagining things, buddy.'

'What do you mean?' the fair one asked.

'There's nothing there but the wall.'

'Don't be ridiculous! She's as clear as day!'

'Are you bullshitting me, Matt?'

'No,' Matt said earnestly. 'I'm telling you, Zak. Believe me . . . she *is* there.'

Carole was there all right. She had long brown hair and was wearing a floral nightdress just as Matt had described. But Zak saw no one and nor was he about to be convinced. The experimenter influenced the experiment, he said, and Matt was seeing what he wanted to see. His own hyped mind had produced the energy reading, *and* Carole. She was a mental projection, not a genuine phenomenon. Matt shifted the tripod and set up the camera. Seeing was believing, he retorted, and he believed Carole was real. And on heat-sensitive film her outline was bound to show. She watched him in annoyance. He did not behave as if she were real. He did not ask permission or ask if she minded, explain who he was or what he was doing there.

'Smile please,' he told her.

And something snapped.

'Get out of my bedroom!' Carole said. 'You've got no right to come barging in here and take my photograph! Who the hell do you think you are?'

Matt seemed to freeze in the flickering moonlight.
Then clutched Zak's arm.
'Did you hear that?' he said.
'What?' asked Zak.
'She spoke.'
'Leave it out!'
'I'm telling you, Zak. Who the hell are we, she said.'

It was a peculiar meeting . . . Matt in the midnight darkness and
Carole in the morning light with the veiled air shimmering
between them. His full name was Matthew Boyd-Hamilton
with a hyphen, he said, and Zak was over from the United States
on a two-year student exchange. They were both studying
parapsychology at the nearby university and Carole was vital
to their experiment. She did not understand the technicalities
of time displacement and psychokinetic traceability, but she
agreed to take part. After all, Matt was very good-looking even
if he was a ghost, and talking to him was better than being bored
and alone.

'So what do you want me to do?' she asked him.

'Scientifically,' he said, 'we need to prove you exist.'

'Isn't it obvious?'

'To you and me, maybe. But say-so isn't enough. It's not
enough to convince Zak, let alone the board of examiners.'

'So what do you want me to do?' Carole repeated.

Zak, who was an electronics expert, set up the equipment and
ran through a series of tests. Portable computers flickered and
buzzed but apart from the original bleep of the energy pulse
Carole failed to register. Nor did she show on the heat-sensitive
video-camera, in infra-red or ultraviolet light. Except to Matt
she remained invisible and inaudible, her existence unproven.
In other words, said Zak, she was not really there.

'Are you calling me a liar?' asked Matt.

Carole took a throat lozenge from the silver box and waited
while they argued. Whatever Carole was, said Matt, a mental
projection or an independent entity, they needed to find out.
And when high technology failed, human minds came into their
own. Zak's machines were not infallible. And what was wrong
with a tape recorder and common sense? If they could verify
whatever information Carole gave them . . .

'*If*,' said Zak.

'It's worth a try,' said Matt.

'Would you like a blackcurrant throat sweet?' Carole asked.

'No!' said Matt . . . then turned towards her, as if he suddenly remembered she was there. 'No thanks,' he said. 'If you touch the circuit you'll probably break it and we're not into experiments of telekinesis.'

'What's she saying?' Zak asked suspiciously.

'She says . . .'

Matt hesitated, regarded Carole thoughtfully, as if for a moment he too doubted her reality or else she had no right to be chewing sweets in his company. She closed the box, saw his eyes following her movements, the pressure of her fingers on the hinged lid.

'What's wrong?' she asked him.

'Nothing,' he said.

'That's what I mean,' said Zak. 'If everything she says is inaudible it's not going to work, is it?'

But it did work. For the benefit of Zak and the tape recorder Matt repeated everything Carole said. It was very mundane, just details of her name and age, where and when she had been born, which Zak intended to check with the Central Records Office. And even that much seemed questionable, as if the date of her birth was not as they had expected. She had to produce the calendar for confirmation. She had been born sixteen years ago, she insisted, and now it was 1987 . . . January 21st 1987. Outside it was snowing . . . Mrs Thatcher was Prime Minister . . . and why on earth should she remember the First World War?

'Zak?' said Matt.

'Yeh,' said Zak. 'I heard.'

'Someone's goofed. Your time displacement machine has got to be faulty.'

'How about your imagination, buddy?'

'If I were making her up she'd fit the preconceived image,' argued Matt. 'She'd have a mop and a feather duster and the date would be 1917. Right? That means . . .'

'OK!' said Zak. 'That *suggests* she's genuine, existing in her own right and nothing to do with you. But *if* she's genuine how come I don't see her? And how come on all this psycho-sensitive equipment she doesn't show?'

Matt shook his head. The moon was gone and infra-red light made all things colourless, stripped him of clarity and dissolved him to a shadow, as if he were hardly there at all. And Zak too was no more than a grey shade restlessly prowling, checking and re-checking the vision screens and print-outs, leaving his footprints on the dusty floor. He made Carole feel responsible, as if she ought to apologize for being what she was. Instead she shivered, not knowing what to say.

The room had grown cold without the convector heater. She could feel the chill of the night wind through the broken window and Matt's eyes watching her, intense and curious, as she reached for her dressing gown. It was pale blue quilted, she heard him tell Zak, and she was obviously sensitive to temperature, reacting to her own space-time environment. And now she was taking a blackcurrant throat lozenge from a silver box . . . similar to a box his mother had at home on her dressing table which had been handed down through the family.

'You want me to go on?' asked Matt.

'No,' growled Zak. 'I've heard enough!'

'But it's odd, don't you think?'

'You ought to be on stage, Boyd-Hamilton!'

'Two blackcurrant lozenges in half an hour . . . why should I imagine that?'

'I've got glandular fever,' Carole told him.

'She says she has glandular fever,' said Matt.

'What?' Zak said sharply.

'Glandular fever,' Matt repeated.

There was a moment of silence.

'Shucks!' said Zak. 'I take it all back.'

'You mean I've finally said something right?' asked Carole.

Matt smiled, picked up a fragment of mortar from the floor and aimlessly threw it. It should have landed at Carole's feet but the shimmering air absorbed it, absorbed the throat lozenge Carole aimed at him. He smiled again at her effort. It was a barrier, he said, which nothing could pass through and it was not just space between them but time as well. He glanced at his wristwatch. One hundred and thirty-five years, six months, two days, and fourteen hours to be precise, he said. In his time it was July 23rd 2121.

Carole gaped at him. Even when Matt explained it was not imaginable. She could not envisage a hundred and thirty-five years into the future. England was ruled from Brussels, he told her. Energy came from the sun and there was no nuclear power, no major world problems and not much political dissension. And the latest American space ship was about to take off for the stars. There was not a soul left alive who remembered when Carole lived. The twentieth century was ancient history and Gossington Square was derelict and due to be demolished.

'That's why we're here,' said Matt. 'There aren't many old houses left. This is the only one in the area which is empty and reputed to be haunted. It's not exactly safe but we had to take the chance. A couple of weeks from now the house will be flattened and its ghosts will be gone.'

'Are you saying you're a ghost-buster?' Carole asked him.

'That's right,' said Matt. 'And you're busted. We were hoping for the housemaid who committed suicide but we'll settle for you.'

'I'm not a ghost!' Carole said indignantly.

'Aren't you?' Matt said quietly.

Her insides lurched. His smile was sad and he was looking at her gently, tenderly, not wanting to distress her but wanting her to understand . . . from where he stood, one hundred and thirty-five years in the future, Carole was dead. She thought she must have died without knowing it, that very morning, before she had even lived. She wanted to scream and deny it, tell him he was wrong, that she was still alive and would go on living, but then Mrs Dawkins came into the room.

'How are you feeling, my dear?'

Carole froze, looked towards Matt, but it seemed Mrs Dawkins did not see him. She simply walked through the curtain of shimmering air and picked up the throat lozenge that lay on the carpet . . . and as she did so, everything vanished. The room was as it had been before, wintry and cold, with snow fluttering against the window pane and the clock on the mantelpiece saying ten past one.

Carole was dead, Matt had said, but she did not tell her mother. Even to her own mind it seemed crazy. Yet she needed to convince herself she was alive. She noticed the heat in the bathroom and the scent of talc, the taste of kedgeree her mother cooked for supper. And that night she lay awake feeling the blankets rough and warm to her touch, remembering the television serial she had sat and watched, hearing the tick of the clock, the rattle of the window, and the whine of the wind in the chimney breast. All those things assured her she was alive. Unless they were illusions?

Maybe, she thought, life was a dream and when she awoke she would find herself dead? Or maybe Matt had been an omen? A cold moon shone on the snow in Gossington Square and she was afraid to sleep, afraid to let go of her awareness of herself and the world. And in the morning, when her mother drew back the curtains, Carole was pale and tired and dark shadows ringed her eyes. She looked like death warmed up, her mother said.

'Maybe it's terminal,' Carole said agitatedly.

'What?' enquired her mother.

'Glandular fever.'

'That's highly unlikely,' her mother replied.

It was a kind of reassurance and Carole's own common sense told her that ghosts didn't need to eat breakfast or write school essays, did not stub their toes on the table leg or suffer from headaches and swollen glands. They did not fancy other ghosts either, but Carole spent the morning waiting and hoping Matt would return, materialize from the thin air of her room . . . a ghost from the future as she was a ghost from the past. Nothing happened. Her eyes grew leaden and heat shimmered above the convector fire . . . and Mrs Dawkins woke her at one o'clock with chicken soup for lunch.

Had it not been for Splodge Carole might have believed she had invented the whole incident. But that cat was behaving very peculiarly, Mrs Dawkins said. He had spent yesterday afternoon and evening crouching behind the sofa and refusing to come out. And earlier that morning, when Mrs Dawkins had picked him up intending to bring him upstairs for Carole, he had sworn and struggled like a wildcat and finally scratched her, fled downstairs to the basement boiler room and escaped through the partly open window.

'I can't think what's come over him,' Mrs Dawkins said worriedly.

Carole knew. A couple of ghost-busters from AD 2121 had scared Splodge half to death. And all afternoon she heard Mrs Dawkins calling across the back gardens. It made her feel guilty thinking of Splodge out in the cold snow, cowering among the cabbages and afraid to come home, while she sat by the convector heater wanting nothing more than for Matt and Zak to reappear and feeling disappointed they did not.

Cats had short memories. Splodge returned the following morning, but as the days went by Carole's disappointment turned to depression. The snow melted and snowdrops bloomed beneath the lime trees in the Square and Matt's absence haunted her. She thought she would not have minded if he *had* proved her to be a ghost because her life, as it was, was hardly worth living. She was sick of having glandular fever, sick of being confined to the house, fed up with everything.

'I might as well be dead!' she announced.

Her mother was marking school exercise books.

'Why's that?' she said.

'Well, what's there to live for?' Carole asked.

'There's next week's episode of *Dallas*.'

'Who cares about *Dallas*?'

'Tomorrow's dinner then?'

'I'm being serious,' Carole said cuttingly.

'So am I,' her mother replied. 'What else do we live for but the little mundane things of life? If we sit around waiting for the few rare, wonderful moments that make it all worthwhile we may as well not live at all.'

'That's what I meant!' said Carole.

'You'll get over it,' her mother promised.

Splodge got over it. Accompanied by Mrs Dawkins he made a few nervous forays into Carole's room and, finding nothing to alarm him, took up residence again on the candlewick counterpane. He was better than no one, Carole supposed. And when February began with two days of freezing rain she followed Splodge's example, sighed and forgot . . . until she awoke that night and saw beyond the wall of shimmering air the room full of sunset light and Matt standing there. It was four in the morning according to the clock on the mantelpiece, and Carole did not know if she were glad or furious, or how to react.

'Where have you been?' she hissed.

'Checking,' he told her.

'Where's Zak?'

'He's checking too . . . at the Central Records Office.'

Carole draped her dressing gown around her shoulders.

'So how long does it take?' she asked him. 'You've been checking for ten days already and all I gave you was my name and address!'

Matt looked surprised. The sunset was brassy behind him and trees drooped in the summer heat. Owls hooted in the derelict Square. When Mrs Dawkins had entered the room the time circuit had snapped, he explained. He had tried to get back to her as quickly as possible but obviously the passage of time in past and future was not the same. Carole's ten days was his yesterday and his early evening was the middle of her night.

'I'm sorry,' he said honestly.

She was glad anyway, glad he was back, but with her mother sleeping in the next bedroom their conversation had to be in whispers. He needed to talk to her, he said, alone, before Zak returned from the Central Records Office. Something had been worrying him, nagging at his mind ever since Carole had first appeared. It was not just the fact that he could see and hear her and Zak could not, nor was it the fact that the machines failed to register her presence . . . it was the fact that her behaviour was inconsistent with any known psychic phenomenon. In other words she did not act like a ghost.

'Nor do you,' Carole told him.

'Well, I'm not a ghost,' he said.

'Yes, you are,' said Carole. 'You don't have any substance and I can see straight through you, so what else can you be? And if I'm dead to you then you're dead to me . . . or rather, you're not yet born. I mean, why should I have to prove I'm real when you're not real either?'

Matt stared at her.

'I don't understand,' he said.

'Now you know how I feel,' Carole told him.

Matt ran a hand through his blond unruly curls. He was as confused as she had been for the last ten days, her mind going around in circles trying to work it out. Now it was his turn to think himself a ghost. She could see the stones of the wall through the catsuit he was wearing, the broken window through his eyes. They were blue, she thought, bright as a midday sky. But the impression faded among leaves of trees and the roseate hues of sunset. She was a ghost seeing a ghost and was tempted to laugh, but maybe it was not so funny. Surrounded by midwinter darkness and all the trappings of her own reality, Carole ached with the sheer impossibility of knowing him.

'What *is* this?' he asked her.

'I don't know,' she replied.

'I'm alive, so I can't be a ghost.'

'In that case I'm not one either because I'm alive too.'

'That's impossible.'

'But it's true,' said Carole.

'Zak's never going to believe it.'

'But you do?' Carole asked anxiously.

'I suppose that's why I wanted to talk to you,' he said.

'So what do we do now?'

'Prove it?' he sighed.

Carole approached the veil of shimmering air. Matt was beyond it, so close that she thought she could touch him if she reached out her hand. Maybe he read her mind and knew her feelings, wanted her to be real just as she wanted him. Or maybe they did not think at all. Time had no meaning until Carole stepped into it and found herself alone. The room was dark. Rain lashed the window glass. Matt and the summer world and the hoot of owls were gone.

Several days passed before Matt reappeared. Carole was sitting in the armchair beside the convector heater writing an essay on the French Revolution, when she heard the hum of the time displacement machine. She held her breath as the shimmering air dissolved the walls and window and the morning faded to a future midnight. Both Matt and Zak were there but she had no chance to speak to them for Splodge, asleep on the bed, suddenly awoke and was aware.

He seemed to go berserk, a madcat spitting and swearing and trying to escape. Ears flattened, tail fluffed and belly touching the floor, he headed for the door, found it shut and fled beneath the bed, emerged on the other side and shot through the time barrier before Carole could stop him. Claws raked the velvet curtains. Jigsaws and the Monopoly set, stored on top of the wardrobe, fell as he leapt. And there he stayed, cowering behind a wicker basket full of dolls' clothes, peering down with green eyes bigger than gobstoppers and a slightly puzzled expression on his splodgy black and white face. He had broken the circuit. The room was as it should be. February sunlight lay bright on the pink patterned carpet and only Carole was mad.

'You great stupid idiot!' she yelled.

She left the door open, spent the rest of the day sorting out thousands of jigsaw pieces, and what should have been a beautiful encounter had been ended before it began. Then her fever, which had abated, returned worse than ever. Her head throbbed, and paracetamols ceased to have any effect, and even in bed she had to wear a woollen scarf tied tight around her neck to ease the pain. Her mother filled hot-water bottles before she left for school and each morning, on her way to the Oxfam shop, Mrs Dawkins looked in and made her a honey-and-lemon drink.

Freezing mist hung outside the window, made ghostly the lime trees that grew in the Square and isolated Carole from the world. Not that she cared. Snuggled in bed with the cat she felt miserable enough to want to be left alone and she was not particularly pleased when the room started buzzing and shimmering, Splodge had another nervous breakdown in his hurry to escape, and Matt and Zak re-established their connections.

'Carole?' said Matt.

Clouds hid the moon and a flashlight shone on crumbling walls, touched the bright elusive blue of his eyes. DON'T BUG ME, the slogan on Zak's T-shirt said. Their voices seemed to come from far away, from a future England in the grip of a heatwave. And how could it be only an hour since Splodge broke the circuit? Only yesterday that Carole had last talked with Matt? Days and weeks were muddled in her head but it was some consolation to learn that she was not about to die of glandular fever. Zak had traced her birth certificate, Matt informed her, but had found no record of her death. Presumably she was going to live and marry and change her name, but as twentieth-century records were not computerized he could not tell her who her future husband would be. Having met Matt, Carole was not really interested anyway, and nor was Zak. Her future was beside the point, he said. And finding her birth certificate might prove she had existed once, but it did not prove she existed now, either as a living person or a ghost.

'If she's real we need evidence!' said Zak.

'We could try some awareness tests,' suggested Matt.

'Right now I don't feel like it,' Carole said.

'Yes,' said Matt. 'Something like that. You feel, therefore you are, and that makes two of us. But I'm not sure about Zak.'

Now and then, Carole could never tell when, but throughout their hot July nights where buff moths fluttered and her February mornings of frost and sun and rain, she tried to convince Zak she was a thinking, feeling, living human being. Her breath made mist on the cold surface of a mirror. She bled when she was scratched, burned when she touched a naked flame. She could deduce, debate, argue, agree or disagree, laugh, cry, hate and love. Yet she could prove nothing because Matt was her only witness and he could be making her up. Not even when she read a passage from a daily paper which checked out verbatim, was Zak convinced. It could be some weird telepathic link-up, he said, Matt's mind picking up vibes from the past.

'What does it take?' Carole asked despairingly.

'After five hundred repeat performances he might be swayed,' said Matt. 'You know what they say about scientists? If they can't dissect something or examine it under a microscope then it doesn't exist. At least you have God for company.'

'And you,' Carole said softly.

'I'm beginning to wish,' he replied.

'If we were really ghosts . . .'

'Don't,' he said gently.

'If there were just some way . . .'

'There isn't.'

But maybe there was, Carole thought afterwards. Flies caught in amber survived through geological aeons and time capsules were sent into space, or buried under concrete for future generations to find. There had to be something Carole could give that would survive a mere one hundred and thirty-five years, something that would reach Matt and prove to Zak she were real. All night Carole thought of it, eager for morning and needing to act. And it was nothing to do with glandular fever that her eyes shone and her cheeks were flushed. She actually felt better, she told her mother.

Later, when the house was empty and Mrs Dawkins had gone with the shopping trolley to collect the weekly groceries, Carole wrote Matt a letter. She enclosed it with a photograph, a lock of her hair, and a blackcurrant throat lozenge, inside the silver box. At home he had one like it, he had said, but this box was Carole's. It was engraved with vine leaves and cherubs and had been given to her by her grandmother before she died. Carefully Carole wrapped it in newspaper and sealed it in a polythene bag. Then she fetched tools from the kitchen, prised away the boarding and placed the package on a ledge in the chimney. Her hands were black with soot and she had to hammer the bent nails straight before she could fix the board back into position. Exertion made her feel ill again but she knew it would be worth it, worth everything to prove herself alive.

February gave way to March. Crocuses bloomed, yellow and purple beneath the lime trees in the Square, and sparrows nested. If the weather was fine, the doctor said, it might do Carole some good to go outside for a breath of fresh air. But she staged a relapse, fearing Matt might appear when she were gone. And the next morning her relapse was genuine. Her head ached, her temperature was up, and the glands in her neck pained something awful. And, spooked once too often, Splodge refused to keep her company, clawed his way from Mrs Dawkins's arms and fled. She spent the day in bed and alone, wondering all over again if she would ever recover.

'Of course you will,' her mother said positively.

'Maybe I don't want to,' Carole said dramatically. 'Maybe I'd rather die and fall in love with a ghost.'

Her mother laughed.

'Love is a symptom of life,' she said. 'But the dead are dead and don't have feelings.'

And that was proof, thought Carole. When Matt read her letter he would know for sure she was alive. Each new day dawned with a kind of nervous anticipation, an experience of relief when her mother went to school and Mrs Dawkins left for the Oxfam shop, a morning of waiting and hoping, another disappointment. Then someone moved into the upstairs flat. A music student with long hair, Mrs Dawkins said disapprovingly. And Carole had something else to contend with. She listened to his footsteps walking the floors overhead, the sound of his radio, the flush of water, and the slam of his door. She heard him practising endless scales on a clarinet. He was not intrusive exactly, not over-loud and inconsiderate, yet he was there and she was constantly aware of him. She felt inhibited and no longer free, afraid that when Matt came back she might be overheard and her secret discovered. She wanted the house to herself again, hoped the ghost of the housemaid would drive him away but, to the plaintive notes of a clarinet concerto, it finally happened.

The still air shimmered and wet grey daylight beyond the window slowly darkened to a July night. Carole forgot about the student. There was a thrill inside her and her heart beat faster, and the music was gone in a rumble of thunder and a deluge of summer rain. White with plaster dust and opaque as milk, it dripped through the ceiling and splattered on to the floor, and behind Matt's eyes she saw the lightning flicker, saw the flash of his smile.

'How are you, Carole?'

'Better,' she breathed.

But Zak was in no mood for preliminaries. He was worried about the effects of the lightning on his time displacement machine, about safety factors and the roof falling in and the fact he was getting wet. Tape recorder at the ready, Zak simply wanted to collect the routine data and return to campus. Never mind how Carole was feeling, he said. All Matt needed to ask was the time and date, what the weather was doing and the main newspaper headlines which they could check with the met. office and archives in the morning . . . then they could both go home.

'Because I'm not hanging around here all night while you chat up the wall,' Zak concluded.

'No one asked you to,' Matt informed him.

'So why don't you stick to the business in hand?'

'Why don't you push off right now?' Matt suggested.

'And leave you in charge of my equipment?' said Zak. 'No way, buddy! Besides, I might miss something.'

Matt sighed, turned to Carole.

'That's the trouble with gooseberries,' he said. 'They're too thick-skinned to understand.'

Carole laughed.

'He will in a minute,' she promised.

'I doubt it,' said Matt.

But Carole had written Matt a letter. It would prove she was real, she said, that she had been aware of him and Zak from the moment she had met them. She had written it down, everything that had happened, all her perceptions and all her feelings. She had put it on a ledge up the chimney, in the silver box. And maybe it was not exactly scientific but it was the only thing she could think of which was part of herself, the only thing she could give Matt which was likely to survive . . . a letter, a lock of her hair, and a blackcurrant throat lozenge.

'What's she say?' asked Zak impatiently.

'She says . . .'

Matt shook his head, grinned, then laughed in delight. His eyes shone blue in the torchlight. 'You're beautiful,' he told Carole, and turned away.

'So what's she say?' Zak repeated.

'Wait and I'll show you,' said Matt.

Lightning flashed on the fairness of his hair, and the ceiling dripped and bulged as he approached the chimney breast. There the darkness absorbed him. Carole heard the rotting wood give way as he tore at the boarding, heard Zak's warning cry. She hardly knew what happened next. There was a noise like thunder and her scream mixed with Zak's as the roof beam fell and Matt was buried under tons of rubble. Then there was only Zak, tearing at the stones and plaster chunks and trying to free him, a ghost in the torchlight unashamedly weeping, knowing, when he found him, Matt would be injured or dead.

Carole wept too, loudly and hysterically, not caring that the door opened or who came into the room. He wore blue denim jeans and all she could do was scream at him . . . 'Help him! Help him!' . . . watch as he walked towards the shimmering curtain of air and Zak dragged out the body.

'Dead!' sobbed Zak. 'Oh, no . . . not you, Matt!'

Then it was over, ended, everything gone. The circuit was broken and Carole was left in the wet grey morning, heart-broken and wretched, with a total stranger.

He spread his hands.

'There was nothing I could do,' he said sadly.

'No,' choked Carole.

'And you don't need to be upset. They were only ghosts and that's how ghosts behave. They relive the moments of their deaths over and over. I've got one upstairs. She walks around my bedroom with a carving knife and there's nothing I can do for her either.'

'You don't understand,' sobbed Carole.

'No one can change the past,' he said gently.

'But Matt lived in the future!' wept Carole. 'And it's my fault he's dead. I didn't need to prove I was real because he knew anyway. If I hadn't put that box up the chimney . . .'

The student was kind and quiet, lending her his handkerchief, making her sit in the kitchen and making her coffee, listening as she talked. He did not say she was crazy or imagining things, or that he himself would have to be mad to believe her. He did not say anything, just listened and waited until she was done. Rain in the ensuing silence fell softly on the roof of the outhouse and the window steamed as Carole wiped her eyes for the thousandth time and finally looked at him. He was staring thoughtfully at the dregs in his coffee cup . . . a young man with fair shoulder-length hair and bright blue eyes. For some reason he reminded her of Matt and once more the silly tears began to flow.

'What'll I do?' she whimpered. 'How can I live with it, knowing that I caused his death? How can I bear it?'

He pushed back his chair.

'Maybe you won't have to,' he said. 'It hasn't happened yet, has it? Not for Matt. For him it won't happen for another hundred and thirty-five years. We can't change the past but we can change the future. Do you have a screwdriver or something?'

Uncomprehendingly Carole dragged her mother's toolbox from the broom cupboard, watched him select a claw hammer and disappear into the bedroom. The nails gave way easily and he prised away the board that sealed the chimney, returned a minute later with the silver box in his hand. If Carole got rid of it, he said, then Matt would have no reason to go to the chimney breast, no reason to be standing there when the ceiling fell. He would not die and she would not be responsible. And was it really as simple as that?

She watched him open the pedal bin.

'Yes?' he asked.

Carole hesitated. The box was an heirloom. It was old and valuable and somehow it seemed wrong to throw it away. Yet she did not want to keep it. It bound her to Matt and her own memories, to the distant future when he would be living and she would be dead. She supposed she could sell it to an antique shop but that seemed wrong too.

'Yes?' the student repeated.

'No,' said Carole.

She took it from him, tipped the contents in the bin, then handed it back.

'You keep it,' she said.

He frowned.

'Are you sure?'

'Please,' she said earnestly. 'I'd like you to have it.'

He smiled then, and his smile was like Matt's. He would treasure it, he promised, use it as a paper weight and think of her. Dull silver it shone in his hand and she felt it belonged with him, that by giving it to him she had not parted with it at all, or parted with Matt. She had the peculiar feeling that nothing had changed because nothing had happened and the future began in his eyes. She was glad she had met him, grateful for all he had done, for his blond hair and his bright blue eyes and the squeeze of her arm when he turned to go. But Splodge, washing his backside on the landing carpet, took one look at him and fled.

'What's up with the cat?' he asked.

'He thinks he's seen a ghost,' said Carole.

And in a way Splodge had.

'My name, by the way, is John Boyd-Hamilton with a hyphen,' the student said. 'Fancy coming for a pizza on Saturday night?'

The Picnic

PENELOPE LIVELY

I hate picnics. There's all this fuss about finding a nice place, and then when you've found it there'll be too much wind, or wasps, or a cow-pat, and when everybody's settled down you can be sure something they can't do without will have been left in the car, half a mile away. And it'll be me that's got to go back and get it because I'm the eldest. 'Just pop back and get the rug, Michael—it won't take you a minute—and while you're there you might get Jamie's windcheater, and Dad's pipe, and my glasses, and the baby's bottle . . .'

I hate picnics.

Our picnics are usually to celebrate something. We're a ceremonial family: anniversaries of this, that, and the other; birthdays—even down to the dog's—nothing gets left out. This was Jamie's birthday. Eight. And Jamie, of course, has to pick Bodmin Moor.

'Draughty,' said Gran. 'I'll stop home in the garden, if nobody minds.'

But they weren't having any of that, the parents. We're a united family, too: positively tribal. One goes, we all go.

'Nonsense,' said Mum. 'It's not going to be draughty in June. Middle of the summer, you couldn't ask for better.'

'The Summer Solstice, in fact,' said Dad, with his pocket-diary open. And then we get a great long disquisition, for Jamie and Gran, about how the solstices are the time of year between the equinoxes when the sun is furthest from the equator and appears to stand still. Yawn, yawn.

And so we fetched up at the Hurlers at half-past eleven on Jamie's birthday, picnic-baskets in hand, dog on lead, baby in pram, sun shoved firmly behind a black wodge of cloud and likely to stay there as far as I could see. Lovely picnic weather.

Gran thought it was a funny place to choose for a picnic. 'Too bare. And it's industrial. All those chimneys.'

I put her right about the chimneys—quietly, not to get anyone upset. 'Does being historic tin-mines make them look nicer?' she said, and we had a bit of a giggle about that. She's all right, Gran. But of course it wasn't the tin-mines we'd come to see. They're great on having an objective, the parents. We never just go anywhere—we go there to see something. Though in this case, as usual, old Mum gave it one quick look and then was off getting settled in. Finding a nice place out of the wind, somewhere for the pram, a bit of dry grass to sit on, all that . . .

The Hurlers aren't all that much to look at, granted. A bit stumpy, the stones are, sticking up out of the gorse and stuff—in fact at first they seem just accidental so that it comes as a bit of a jolt when you realize they are in fact arranged in circles. Even so, they're not on nodding terms with Stonehenge and that lot. We all dealt with them in our own way: Mum didn't bother, Gran had a look round, found herself a nice comfy one to lean against and got her knitting out, Jamie climbed three of them and jumped off again, Toby (the dog) lifted his leg against the biggest and then went rabbiting, Dad held forth to me because nobody else was listening.

'Prehistoric.'

'Yes, Dad. How old?' Politely.

That had him floored, as I knew it would, so I told him, because as a matter of fact I'd looked them up in the Cornwall book at school, the day before. 'Bronze Age, they think, but nobody's all that sure exactly when. The Beaker People or the Urn People or one of those lots.'

'Taken over now by the Picnic People,' said Dad. Not all that good a joke, but we enjoyed it until Mum called out—wait for it—that she'd left the newspaper and the baby's feeder in the car and would Michael just pop back for it.

So off I trailed. Mind, it wasn't that far—I've known worse. You could see the car, and the other one that had been there when we'd come. Mum was annoyed about that—she likes having places to herself. We're a territorial family, too. She gave it a few nasty looks, but when we got up to the stone circles the other people were some way away, camped on the rising ground nearer the Cheesewring, with *their* picnic and *their* folding-stools and *their* rugs and cameras and newspapers.

'That's all right,' said Mum. 'They're nowhere near. And they look nice.' Mum's an expert in niceness. It conducts itself for her, like electricity. She knows if people moving into our street are nice before they've got the removal van unloaded.

'Anyway,' said Gran, 'you like to know there's someone else around. You don't want to be on your own, do you, not really.'

'Why not?' said Jamie.

'Well—if one of us had an accident or something . . .'

'Listen to you!' said Mum. 'I thought this was a celebration.'

Coming back from the car I had a bit of a think about the stone circles, and what they were for, and all that. Which nobody really knows, of course. *Of religious significance*, the book said, vaguely, and then it waffled on a bit about rites and rituals, meaning, I suppose, that it hadn't a clue really. Of course it's a ritual—any fool can see that. Just like you draw squares on the beach and play hopscotch in them. But what ritual? You couldn't guess hopscotch from the squares, not in a hundred years. There was a slightly gruesome bit in the book about the bones of sacrifices being found near similar stone circles on Dartmoor, and a lot about tribal warfare which made you realize that it must have been more than somewhat dicey living in those days. It's bad enough now, with cars zooming at you and pollution and all that, but at least I know Mr Davidson next door isn't likely to stick a knife in me.

I was wrapped in thought, as they say (they actually do—'Wrapped in thought, Michael?' Dad says. Mind, he's got a point, I daresay—it's something I'm known for and apparently it can be more than a bit irritating), and dawdling, I suppose. When I looked back at the Hurlers I could see Mum standing up waving. Hurry up, she meant, not hello, how nice to see you again. It was twelve exactly, my watch said—I hadn't been gone that long—but I ran a bit, or at least I trotted because I'm in favour of a quiet life and Mum can get stroppy if she's kept waiting.

I tripped over a stone or something once, and came down a cropper on the grass. Just as I got up, the sun came out. At least it came out in one place but not in another, if you see what I mean, so that where I was it was still grey and dull but over there at the Hurlers, and beyond, all the way up the slope beyond, it was bright sun. Funny. You could see the shafts of sunshine streaming down onto Mum and the rest of them, and the other family in their picnic place. I could see them very clearly, all standing or sitting quite still, as though they were kind of frozen by sun, I thought. Silly idea.

And then the wodge of cloud plonked itself back again and it went grey. I arrived at where the family were and gave Mum the paper and the feeder, but she seemed abstracted. She didn't even say thank you, which was odd, because one thing you can say is that Mum's got nice manners. Outside the family as well as in. Everybody likes Mum. She'd got the picnic all laid out but she was staring over towards the other family all the time.

We sat down and Mum began dishing out sandwiches. After a minute she said, 'You know, they've moved. They've come a bit nearer.'

And Dad said, 'Yes, I think they have.' He was staring too.

I looked. They'd put themselves into a bit where the gorse made a wind-break, the other family.

There was a pause. Mum was unscrewing thermoses. And then all of a sudden she said, 'They've got no business.'

I looked at her. Her voice sounded most peculiar—kind of strangled. She really meant it. She minded.

'Oh, come on, Mum,' I said. 'They've got as much right here as us.' She took no notice of that and what's more neither did anyone else. They were all looking over at the other family. Gran had put down her knitting and was muttering to herself. It was extraordinary.

They weren't eating yet, the other family. You could see all their stuff, in baskets and that, but they hadn't unpacked it. There were four of them—parents and two kids, around eleven or twelve, and the inevitable dog. And then while we were looking at them they got up and wandered off up the slope, as though maybe they were going up to the Cheesewring. Before they went they all stared over at us. It seemed to be catching, this business.

We ate our sandwiches, and drank our tea, and nobody said anything much. Not even Jamie. Once Dad asked if there was anything more to eat. 'No,' said Mum. 'That's the lot. Sorry. I should have brought more.' Once or twice I tried to jolly things up a bit, but nobody was having any.

And then all of a sudden Mum said, 'Jamie. See if you can get some of their sandwiches.'

Once upon a time, a long time ago, when Jamie was about four, he nicked a brass screw from Woolworths. He thought you could help yourself, you see—all those nice trays with shiny things in them. And Mum just about went through the roof. She took it back to the manager herself, personally, and Jamie had to come too, so he'd know what was what for ever and ever about taking things that aren't yours.

I thought I couldn't have heard right. I gaped at her with my mouth open like someone in a bad telly film.

Not so Jamie. 'OK,' he said. And he got up and went off through the gorse and stones and bushes towards the other family's picnic place. He went off, I say, but he went in a way I'd never seen him go before. He kind of slid from bush to bush and stone to stone, rather like he'd do if he was playing stalking, or tracking, or like I did when I was his age. Only he was doing it properly. Professionally, as it were. As though he'd been doing it all his life. Most of the time I couldn't see him at all, myself, even though I knew where he was. He melted, somehow, from one place to the next.

I watched, not saying anything because I was still too shocked to say anything. And the others watched, but they weren't shocked. Just interested. 'Good boy,' said Gran, once. 'Good lad.'

I took off my glasses and scrubbed them around on my sleeve. It's a thing I do when I'm fussed about something. You always feel as though things might clear up if you can see better. But even when I could see the moor unsmudged and unspotted, Jamie was still tracking over to that patch of rug on the hillside, and the parents and Gran were still sitting there watching him, cool as cucumbers.

The other family stopped and looked back once or twice. It

was almost as though they had a feeling there might be something going on. But every time they looked Jamie melted into a stone or a bush, and they didn't seem to see him.

And then he darted at their basket, whipped something out, and was gone again, so quick it hardly seemed to have happened.

He got back. With half a dozen sandwiches wrapped in silver foil. 'Ham,' said Mum. 'Nice. Bread's from a cut loaf, though.' She passed them round. Everyone took one except me. I said I wasn't hungry, thank you.

'Anything wrong, Michael?' said Mum, quite ordinary and calm. 'It's not like you to turn food down.'

I said angrily, 'Of course there's something wrong. I don't know what you . . .' But they weren't paying me any attention.

'What else have they got, Jamie?' said Dad.

'Bananas. Some cans of Coke. Tart things—shop ones. Lyons, I think.'

'Not worth it,' said Mum. 'Anyway, they're coming back.'

They were walking quite fast down the slope now, the other family, back to their things. It was overcast now. Grey, chilly. It felt as though it might rain.

I said, 'Let's go home. It's going to rain.'

'What?' said Mum. Not meaning, 'I didn't hear you', but 'I'm not listening to you'.

The baby started fussing. Mum reached into the picnic basket and gave her a chicken bone.

If I hadn't seen it with my own eyes I'd never have believed it. Pampered, that baby's been, from birth. Orange juice, strained messes, sterilized this and that.

As soon as Mum wasn't looking I took the chicken bone away. And the baby started yelling so I had to give it back. I took my glasses off again and had another scrub round the lenses.

The other family had got back to their place. They sat down on their folding chairs and on the rug, half out of sight now behind some bushes, though the father seemed to have put himself deliberately so that he faced out towards us. Presently, though, he moved, and we couldn't see any of them—just a corner of the rug.

We were on a grassy bit at the top end of the stone circle. Mum had picked it for flatness and absence of gorse, after a slight argument with Gran, who had wanted to stay by her personal choice of stone. Now Dad said all of a sudden, 'It won't do, here.'

So they were seeing sense at last. 'No,' I said. 'And it is raining now, anyway. Let's get off home.'

'What do you mean, Michael? Don't be silly,' said Mum. And then she said to Dad, 'You're right. Too enclosed. You can't see the approaches.'

Gran and Jamie had joined in now. They were on about cover, and that line of scrub over there, and having someone on the higher ground as a look-out. I just sat there. It was like a bad dream. And the rain was serious now.

'Come on,' said Mum. And suddenly there we all were, collecting everything up—thermoses, rugs, the lot—and moving them into a place just beyond the stone circle where there was a hollow in the ground and, just above it, a crest with wortle bushes and stuff. The bushes hid the hollow from the opposite slope. Dad lay on his stomach and stared through the bushes for a moment.

'Fine,' he said. 'Good view of their site, but they can't see us.'

'They'll have a look-out,' said Mum.

'True enough.'

I said, 'Look, I don't know what's the matter with everybody. They're just another family, those other people. *Another family*. Like us.'

'Don't shout so, dear,' said Mum.

'Should get one of them,' said Gran.

'Hostage?'

'Maybe. We'll see.'

Or else I'd gone barmy. Stark, raving mad. There they all were, sitting in the rain, looking out through the bushes every now and then, and going on like this. That was another thing—sitting there in the rain. We're a rain-allergic family, we are. One grey cloud on the horizon and we strike camp. Two drops and we're off the beach for the day. A doubtful weather-forecast and we stay at home. And there they were just sitting with the rain running off them, taking no more notice than a lot of horses in a field would.

I said, 'I'm getting wet.'

'What?' said Mum. 'What' meaning 'Don't bother me', again.

'I know,' I said, all bright and breezy. 'It's a game. It's some sort of joke you thought up between you while I was down at the car. Jolly funny. But let's stop now.'

Nobody paid the slightest attention.

'Ssh,' said Jamie. 'I can hear something . . .'

I couldn't. At least only birds and the usual kind of outdoor noises. And the rain.

'Downwind,' said Dad. 'There's one of them coming downwind.'

They were all staring through the bushes now, lying on their stomachs. 'It's one of the children,' said Mum. 'I saw a bit of jersey just then.'

Dad slid back into the hollow and rummaged around in the grass. He picked up a lump of stone, fist-sized, and then he stood up, looked quickly round, and threw it. Then he ducked down again.

There was a kind of gasp, from not far away. The noise you make when you've stubbed your toe or something.

'Got him,' said Dad.

'That'll teach 'em,' said Gran.

'Stop it . . .' I said. I was almost in tears, I can tell you.

'Be quiet, Michael. Raid, do you think, or full-scale attack?'

'Raid,' said Dad. 'He's going back.'

I said, in a silly, high-pitched voice, because I was getting in such a fuss I hardly knew if I was coming or going, 'If you do that kind of thing to people they're likely to do it back to you.' I sounded like Mum, when I was three or four, and having a spat with one of my mates. 'Oh, *please* can't we go home,' I said, since nobody so much as listened to that one. And I looked at my watch.

It said twelve exactly. But it had said that a quarter of an hour or so ago, when I was coming back from the car, so I listened to it. It hadn't stopped, at least only the hands had. I shook it, but the hands stayed stuck. It's a rotten watch, anyway: seven and a half books of Green Shield stamps. 'Where's Toby?' said Jamie, suddenly.

Mum humped herself up to the top of the ridge, very cautious, and whistled. He always comes best for Mum. Knows where the food-supply is.

Nothing happened. No Toby bouncing through the grass. Mum knelt up so that she could see better and whistled again.

And a stone whizzed past her ear and thumped down onto the rug.

'Get down!' said Dad.

'They've got within range, somehow!'

'We'll have to move.'

'Not if I can find out where he is,' said Dad grimly.

He went up on the ridge, and stood, and then ducked. At once another stone flew past him and smack into the side of the pram.

'Behind that big rock over there. Only one of them.'

They were all grubbing around for stones. 'Come on, Michael,' said Mum. 'Don't just leave everything to everyone else.'

I grubbed, miserably, and found a bit of granite and then lost it again. The rest of them had got a good supply, including Gran. She was getting together a nice little store.

'I'm going to winkle him out,' said Dad. He was filling his anorak pockets with stones. 'Have we got a knife?' Casually.

'Dad!' I said. At least I meant to. It came out as a sort of squeak.

'Only the plastic ones,' said Mum.

'Pity. I'll have one of them, all the same.'

He went out of the hollow the back way, as it were, and for a minute or two we could hear him rustling along from bush to bush. Then silence for what seemed a long time.

Then a grunt, crashing noises, a yell, someone running, more thumps. And Dad came back, panting, a dirty great swelling on the side of his cheek.

'Sent him packing!'

Nobody but me paid any attention to the bruise.

I said, 'Did he do that?'

'What? Oh, he clipped me with a stone before I could get to him.'

Mum didn't even look at it. Mum, who's brandishing the antiseptic and the plaster around at the merest hint of a scratch, normally.

'Which of them was it?'

'Young one, again. The rest have stayed put.'

'Now what?'

'Now we go home,' I said, hopelessly.

'I reckon,' said Dad, 'we use Jamie as a decoy. Try to draw one or two of them off, and then go in. Drive them back up the hill.'

'What about me?' said Gran.

'You stay here. You and the baby. Retreat if you have to.'

Gran nodded.

'Why did you have to interfere with them in the first place?' I shouted. 'If you'd just left them alone all this wouldn't be happening.'

Mum stared at me. 'They'd got things we wanted, hadn't they?' she said. 'Do get on and collect some stones, Michael. I don't know what's got into you today.'

Dad was explaining things to Jamie. He was to get out of the hollow and work his way round till he was on the far side of their site, and then he was to attract their attention, show himself, and make off fast. With any luck one or two of them would come out after him.

'Look,' I said. 'He might get *hurt*. If they're carrying on like this too. You can *kill* people, throwing stones.'

'Then we'll have to hurt them back, won't we?' said Dad, reasonably.

'But we've only got to go somewhere else . . .'

'Our place,' said Gran. 'Got to keep it. Silly boy.'

There wasn't any point in going on.

Jamie was getting ready to slip away. 'Don't be long,' said Mum. I looked at my watch; reflex action. Still stuck at twelve; still ticking. Stupid cheap watch.

And just as Jamie wriggled through the first few yards of cover it happened. A whole hail of stones, banging down on the rug and the thermoses and the grass. 'Take cover behind the chairs,' said Dad to Gran. 'The rest of you up on the ridge.'

We flattened out along the top, clutching stones. Thirty yards away or so a head came out from behind a slab of rock. A stone came flying towards us, and fell short. There was movement in several different places.

'It's all of them,' said Dad. 'Michael, you look after that one on the right.'

I threw a stone in that direction, half-heartedly. It bounced off a rock. And just as I'd got my head down again one came back and caught me on the arm. It hurt. And suddenly I wanted to do it back to somebody, like when you're about five. I took the biggest stone I could see from the pile behind us that Gran was busy stoking up all the time, and I stood up and chucked it at something red I could see beyond the next big boulder. Meaning not to miss, that time.

And somebody yelled.

'Good shot!' said Dad.

That made me see sense again.

'Stop it!' I yelled. 'Look, just stop it, all of you!' And I slid back down off the ridge. I wasn't having any more to do with it.

Gran was sitting on the grass behind the folding-chairs, with the baby beside her. The baby was watching what she was doing and making the daft 'Ooo' and 'Aaa' noises that babies make (rather nice, in fact, but I was in too much of a state to stop and have a chat like I would normally). What she was doing, Gran, was making a fire out of paper bags and dry grass (it kept going out, of course, because of the rain) and putting chicken bones on it and kind of mumbling at it. Barmy. Just clean, honest-to-goodness barmy. No wonder the baby was interested.

There wasn't time, though, to ask her what precisely she thought she was doing because first Jamie gave a yell and said, 'Oh, look, look!' and started waving Toby's collar around, which had come hurtling onto the ground beside us tied onto a stone, and then pebbles and things were coming down so thick and fast that Dad and Mum came sliding down and Dad said, 'Out! Get out, all of you. Back to the circle, and into the gorse beyond.'

Jamie was wailing, 'They've got Toby!' and Gran was chanting away now at her stupid fire, for all the world like somebody in church, until Dad bundled her up and off, and we were all scuttling over the grass, dragging things with us.

'Stop!' said Dad, and they all got down behind a big lump of granite on the edge of the circle. Not me, though.

'Michael! I said *stop*—come back here!'

'No.' I'd had enough. I began to run, the wet grass snatching at my feet so that I tripped and I could hear Dad yelling still, and Mum, but I got up again and went on. I could see the car and that was where I was going. After that I didn't care. I wasn't staying another minute in that stupid, crazy place with everyone behaving like lunatics.

I ran, with whatever I'd picked up (the newspaper and the baby's feeder, of all things) clutched in one hand, and the rain streaming down on my face. I couldn't hear them any more. Nothing. Just me, panting, and birds and things.

I fell over again. I think I banged my head or something because for some reason I didn't get up at once. I lay there face down for a minute, heaving and blowing, and expecting someone to throw a stone at me, or jump on me.

I lifted my head and I could see them, Mum and Dad and Jamie and Gran and the baby. They were sitting about in the middle of the stone circle, and the sun had come out. They were just sitting in the sun. And Mum was waving.

I arrived at where they were and Mum took the paper and the feeder.

'Thanks, dear. What's the matter?'

'Nothing,' I said.

'You didn't have to rush so. It's only just gone twelve.'

It had, that stupid watch said so. About thirty seconds past.

'What were you doing?' said Mum. 'Just lying on the grass there?'

'Wrapped in thought, eh?' said Dad.

'There's something wrong with my watch.'

'Let's see.'

'It doesn't matter,' I said. 'It's going again now.'

'And it was raining down there,' said Mum. 'We could see. You've let yourself get soaked.'

'When are we having my birthday picnic?' said Jamie.

Mum started dishing out the sandwiches. The sun was out; the baby had gone to sleep; Dad was reading the paper. All right, I've got a vivid imagination. It's not a crime.

'There's someone coming,' I said.

'No need to sound so put out,' said Mum. 'It's just one of that other family.'

'He's got Toby,' said Jamie.

'So he has.'

The man had his tie knotted round Toby's neck. 'This little chap belong to you, by any chance?'

'He's slipped his collar,' said Jamie. '*Bad* dog.'

'That's very kind of you,' said Mum. 'We're most grateful. Thank you very much.'

'Not at all. Wonder if I might ask you a favour, in fact. Loan of a tin-opener for five minutes.'

Mum was rummaging in the picnic basket.

'Exchange is no robbery,' said Dad.

'Fair enough,' said the man. 'Seems to be turning out fine after all.'

'Lovely.'

Mum found the tin-opener.

'Very kind of you. Spoils the day a bit if you can't get at the food.'

'There's always something,' said Mum.

'Too right. We already had one of the kids get in an argument with a rock.'

'My husband's just had a bit of a fall. Nothing much.'

It was the first time I'd noticed the swelling on the side of Dad's face.

'Dangerous place,' said the man.

Everybody was smiling away, except me.

The Man
from When

DANNIE PLACHTA

Mr Smith was about to mix a moderately rationed Martini for himself when a thunderous explosion quaked through his house, upsetting the open bottle of Vermouth. After applying a steadying hand to the gin bottle, and while the ice cubes still tinkled maniacally in their shuddering bowl, he sprinted outside. An incandescent glare a hundred yards from the house destroyed the purple sunset he had been admiring not five minutes earlier. 'Oh, my God!' he said, and ran back in to phone the state police.

As Smith was procuring a heady draught of gin directly from the bottle, he was further alarmed by a steadily gushing hiss from beyond his open front door. When the sound persisted for a full minute, he went cautiously to the porch to find an intense mist rising from the area of the fiery thing he had viewed moments earlier. Somewhat awed, and thoroughly scared, he watched and waited for about five minutes. Just as he was about to go inside for another belt of gin, a man walked out of the fog and said, 'Good evening.'

'Good evening,' said Mr Smith. 'Are you the police?'

'Oh, no,' answered the stranger. 'I'm from that,' he said, pointing a finger into the mist. 'My cooling equipment finally kicked into high.'

'You're a spaceman,' Smith decided.

'I only came a few hundred miles,' shrugged the stranger modestly. 'Mostly, I'm a time traveller.' He paused to light a dark cheroot. 'The one and *only* time traveller,' he added, with a touch of pride in his voice.

'The real McCoy, eh? Well, come on in and have a drink. Vermouth's all gone, but I saved the gin.'

'Be glad to,' said the stranger, as they walked in together.

'Past or future?' wondered Smith, handing the bottle to his guest.

'From the future,' replied the time traveller after a satisfying pause. 'Hits the spot,' he smiled, returning the bottle.

'Well,' said Smith, sitting down and making himself comfortable, 'I guess you'll want to tell me all about it.'

'Yes, thank you, I would.'

'Feel free,' said Smith, passing the bottle.

'Well, I had my final calculations, with the usual plus or minus . . .' He paused for another sip of gin. 'And of course it was the minus that had me a little worried.'

'But you took the chance,' interjected Smith.

'Naturally. And as it happened, there *was* some minus. Just enough to destroy the world.'

'That *is* too bad,' Smith commented, reaching for the bottle.

'Yes. You see, there was such an expenditure of energy that it completely wiped out the Earth of my time. The force blasted me all the way through space to this spot. By the way, I *am* sorry if I disturbed you.'

'It was nothing, nothing at all. Forget it.'

'Well, in any event, I took the chance and I'm not sorry. A calculated risk, but I proved my point. In spite of everything, I still think it was worth it. What do you think?'

'Well, as you said, you took the chance; you proved your point. I suppose it *was* worth it.' Smith took a final drink, saving a few glimmering drops for his guest. 'By the way, how far from the future did you travel?'

The time traveller grabbed the gin bottle and consulted his watch. 'Eighteen minutes,' he replied.

'It wasn't worth it,' said Smith.

Fire, Fire

ALISON PRINCE

'London's *burning*, London's *burning*",' Roland sang emphatically as he tramped up the forestry path to the Giants' Graves. He glanced over his shoulder and instructed, 'Come on, Emma. "Fetch the engines, fetch the engines"—'

Emma was too out of breath to join in her father's song. Midges danced before her face and the sun beat down in dazzling patches between the trees as she trailed behind her parents. She thought wistfully of the beach and its weedy rocks.

'"Fire, fire . . . fire, fire",' chirped Rosemary, hard on her husband's heels. '"Pour on water, pour on water".' She paused, giving a hitch to the backpack in which she carried Luke, Emma's baby brother, and looked back at her daughter. 'Emma, do try and keep up, darling,' she said.

'Never get your second wind if you keep stopping,' Roland advised. 'The trick of hill-walking is to maintain a steady pace.' He strode on, stabbing at the ground with the long stick he had cut from a hedge. Stripped of its bark, it was as pale as his bare legs.

Emma flapped at the midges and toiled on reluctantly. The close-planted spruces on either side of the path were dark and silent, shutting out the sky. Nothing grew on the soft bed of brown needles between them. The steep slope where Emma walked had been cut into steps, each one edged by a pine log, and the climb seemed never-ending. Emma counted her strides;

one-two, *one*-two. It was irritating that her short legs had to take an extra pace to each step, thus meeting every riser with her left foot. She paused again, panting. Her left leg ached. Her parents were hopelessly far ahead now, still indomitably singing. Their voices drifted back to her. ' "Fire, fire . . . fire, fire . . .".' And then the tune was swamped by a far more strident sound as a group of youths appeared at the top of the path with a blaring transistor radio. Emma saw her father turn to stare furiously after the boys as they galumphed down the steps, irreverent in jeans and trainers and old T-shirts. Emma stood out of their way as they charged past her in a pulsating gale of amplified sound. Then she started slowly up the steps again, leading with her right foot this time; *one*-two, *one*-two.

She came to a tree that had an iron ring hammered into its trunk, embracing a group of birch brooms—an umbrella-stand full of witches' broomsticks, Emma thought. Glad of a good excuse to stop again, she stood still and stared at them.

'Come *on*, Emma!' her mother called despairingly from the top of the steps.

'What are these broomsticks for?' Emma shouted up to her.

'They're fire beaters. In case—'

Roland interrupted. 'Emma, we can't keep waiting for you all the time. We're nearly at the top—see you up there, all right? It's not far.'

'All right,' agreed Emma, relieved. Fire beaters, she thought, and turned to look again at the broomsticks which leaned together within their iron band. The dark trees above her were ominous, shutting out the sky like the buildings in a great city, though the light did its best to break through in little twinkling bursts between the branches. Could broomsticks really put out a fire? What if it spread too fast, engulfing the people who beat helplessly at the flames? What if it became a forest Fire of London, roaring from tree to tree and turning each one into a blazing torch? Emma shivered, and touched the iron ring which held the beaters, as a kind of reassurance. Perhaps the broomsticks were not meant for practical use. Perhaps they worked as a charm against fire, a modern, man-made effort to invoke the power of ancient magic.

Emma began to plod up the steps again, thinking of what her father had said about the forest. 'A rural slum,' he had declared, jabbing at the pale green, tree-dotted area on his Ordnance Survey map as they sat over breakfast that morning in the guest house. 'Ruining the environment. Nothing lives in close-packed Sitka spruce, it's a plague on the landscape.' Rosemary, spooning something into Luke's mouth, had continued to make encouraging noises to the baby, but Mrs Kerr had given Roland a motherly smile as she cleared away the egg-and-bacon plates.

'There's a lot of folk don't like it,' she said. 'The Forestry have made some good paths, right enough, but they've planted their trees awful close round the Giants' Graves. You could see right across the Bay from up there at one time, but now it's all shut in.'

That was why Roland had decided on this expedition, so that he could see for himself what the Forestry Commission had been up to. Emma had been enthusiastic at first. The Giants' Graves. She imagined vast, oblong tombs on which lay carved stone figures with their huge, blank-eyed faces staring at the sky. Their clasped hands would be the size of boulders and their upturned feet would tower above Emma, pointing tree-high at the sun.

Perhaps there were still giants in the wood, Emma thought suddenly. Somewhere up the dark slope, maybe they trod their way through the forest, with legs thicker than tree trunks and colossal feet silent on the carpet of pine needles. With a gasp of fear, she began to run, scrambling desperately up the last of the wooden-edged steps. Her father had said there was no such thing as a giant, but she was not sure.

The path climbed steeply here, among the gnarled roots of an older woodland, leaving the monotony of spruce behind. Light filtered down more freely through the leaves of chestnut and ash and rowan, but Emma could not see through the tangle of bushes which grew in dense profusion between the taller trees. Was somebody watching her from above the branches, a dark presence against the sky? Panting as she clambered on, she glanced fearfully up the slope on her left, hearing the creak of a branch which might mean that a huge hand had parted the trees to look at her. The moment of inattention took its toll. Emma's foot caught in an arching tree root and she stumbled and lost her balance. She grabbed at a clump of ferns, but the fronds came away in her hand and she pitched down the steep slope on the right of the path, slithering and rolling through the thick undergrowth. Dark trees and flashes of sky somersaulted across her vision, alternating with the bruising closeness of leaves and earth in her face.

Then she was lying on her back. She felt sick and dizzy, and she seemed to hurt all over. Cautiously, she raised her aching head, and found that she lay beside a narrow stream of water which cut its way between grass and ferns, running fast over brown stones. Her left ankle hurt worst of all, with a violent pain which made it seem impossible to move her foot. She gave a choking sob.

A shadow fell across her face and she gasped. Somebody stood above her, tall and dark against the sky, and for a moment it was a nightmare come true. A giant had found her. Then the figure crouched down, and Emma saw that it was not a giant at all. The face which gazed with concern into hers belonged to a young woman whose long hair hung loose, the dark strands of it brushing Emma's arm with a touch as faint as feathers. Her skin was deeply sun-tanned, almost as rich a brown as the stones under the water, and she wore a rather shapeless dress which reminded Emma of her mother's suede waistcoat, old and a little scruffy. It seemed an odd thing to wear on such a hot day, and Emma felt a fresh pang of alarm. Although this person was not a giant, could she be one of the strangers against whom her parents had warned her? Some people, they had said, were not quite normal, and although they were to be pitied, they should be carefully avoided. Emma tried to scramble to her feet, but her ankle gave a stab of pain and she collapsed on to the grass again. The woman sat back on her heels and watched her, as if trying to guess what she would do next.

Emma risked a glance at the woman's face, and met the steady gaze of blue eyes. There was a sense of sadness about her expression, and Emma felt reassured. This was not a person who wished her any harm—and Emma knew she needed help. 'I hurt my ankle,' she said.

The woman nodded, reaching out a brown hand to touch the swelling above the strap of Emma's sandal. It was a gesture so motherly that Emma felt an ache of childish, dependent tears well up, stinging her eyes. She felt her lips tremble and ducked her head, trying hard to be sensible and rubbing with one finger at a streak of earth on her knee. She saw that there was a triangular tear in the skirt of her blue dress, and put the frayed edges together carefully, wishing she was still climbing the wooden-edged steps, one-two, one-two. She began to cry.

The woman dipped her hand in the stream then gently put a finger under Emma's chin to lift her face and wipe the tears away with cool, wet fingers. With her eyes closed gratefully, Emma heard the woman speak for the first time. The words she used were not English, and yet Emma knew their meaning. 'Don't cry,' the woman was telling her. 'You are alive.' Then the touch of her fingers was gone and Emma opened her eyes to stare at her, and saw that she, too, was struggling not to weep, hugging her knees and rocking a little, staring up through the trees at the leaf-dappled sunlight in an anguish which Emma did not understand. And then, like the words she had spoken, the meaning was clear. Emma was alive, but someone else, whom this woman had loved, was dead.

This is a dream, Emma thought. Otherwise I could not understand. Perhaps I hit my head when I fell, and this is not really happening. Soon I will wake up.

Reassured by this idea, she shifted into a kneeling position and put her arms round the woman's neck to comfort her. They clung together in a close embrace in the quiet company of the trees, and Emma gave a contented sigh, relaxing into a closeness which reminded her of what she now thought of as her childhood. Since the birth of Luke, she had felt very grown-up, and a little lonely.

I shall remember this dream all my life, Emma thought. The smell of the bruised grass, the closeness of the arms which held her and the broken, sparkling light above the trees joined in a completeness which included her aching head and the pain in her injured ankle, and made their throbbing almost comfortable.

Gradually, the moment passed. The long-held position began to produce little cramping sensations of its own, and Emma was aware of a dawning uneasiness. The voices of her parents broke into the dream, calling her. 'Emma! Where are you? Emma!' And then her mother's voice, distant, but sharp with anxiety. 'I *knew* we should have waited.'

'I'll have to go,' Emma said. 'They're looking for me.' The thought of the climb which lay ahead was daunting, even if her new-found friend would help her.

The woman reached out a quick hand as Emma tried to get up, gripping her wrist with such a firm strength that it was almost painful. For a moment, Emma was alarmed again, but then she found herself being swung on to the woman's back, to ride there just as she had done when her father used to give her a piggy-back, out on walks when she was smaller.

With her arms tight round the woman's neck, Emma buried her face in the dark hair to protect herself from the whipping twigs as she was carried quickly up the steep slope. Eyes closed, she inhaled the smell of the thick, coarse hair. It was sweaty and yet curiously sweet, reminding her of the pony she had once ridden on an Outdoor Pursuits holiday two years ago.

At the top of the path, the sun blossomed suddenly on Emma's bare arms, and she sensed that the trees had given way to an open space. She heard voices, blending together in a slow chant which was very different from her father's punchy rendering of 'London's Burning'. She raised her head and flapped at the ever-present midges.

For a moment, the blaze of the sun dazzled her. Then she saw that she was on a smooth, grassy place high above the trees, with the sea sparkling far below. And she was circled by dark-haired people who stood motionless as they joined in the chant, many of them with closed eyes. All of them were bare-footed, dressed in brownish garments like the one Emma's friend wore, but their stillness and the gravity of their faces made it clear that something important was happening.

If this was real, Emma thought, then these must be actors, playing their roles in some strange pageant. Or was it just a continuing part of the dream? She stared round her from the height of her piggy-back ride, across the woman's head, and saw a low stone building in the centre of the grassy place, rising with massive solidness from the close-nibbled turf. The woman moved closer into the circle, and heads were raised to glance at her with respect and sympathy. Nobody gave any sign of noticing Emma's presence.

The narrow doorway into the stone building showed nothing inside it but pitch blackness. Emma stared at it in horrified fascination as her preconceived idea of the Giants' Graves was taken over by this new reality. Her vision of the great carved figures slipped away into the past, replaced by the understanding that, instead of graves, there was this single tomb, built, not by giants, but by the ancestors of these real people who stood quietly round her. Except for the sense of awe which hung in the still, hot air of the afternoon, it could have been a disappointment.

The woman turned and gently lowered Emma to the ground, keeping an arm round her in mindfulness of the injured ankle. And in that moment, Emma knew the reason for the ceremony which had brought the people together. A long stack of cut wood stood in front of her, the billets carefully arranged so that they formed a solid, high table like an altar. On top of this, a girl of about Emma's own age lay on her back, with her face turned to the sky. She was utterly still. A circlet of starry white flowers crowned her dark hair and her eyelids were not quite closed, but as Emma stared at the motionless face she knew that the eyes saw nothing. With a tingle of coldness under the dark blue sky, she was aware for the first time of the meaning of death.

The woman bent down and kissed the dead child on the lips, then turned to Emma and kissed her with the same gravity. In the heightened awareness of the dream, Emma again understood. There was a continuance. The kiss made a link between the dead girl and a living one, so that both of them were part of all time and of all people.

Reaching out to the child once more, the woman detached a single small flower from the garland which encircled her head, and gave it to Emma, who stared down at it and smelt the pungent scent which it gave off. An ache of tears began to gather in her throat.

A small fire burned in a circle of stones nearby, and the heat from it shivered the blue air and broke the straightness of the horizon. As Emma watched, an older woman moved towards this fire and stooped to ignite a bundle of twigs. The chanting began again and grew louder as the blazing twigs were carried to the stack of wood on which the child lay, and a first wisp of smoke curled upward against the sun.

Emma released herself from the woman's supporting arm and sat down clumsily on the grass, staring at the little flower which she held and seeing the precision of its white starriness blur behind the pall of her tears. She did not want to watch the fire engulf the girl and her garland of flowers. The dream was too real to bear any longer, and she wanted it to stop. Distantly, she heard her mother's voice again. 'Emma! *Emma!*' She sounded frantic.

'*Mummy!*' Emma screamed. 'I'm here!' She turned away from the sight of the mounting flames, with her hands on the short turf, crushing the small flower, and, thankfully, she could feel approaching footsteps vibrating through the earth.

'Emma!' Her mother was kneeling beside her, hugging her. 'Wherever did you get to? What happened?'

'The fire,' Emma sobbed. 'I know she's dead, but it seems so awful.' The pungent, oniony smell of the white flower was strong as she covered her eyes with her hands.

'Fire? Darling, what are you talking about? And you've torn your dress.'

Emma looked down and, once again, brought the frayed edges together. So it was not a dream. She turned her head

bravely to look at the doomed body of the child—and gasped. Tall spruce trees stood only a few paces away, as dense and close as the walls of a room. The people had gone, and where the dark-doorwayed building had stood, there was nothing except ancient stones, half-buried in the rabbit-nibbled grass. The shock was such a mental somersault that Emma felt the colour drain from her face.

'Darling, are you all right?' asked Rosemary in concern.

Emma could not answer.

'Come on, we'd better find Daddy,' her mother went on. 'He's down the path, looking for you.'

'I hurt my ankle,' said Emma, certain at least of this. And, for a second time, fingers reached out to touch the puffy swelling above the strap of her sandal.

'Oh, my goodness,' said Rosemary, sounding worried. 'Can you wriggle your toes?'

'I don't know,' said Emma. 'Yes, a bit.' She felt strangely tired.

Her mother leaned over her to inspect the ankle again. 'You may have broken it,' she said, then added, 'You do smell of garlic. Have you been picking the wild garlic that grows down by the burn?'

Emma shook her head, and wondered if the little flower lay somewhere on the grass. Her tiredness made it seem too difficult to look.

Rosemary thought of something else. 'How on earth did you get up here?' she asked. 'You can't have walked.'

'A lady carried me,' said Emma. 'Piggy-back.'

Rosemary frowned. 'You shouldn't go off with strangers, Emma,' she said. 'I've told you before.'

'She wasn't a stranger,' said Emma, and felt her eyes fill with tears again.

Roland strode into the narrow clearing and said, '*There* you are! Didn't you hear us calling?'

There were explanations and hugs and apologies, and then Roland said 'Upsy-daisy!'—and, for the second time that afternoon, Emma found herself riding piggy-back in the hot sunshine.

As they set off down the hill, Roland ranted volubly about the villainy of the Forestry Commission in planting conifers so closely round a historic site. 'It's a desecration,' he said to

Rosemary, who preceded him down the path with Luke's head resting against the back of her neck as he slept in his backpack. 'An act of utter vandalism.'

'Absolutely,' Rosemary agreed.

Emma hardly listened. With her arms round her father's neck, she remembered the pony-smell of the dark hair in her face on that other ride in the tree-dappled shade, and was not sure which one was the dream.

Much later, Emma lay between the cool sheets in her bedroom at the boarding house, feeling the throbbing of her bandaged ankle which the doctor had declared badly sprained but not broken. The flowered curtains had been drawn across the window, shutting out the evening sun.

It was all very puzzling. Emma's head hurt when she tried to work out the logic of what had happened, almost as if in warning not to battle with the unfathomable. It was easier simply to relive the encounter and be carried again up the steep path to the open place under the wide sky, where the sea sparkled and a wisp of smoke rose towards the dazzling sun. And then she seemed to be not carried, but climbing, toiling behind her parents and hearing their voices raised in cheerful song. '"Fire, fire . . . fire, fire . . .".' She drifted off to sleep.

Flickering light filled the room, glowing through the curtains, and there was a confusion of noise. Somebody was banging on the front door downstairs. Emma heard Luke splutter into a waking cry in her parents' room next door. After a little while, her father came in, wearing his anorak over his pyjamas. 'Forest fire,' he said with a kind of satisfied excitement. 'Mrs Kerr says they've turned out the helicopter to try and deal with it. Her husband's in the fire service volunteers, so they came and knocked him up.' He crossed to the window and parted the curtains, silhouetted against the reddish light as he stared out. 'Actually,' he admitted with a glance back at Emma, 'if it opens up that Neolithic burial site, I shan't be sorry. It serves them right. Should never have planted there in the first place.'

Emma closed her eyes. Flames licked up into the dazzling sky as she stood again in her imagination beside the stack of wood and saw the child's face, empty of all expression, shiver in the heat. Emma knew now, since a conversation with her perplexed parents, that thousands of years separated her from the people who had stood in a circle by the tomb which held the ashes of their dead; and yet, for a little time, there had been a link between them. Perhaps that link had worked both ways, she thought. Perhaps the woman who had dipped her hand in the cold water and wiped away Emma's tears had been dreaming, too. And if that had been so, did she now remember Emma, the child who was still alive? Did she and her people know that the forest was burning?

Seeing again the flaring bundle of twigs applied to that carefully-stacked altar of cut wood, a new possibility leapt into Emma's mind, and she opened her eyes with a little gasp. Was it the flames of that fire which had spread to the present-day forest?

Roland turned from the window at the sound of Emma's gasp and said, 'It's all right, love. Nothing to be afraid of. They'll soon have it out. Young vandals like those ones we saw with the transistor radio started it, I expect. They're the kind who would be careless with matches.'

Somewhere at the back of Emma's mind, a dark-haired woman smiled, and Emma, too, hearing the crackle of the rising flames and the chant of the circled people, knew that her father's suggestion was absurd. She put her hands over her face to hide the twitch of her lips—and, lurking behind the soapy fragrance of bedtime washing, there was the faint, pungent reek of a flower as white and as timeless as a star.

Even if the fire swept down the hill and engulfed the houses, Emma thought as her limbs slackened in sleepy warmth, it did not really matter. Death was not the end of everything. There were always dreams.

Master Ghost and I

BARBARA SOFTLY

Nathaniel Dodd, the steward who had served our family for as long as I could remember and who had not seen me for close on five years, stared disapprovingly over the roll of parchment in his hand. His eyes, squinting in the sunlight that danced through the window to make a mockery of the sullen atmosphere, became mere pinpricks that tried to pierce my thoughts. His stare moved from my tanned features to the buff coat of my officer's uniform, travelled down the sleeve and paused on the edge of plain linen at my wrist. Involuntarily, and immediately ashamed of the action, I curved my fingers under my gloves so that he would not notice the nails I had split that morning while mending a broken bridle. From my hands the stare glided to my sword, slid from hilt to tip and came to rest on the spurs of my muddied riding boots.

'I left as soon as I received your message,' I began in weak apology for my unkempt looks, and feeling momentarily like the refractory schoolboy he still considered me to be.

The squinting eyes swung from my boots to my face again.

'You may sit down,' he said.

Four cold words; not 'Good day' or any remark on the change in my appearance which the half decade of soldiering with the Parliamentary Army must have made. I checked the rising comment, for I had no wish to make a greater enemy of the man who was the sole link with my family who had disowned me.

What had I done? Rebelled. The only one of my parents' four children who had dared to disobey their wishes. My two brothers had, not willingly, directed their lives into the ways chosen for them and my sister, at an early age, had been given in marriage to an elderly landowner of wealth in order to provide him with much-wanted heirs. But I, at fifteen as I then was, had seen little glamour or excitement in the life of a priest when I learned that I was destined for the Church. Glamour, life, excitement were to my mind to be found in my youthful pleasures, my sword, my horse, and the prospect of fighting; but not fighting for King Charles, who had just raised his standard at Nottingham, and who was head of that very Church from which I wished to escape.

A few months after I had run away from home I was tracked down by Nathaniel Dodd. That was the first time I was summoned to receive his disapproving stare and the four cold words—'You may sit down.' On that occasion I had remained standing, a silent but defiant fifteen-year-old, my hair cropped as short as the most fanatical Roundhead's, determined to retain my freedom. It was not my freedom that Master Dodd wanted. It was to tell me that I could go the way I had chosen and live on the meagre pay of a common soldier because my family had disowned me, and there would never be any forgiveness for me.

'Callous young puppy,' Nathaniel Dodd had hissed at my apparent composure.

'What do you expect me to say?' I had asked, goaded into speech by his contempt. 'If I show sorrow now for the distress I have caused my parents for not entering the Church, you will be the first to tell me my repentance is too late. The Church is not for me. Why should a boy's life be stunted to suit his parents' whim? If they prefer to exile me and make me homeless, they are to blame for their own unhappiness now, not I.'

They were hard words, and they came from a heart that was steeling itself to do without kindred and home for the bitter years of civil war.

Now, five years later, Nathaniel Dodd had sent for me again saying that he had important family matters to divulge. By this time there was a lull in the fighting and I, no longer a common soldier but a captain of a troop of horse in the New Model Army, was able to leave my quarters without a moment's delay.

Believing that my father or both my parents were dying, if not dead, I covered the many miles to Master Dodd in two hot summer days, to arrive tired and travel-stained on a well-nigh lamed horse in the mid-afternoon.

'You may sit down.' The words were repeated.

'Thank you,' I replied, and obeyed, flinging my hat and gloves on the floor beside me.

For an instant the pinprick eyes wavered, then dropped to the parchment and began to read. I was conscious that, at the end of every line, Master Dodd's attention wandered from the black script to my relaxed figure, noting my hair, now long like an ordinary officer's, not shorn like a fanatic's, and the air of maturity and experience.

'Are my parents well?' I asked.

He started as if he had not expected me to have the temerity to address him first.

'In exceptional health, I believe,' he said, and there was a hint of acidity in his voice showing that neither I nor what he read on the parchment was to his liking.

'This is your uncle's will,' he continued in the same sour tone. 'Your father's only brother Edward Knapton, who, until within a few months of his death fought loyally at the King's side.' He glared at me over the parchment again and I wondered why he was at pains to tell me this. 'He has left his fortune, which was considerable, not to your father, your brothers or your sister—but—to a rebellious, ill-favoured, traitorous'—and here his list of adjectives failed him—'ne'er-do-well—to yourself.' He tossed the document in contempt on to the table in front of him.

I hid my amazement at his news and replied with as little sarcasm as possible that my uncle must have known the others were well provided for. If Master Dodd had been a common soldier he would have spat out his disgust.

'The man was mad,' he exploded, 'mad! He destroyed his previous will and made that—that travesty—only a short while ago.' His fingers quivering with fury, he pulled some keys from a drawer and went to a small coffer under the window. 'If you need money now I can let you have some, and the rest can be sent when and where you want it later. The house can be sold and then I—'

'What house?' I interrupted.

'Your uncle's,' he barked. 'Now yours. A new house—' And he named a village deep in a part of the West Country which had been torn by the campaigns during the early years of the war. 'He finished building it this spring and planned to live in it at once, but—' He hesitated, lifting the lid of the chest and burying his hands in its contents. 'It's no place for anyone and you'll not be needing a house when you are on the march all the time—you chose to give up one Royalist home and this will only be another. It will fetch a good price and—'

'I do not wish to sell it,' I replied firmly. His ready acceptance of the fact that I neither needed nor wanted the house roused my obstinate nature, although I was not really inclined to be saddled with the property. 'You can give me the keys and I will go down there.'

He straightened up, his eyes blinking nervously.

'You'll not like it. Your uncle could not abide it in the end.'

'No doubt that was why he left it to me,' I said. 'If he had been fond of it he would have given it to a more worthy recipient. In any case, I should like to see the servants. They might not be willing to serve a rebel master after a Royalist one.'

'There are no servants.' He spoke slowly in order to convey some deeper meaning. 'The place is empty, no one will stay there. Your uncle was driven from it—by some power, some evil—he believed the place was haunted.'

'Haunted?' I laughed. 'What—a house not a year old with a ghost? Who is it? One of the bricklayers fallen from the scaffolding or did they wall up the master carpenter in the chimney because of his prying ways?'

Nathaniel Dodd eyed me with awe and a strange fascination.

'Heaven be praised you never entered the Church,' he muttered. 'The supernatural is to be feared not mocked.'

He passed a bag of money and some keys from the coffer to my outstretched hand. Then he smoothed his glistening forehead with a damp palm.

'I shall be ready to sell the property when you have changed your mind,' he said.

I slipped the bag and keys into my pouch, swung my hat and gloves from the floor, and bowed my thanks.

'Maybe I won't change my mind,' I smiled, and I was conscious of the shaft of sunlight dancing joyously across the sombre room. 'For perhaps Master Ghost and I will become well acquainted.'

Forty-eight hours later, on a day that had turned from high summer to the cloud and steady wind which had prevailed for most of the season, I sat surveying my inheritance—or what I could see of its chimneys showing above a high, uncut hawthorn hedge and an iron-studded gateway. Dismounting, I glanced all round, back along the grassy track which had led from the road a mile away; to the right where the deep hills were folded in peace, and to the left where, from a distant, tree-lined hollow, the smoke from hidden cottage fires was being swept like pennants across the countryside.

I hitched my horse to a stake in the hedge and, leaving him there to graze, fitted one of Master Dodd's keys to the lock on the gate. The key grated, the lock was stiff and the gate had to be pushed over uneven ground where I had thought there would be a smooth drive. There was no drive and I stood staring in bewilderment. There was nothing, nothing but grass, rough and knee-deep or in hummocky tufts and the whole vast hayfield, in which the house and outbuildings seemed to have been dropped, was scattered with mature trees. Only under the nearest line of windows was there a terrace of freshly laid flag-stones, and even they were edged with weeds, littered with wisps of straw and flutterings of dead leaves.

What is it that is so uncanny about an empty house? As I moved softly on the carpet of turf every window seemed to be watching, every stone to be listening, and the air of desolation was so heavy and still that my ears were oppressed with it. Yet there was no stillness; the silence was full of the wind of that dull, clouded summer day, a wind that swept the dry leaves on the flags, that bent the branches of the limes into brooms and brushed them in never-ending motion; a wind full of unseen voices.

The clattering of my spurs striking the terrace steps was enough to unsteady my nerves; my hand flew to my sword while my heart pounded as it had never done in battle.

'Coward,' I muttered, remembering Master Dodd's words. 'But it seems a day of ghosts; the air could be full of them, crying like lost souls.'

'Will you be wanting anything sir?'

I spun round, back to the wall, sword half drawn, ready to defend myself against the supernatural if need be.

A most unghostlike face, balanced on the haft of a scythe, was glaring at me through the overgrown bushes.

'I be here to cut the grass,' it said.

'A pity you did not come sooner,' I retorted, angry with myself. 'It has not been cut for months.'

'I come once a year—the master only wanted me once a year.' The shrubs quivered and a man wriggled on to the stones in front of me. He stood up slowly, stroking the blade of the scythe and eyeing my buff coat with the same look as Master Dodd's—disapproval verging on hatred. 'I'm Mallet,' he said, 'Ned Mallet—and you're a soldier, bain't you.' It was a statement not a question. 'We don't hold with soldiers in these parts; you'd best be off before anyone else sees you.' The scythe tilted in the manner of a battle-axe.

'This is my house,' I told him. 'The master of whom you speak was my uncle and he has left this property to me.'

'That's as maybe,' he growled. 'Master or no master, you're a soldier, and we've had enough of soldiery in these parts whether they be King's men or Parliament's. You leave peaceful folks be.'

'The previous owner, Edward Knapton, was a soldier, too,' I replied.

'Maybe he was.' The man's attitude became more threatening. 'But we don't want no more of you, trampling our crops, eating our food, burning our barns, taking all, and paying nothing. We fought you once with pitchforks and clubs and we'll fight you again whether you be the master, the King, or the Parliament.'

I knew what he meant. Villagers all over that locality, driven to desperation by the plunder of war, had banded together to fight the common enemy, Royalist and Roundhead. Both sides had tried to woo their friendship with promises of better-disciplined troops and gifts of muskets and carbines. The Clubmen, we had called them, because of their primitive weapons.

'You'd best be going,' he said again before I could speak. 'Master Knapton wouldn't stay here. Worried wellnigh out of his wits, he was, though it wasn't us what drove him away. It might have been,' he added menacingly, 'if the devil hadn't done it for us. "I'll not come again" that's what he told me. "Ned Mallet," he said, "the place is evil and I'll not—"'

'Never mind what he told you,' I interrupted, my temper rising. 'You and your Clubmen, the devil and all his demons, I am staying here the night at least. So you "had best be off" down to those cottages and find someone who can come up and cook my supper for me. My horse needs stabling, too, and you can do that on your way back.'

He wavered under the decisive tones, but, as his eyes shifted swiftly over my shoulder, something more like cunning crept into his voice.

'My missus'll come up like she did for Master Edward,' he muttered. 'She'll do the fires and air the linen—though she'll not—'

'I am not asking anyone to sleep here,' I forestalled him, and immediately thought that I should feel safer in my bed with my hostile neighbours on the other side of a barred door. 'I am not afraid of being alone.'

Without another word, he jerked the scythe into his hands and went towards the outbuildings on a path that was evidently the shortest route to the cottages in the hollow. I moved to recross the terrace to the main porch, intending to explore the house, for I was anxious to examine it thoroughly before the man and his wife returned or darkness fell.

With an exclamation of annoyance, I saw another prying villager standing behind me, a boy of about fifteen years of age.

'Who are you?' I snapped.

'Ro-Roger,' he stammered.

'And you live here, too, I suppose?'

'S-sort of.'

We looked each other up and down.

'You—you're a soldier,' he said. 'A soldier in the New Model Army, an officer.'

'A captain of a troop of horse, and before that I served under Waller in most of his campaigns here in the West; and I have been a soldier for the past five years.'

I rolled the words out in fury, waiting for the inevitable disapproval, but it did not come. The boy was staring at me with an odd mixture of incredulity, wonderment, and admiration. His hair was cropped shorter than mine had ever been and he was wearing a shabby doublet and breeches of a faded blue-grey colour. On second thoughts, as I continued to study him, I decided that his clothes were not shabby with the wear of work as Ned Mallet's had been. They were faded with disuse, the lace of his shirt yellowed, dust lines in the creases of folding, and it seemed probable that he was dressed in a discarded suit of my uncle's.

'You knew Master Knapton?' I asked. 'Master Edward Knapton who lived here?'

'He only came once, a short while ago. I met him then,' was the quick reply.

'And he gave you those clothes.'

A momentary glimmer of astonishment showed in the boy's eyes and he glanced down at his doublet.

'They came from the chest at the foot of his bed,' he explained, and then more eagerly, 'Why are you here—you're a soldier, and there's no fighting now—'

'Because the house is mine.' Soon these villagers will be aware of the fact, I thought. 'Edward Knapton was my uncle, and I am John Knapton, his nephew, who—'

'John Knapton?' he broke in. 'You are John Knapton? But—but you're a soldier—a captain in the Army—' His astonishment was not hidden now. 'But no one would ever have dreamed you were a Roundhead soldier as well.'

'As well as what?' I asked.

He flushed, hesitated, and shrugged his shoulders.

'As well as—being—being—'

'As well as being the nephew of a loyal subject of the King,' I finished for him.

He smiled and the flush deepened.

'That's as good a reason as any.'

He laughed, and I could not help liking the boy; his disarming friendliness and his quaint, clipped way of speaking, which was quite different from Mallet's broad dialect or my slight country drawl.

Taking out another of Master Dodd's keys, I went towards the door at the front of the house, and as I reached the porch I heard Roger padding softly after me.

'This is tansy, isn't it?' he asked.

I turned and saw him running his hands up a feathery-leaved yellow flower which was growing in a straggling clump at the edge of the steps. He buried his nose in his palm.

'What a scent!' he exclaimed. 'It reminds me of blazing borders and summer gardens.'

'It reminds me of fleas,' I said, 'and doses of bitter physic when I was a child.'

His guffaw of laughter warmed me. It was good to hear such a sound in the atmosphere of cheerlessness which had so far been my greeting. When I opened the door, wrinkling my nose at the musty smell, Roger was close at my elbow.

He wriggled past my arm. 'Look,' he whispered in excitement. 'It's new—so new. Look at that panelling and this floor.' He darted across the hall to smooth his fingers down the freshly carved woodwork on the walls.

'Of course it's new, boy,' I replied. 'It was only finished this year. Didn't you see it when my uncle was here?'

He shook his head. 'I—I didn't come in,' he murmured, and with an effort seemed to check his eagerness.

After that, with firmly compressed lips, he followed me like a dog, through the living-rooms and kitchens, stopping when I stopped, and pausing to look out of a window whenever I opened one. Upstairs, in one of the bedrooms which was more fully furnished than the rest of the house and had obviously been intended for my uncle's use, the sour staleness was overpowering. As I strode to the window, out of the corner of my eye, I saw Roger drop on his knees in front of the linen chest at the foot of the four-poster bed. With a sigh of pleasure, he let his fingers caress the dull wood as they had caressed the panelling and the yellow herb.

'It's the same,' I heard him hiss. 'It's unbelievable that it's still the same only so much darker.'

'If it's the one Master Knapton took your suit from I'm not surprised it's the same,' I said, glancing round at him. 'But as you did not come indoors when he was here, I don't see how you can recognize it.'

He dropped back on his heels as if caught in some guilty thought or action.

'The date is on it here,' I said quietly, for he did not reply, and I seemed to have damped his enthusiasm. 'On the lid—1620. I've no doubt it was made for my uncle when he was a young man. It's old by his standards now, over twenty-five years.'

'Twenty-five years! That's not old,' Roger protested. 'It won't look like that in over three hundred years, that I know.'

'Neither will you,' I retorted.

He stared at me. There was silence, a second's silence while the wind of that dull, clouded summer day blew in the narrow window and sent only its voices sweeping through my uncle's room.

'"*Tempus edax rerum*",' I commented.

'What?' asked Roger sharply. 'What does that mean? It's Latin, isn't it?'

'Latin, boy!' I exclaimed. 'Of course it's Latin, and at your age you should know what it means.'

'I don't,' he confessed. 'I don't take Latin at my school. I take other subjects.'

I refrained from another exclamation. For all I knew he might be some ignorant local lad that my uncle had befriended and he was trying to cover his lack of knowledge by blaming it on to his schoolmaster.

'"Time, the devourer of all things," is a fair enough translation,' I explained.

Roger's eyes met mine, and again I was conscious of the wind, the rustle of the dead lime flowers on the flags. Then he chuckled—and the sound of hoofs clopping on the terrace beneath us told me that Ned Mallet had returned to stable my horse. I hurried to the head of the stairs to see if the man's wife was with him, too. Before I called down I glanced back at Roger. He had not moved but he was watching me, that strange look of wonder, near affection on his face. Although I pretended not to have noticed, it was with growing feelings of uneasiness and foreboding that I made my way to the kitchen.

Who was he, this boy? He seemed familiar with my uncle's possessions, and yet he said he had only met him once. Was his friendliness genuine or was it a cloak for something deeper? Ned Mallett's antagonism had unsettled me. I recollected his hasty glance to where the boy must have been standing behind me and I began to wonder if, ever since Edward Knapton's death, the villagers had set a spy to wait for the new unwanted soldier-owner of the property; a spy who would gain his confidence, as this boy was gaining mine, and then, at the chosen moment— My fingers sought the hilt of my sword. With that alone, for I now realized my foolishness in leaving my pistols on my saddle, I reckoned I could withstand any treachery.

In the kitchen Mistress Mallet had already lighted the fire and blown it into a blaze. There were clean sheets, which she told me she had brought herself, draped across a bench; but her sullen greeting added to the wave of depression that had come over me at the top of the stairs.

Strong hands smoothed the folds of her petticoats down her broad hips as she regarded me with the eyes of Nathaniel Dodd and Ned Mallet.

'So—you're a soldier,' she sniffed. 'We've seen more than enough of the likes of you.'

'So I understand,' was my quick rejoinder and, leaving her at the oven, I went into the living-room.

'There's bread and cheese and ale for your supper,' she called out. 'I'll make up the beds and then you must shift for yourself. I'll not stay after dusk in this God-forsaken place.'

I did not trouble to reply, but dropped my hat and gloves on the settle as I passed and dragged a high-backed chair up to the table in the window. Sitting there, gazing out over the windswept terrace and the unending grass of that vast field, my depression deepened. Master Dodd had been right; I should have to sell 'the God-forsaken place'. The villagers, even if they intended me no real harm, would never accept me without a struggle, and no doubt, one night spent alone in the house would be enough to drive me away. It would not be difficult to decide which had the most power, the supernatural or the ill-wishes of Master Mallett.

And what of Roger? Was I to be completely alone? It was unlikely after Mistress Mallett's use of the word 'beds'. As far as I could see the boy had no intentions of leaving me, which seemed further confirmation of my suspicions. He had followed me to the kitchen, through to the living-room and now, without turning my head, I was able to watch his form, grey-blue in the growing shadows, where he was crouching on the settle. My hat and gloves were in his lap and he was engrossed, examining both in minute detail—furtively fingering the felt, the leather, even the lines of stitching.

'It's getting dark in here,' I said abruptly.

He started in alarm.

'D-dark?' he stammered. 'I'll switch the light on.'

He sprang across the room to the door and put his hand to the wall. Then he stood still, his hand slipping to his side.

'What's the matter?' I asked, shaken by his words and attitude.

'Candles—I'll fetch the candles,' he murmured.

I stood up to follow him, but hesitated at the strident tones of Mistress Mallett's voice.

'There's candles and tinder in the dresser in the living-room, I'll be bound. Don't you be bothering me, now. The supper's out here and I'll be gone in less than a minute.'

Roger returned. He walked past the dresser, straight to the table, and sat down.

'She doesn't want me in the kitchen at the moment,' he explained. 'There are plenty of candles out there and I'll light them from the fire when she has gone.'

It was a barefaced lie.

'One candle will be sufficient,' I remarked coldly, and sat down opposite.

'I don't mind being in the dark,' he said.

No, I thought in agreement, I do not suppose you do. So much can be accomplished in the dark with an unwary opponent, but I am as watchful as you, my lad.

Suddenly he leaned across and looked searchingly up into my face.

'You know what you said just now, about time,' he began. '"Time the devourer of all things"–"*tempus*", something or other?'

'"*Tempus edax rerum*",' I repeated, wedging my knee under the table so that it could not be tipped unexpectedly and send me off my balance.

'Do you believe that?'

'That time devours everything?' I asked, and I heard the click of the latch as Mistress Mallett left the kitchen. 'It is obvious it does. Look at the grass out there and the hedge. A few months and the place is a wilderness, a few years more of neglect and the whole house will be a tangle of briars, the woodwork rotten and the plaster fallen in. That's time; time devours and—'

'I know,' he interrupted impatiently. 'That's one sort of time —but I'm trying to talk about something else—a—a time that is only a cover, that we have to live by in hours and days, but which doesn't really exist.'

If you are spinning out the time, I thought, you are going about it in a very odd way.

'I'm so hopeless at expressing myself,' he went on with a hint of desperation. 'Something like it comes in a piece of poetry, though I'm not much good at the stuff and I can never remember it properly—

"In every land thy feet may tread
Time like a veil is round thy head.
Only the land thou seek'st with me
Never hath been nor yet shall be—"'

An uneasy cold crept over my whole body as I listened, held against my will by his glowing eyes and the tense face so white in the half light. If he had wanted to put me off my guard, he had succeeded.

'Don't you believe that time is only a veil and if you lift it, you can be anywhere at any period of existence?' he whispered.

Uncertainty, vague fear, and a presentiment of some unknown power gripped me.

'"Time like a veil is round thy head."' The slow words he repeated dropped into the hollow stillness of the empty house.

My question hovered on the air.

'Who wrote that?' I breathed.

'Henry Newbolt,' he said, and even before he spoke I sensed it would be a poet of whom I had never heard.

A sudden flicker of light beyond the hedge in the darkening garden jerked me from my stupor. One hand flew to my sword, the other instinctively closed over Roger's slim wrists on the table.

'Don't move,' I hissed as I pressed him to the chair.

'I can't,' he growled. 'And there's no need to hold me down. I'm not frightened of them.'

The injured tone was reassuring. The boy was no accomplice, of that I was sure, though what he was I had not the courage to admit. I was only concerned at that moment with the need for speedy action.

'I'll wager it's Ned Mallett with his scythe and half the village too, come to drive the soldier from his stronghold,' I muttered in rising anger. 'And this soldier will not be driven. I'll go of my own free will, and neither man nor devil shall frighten me out of my own house.'

I released Roger who was writhing under the strength of my arm.

'Get down to that gate opposite the terrace steps. See that it's locked and bolted,' I commanded. 'They'll not venture over this hawthorn hedge without ladders yet.'

'Can't we barricade the house?' he asked eagerly. 'We could block all the doors and shutter the windows and pour buckets of blazing tar on their heads. That's what they do in sieges—'

'This isn't a siege,' I snapped, ignoring his flippancy although he appeared to be in earnest. 'And it is not going to be one. Attack first, defence afterwards is the order in my troop of horse. There must be another gate behind the stables and I'll wait for you there.'

He darted away and sent the chair flying in his impetuous dash.

'Don't be foolhardy,' I called. 'If they are armed they'll fire.'

'What?' He paused in the doorway. 'With one of those old carbines? Those things wouldn't hit a cow at five yards.'

'They've been known to kill a man at twenty,' I retorted.

'Oh for a Winchester, and I'd pick 'em off like flies,' he cried.

'I want no bloodshed,' I ordered. Again his remark was incomprehensible, but time enough to ask him what he meant later, I thought. 'If they want to live in peace, far be it from me to start a fight, but they must learn to leave me in peace, too.'

If I could retrieve my pistols—if Master Mallett had not had the wits to remove them from the holsters in anticipation of this attack—and could fire over their heads to frighten them into parleying, we might be able to come to amicable terms after all.

As the outer door banged behind Roger, I groped through the dim kitchen to make my way to the stables and barns—but I never reached either. The moment my foot stepped into the sullen darkness of that clouded evening, a bullet shattered the window at my side. I ducked, slid beneath the covering bushes, and flattened myself against the wall waiting for the next shot. None came; no sound, no movement but the trees in the wind and my own shallow breathing. So much for the prospects of peace without bloodshed, I thought, and this was a form of fighting I despised. With my pistols or sword, even my bare hands, I would tackle any numbers if they refused to listen to words of reason, but this game of hide-and-seek, with an enemy who had already spotted me, was not to my liking.

Cautiously I edged sideways, aware that my disadvantage lay in the fact that I was not familiar with the courtyard, and that the stables might be any of the shapes that rose up in the gloom.

If my enemy meant to kill, once I was in the open I was an easy target, and so until I could catch a glimpse of him, it was wiser to hug the wall. My fingers, spreading along the bricks, touched first climbing tendrils, a snail—then, something warm and rough—a hand! I froze. My fingers crept upwards to touch a sleeve. With an exclamation of alarm the owner of the sleeve jerked backwards, and before another hand could drop on mine I sprang at the hidden figure. Nose to nose, knee to knee, we struggled under the bushes betraying our whereabouts to the unseen marksman. His second shot speeding through the branches over my head so startled my antagonist that, in his momentary hesitation, I wrenched myself free, swung my fist and gave him a crushing blow on the jaw. As his sagging body toppled another shape leapt for my throat, received the toe of my jackboot in his stomach and fell winded and writhing to the ground.

Two, I thought quickly, and how many more? Off balance and reeling from my shelter I nearly slipped beneath the double onslaught of a burly figure in front and little, leech-like arms which clasped my wrists behind me. With a vicious kick to the rear, I felt my spurs gouge deeply into a stockinged shin—there was a scream of pain and the third assailant dropped from the fight. But the fourth was taking all my strength; he tripped my feet and sent me sprawling to the dust, bruised and entangled by my own sword, and there we rolled, locked in each other's arms until I became conscious of a light wavering towards us from the darkness of the hedge. It was Master Mallett, a flaming torch held high, and at his side was the marksman with his carbine.

'This is your doing,' I bellowed in a brief moment when I was uppermost. 'I came in peace and if any of these men are dead, may it lie on your conscience for ever.'

I saw the light glinting along the raised barrel and I saw Roger leaping into the circle of yellow flame.

'Get down—he'll fire!' I gasped.

For a moment he stood there poised, a pace from the carbine's mouth—a shot—silence—a feather of smoke—a quiver from the torch as Ned Mallett turned, too late, and struck the gun from the man's hands. The fellow gripping my shoulders loosed them, sat back and eased his bruised muscles; other shapes rose and shambled towards the gate. I lurched to my feet and stumbled forward.

Roger had not moved; upright and as firm as a rock, he watched me coming, a faint smile on his lips. His eyes, as he glanced up into my face, wore an odd, distant look.

'That must be like the silver bullet in the fairy stories that's supposed to kill the devil,' he said quietly. 'It doesn't really kill him, it just gets rid of him for a while.'

'You're hurt,' I said.

I slipped my arm round his shoulders and he did not resist. Slowly I led him to the long grass at the edge of the terrace, where I pulled off my coat and spread it on the ground. He sank down and let his head droop on to the improvised pillow. Kneeling by his side I fumbled with the worn cloth of his doublet, feeling through his shirt to his chest. There was not a mark on him nor a speck of blood.

'There's no wound,' I whispered.

'There won't be,' he murmured. 'I'm not going to die yet. I shall be alive long after you are dead—more than three hundred years.'

I gazed into that still face which glimmered among the grasses like a white moth at rest.

He raised one hand; his fingers touched my hair, my cheek, my linen shirt, the hilt of my unused sword.

'John Knapton—Captain John Knapton,' and I sensed that he was smiling. 'I have always wanted to know what you were really like—and now I know you were a Roundhead soldier as well, while everyone else just believes you to be the man who laid out the gardens.'

'What gardens?' I asked, a great fear gripping me.

'The gardens here,' he replied. 'Gardens that everyone comes to see—the sundial on the terrace where you carved your name and put those strange words along its rim, in English, too. I wonder why you did that; most people of your time would have put them in Latin. It's so short, so short a time,' he whispered desperately. 'There was so much I wanted to see, to know, to ask—and I never guessed how it could end—I—I thought I could be here for ever, if I wanted. The suit was in the chest; I found it there, all folded and old just as he had put it away and then, I hoped I might meet you.' He chuckled. 'I frightened

him, the old man, your uncle, though the villagers thought I was some boy of his. It was too soon and I pestered the life out of him asking what he was doing in your house—everyone knew it was yours—they hadn't a clue it belonged to him first—they even thought you built it.'

His fingers slipped from my sword and lay, a featherweight on my own.

'He was afraid of me,' he murmured. 'I was something out of this world to him, I suppose.'

I heard the wind bending the lime branches, the leaves tapping the flagstones, but there were no voices, only peace in that clouded night.

'The supernatural is to be feared not mocked,' Master Dodd had said—and I was not afraid.

I watched him, how long I watched him, I cannot tell. His slight form lay, a shadow in the flattened grass, his face fading, until, as the moonless hours crept by, he drifted like a moth into the darkness.

My coat was warm when I took it up and stumbled into the house. I lit a candle with the tinder that I believed Roger had not known how to use and mounted the stairs to my uncle's room. There I opened the chest and there I found the blue-grey doublet and breeches, the fine lace shirt, fresh-folded in lavender, just as my uncle had laid them away a few months ago; the dust and creases, the yellowing of age and faded colours that Roger had put on would form with the years, three hundred years of time.

I knelt there, my head bowed in my arms while the candle

burned low in its socket. I, who had never allowed myself to feel the need for a home, now wanted this, my inheritance, though willed to me in fear; and wanted to create out of its wilderness something living to take the place of the destruction which had been five years of my life.

Was it possible, I asked myself, to raise a memorial to a ghost from the future, to a boy not yet born, a memorial that would endure until he came?

'A wall would last longer than that hawthorn hedge,' I thought. 'And oaks are slower growing than limes or elms; flagged paths and stone seats would weather the centuries; shrubs of rosemary and lavender—they spring from slips quick enough although the mother plant may not thrive more than a decade and—'I laughed aloud—'he shall have his tansy and as many herbs as he wants, descendants of the ones already here; and his blazing borders, banked by yew—that's almost everlasting.'

I stubbed the flaring candle in its pool of grease and, fired with enthusiasm, strode to the open window. The limes were still, only an early thrush was rustling the limp leaves.

'A dial on the terrace,' I mused, 'where it will catch the sun most of the day; and my name on it with some Latin maxim carved along its rim, *Tempus Fugit* or—' A chuckle of merriment burst from me. 'But the boy doesn't know any Latin!' I exclaimed. 'Roger, Roger, what an ignorant lad you are—but for your sake, I'll put the words in English.'

I gazed out across that vast field of rampant grass, already seeing in my mind the beauty it was to become. And Roger? I should look for him in vain, for he would not come in my lifetime any more; but come, at last, he would, and love that garden as I was beginning to love it.

'"Long looked for—come at last".' I breathed into that first dawn the words which were to be inscribed in stone.

The sun's gold touched the latticed panes.

I have lived three centuries in half a day, I thought, and then a mischievous smile curved my lips because I knew I should have to write to Nathaniel Dodd.

The house would not be sold—for Master Ghost and I had become well acquainted.

The Doctor

TED THOMAS

When Gant first opened his eyes he thought for an instant he was back in his home in Pennsylvania. He sat up suddenly and looked wildly around in the dark of the cave, and then he remembered where he was. The noise he made frightened his wife and his son, Dun, and they rolled to their feet, crouched, ready to leap. Gant grunted reassuringly at them and climbed off the moss-packed platform he had built for a bed. The barest glimmerings of dawn filtered into the cave, and the remnants of the fire glowed at the mouth. Gant went to the fire and poked it and put some chips of wood on it and blew on them. It had been a long time since he had had such a vivid memory of his old life half a million years away. He looked at the wall of the cave, at the place where he kept his calendar, painfully scratched into the rock. It had been ten years ago today when he had stepped into that molybdenum-steel cylinder in the Bancroft Building at Pennsylvania State University. What was it he had said? 'Sure, I'll try it. You ought to have a medical doctor in it on the first trial run. You physicists could not learn anything about the physiological effects of time travel. Besides, this will make history, and I want to be in on it.'

Gant stepped over the fire and listened carefully at the mouth of the cave, near the log barrier. Outside he heard the sound of rustling brush and heavy breathing, and he knew he could not leave now. He drank some water from a gourd and ate some dried bison with his wife and son. They all ate quietly.

Dawn came, and he stepped to the mouth of the cave and listened. The great animal had left. He waved to his wife and Dun, dragged aside the barrier, and went out.

He went along the face of the cliff, staying away from the heavy underbrush at its foot. He would go into it when he returned, and he would look for food.

In the marsh that lay beyond the underbrush was one of the many monuments to his failures. In the rocks and tree stumps there, he had tried to grow penicillium moulds on the sweet juices of some of the berries that abounded in the region. He had crushed the berries and placed the juices in a hundred different kinds of receptacles. For three years he had tried to raise the green mould, but all he ever produced was a slimy grey mass that quickly rotted when the sun struck it.

He hefted the heavy stone axe in his right hand. As he approached the cave he was looking for, he grunted loudly and then went in. The people inside held their weapons in their hands, and he was glad he had called ahead. He ignored them and went to a back corner to see the little girl.

She sat on the bare stone, leaning against the rock with her mouth open, staring dully at him as he came up to her, her eyes black against the thick blonde hair that grew on her face. Gant whirled at the others and snarled at them, and snatched a bear-hide from the bed of the man and carried it to the girl. He wrapped her in it and then felt the part of her forehead where there was no hair. It was burning hot, must be about 105 degrees, possibly a little more. He put her down on the rock and thumped her chest and heard the solid, hard sound of filled lungs. It was full-blown pneumonia, no longer any doubt. She gasped for breath, and there was no breath. Gant picked her up and held her. He sat with her for over an hour, changing her position frequently in his arms, trying to make her comfortable as she gasped. He held a handful of wet leaves to her forehead to try to cool her burning face, but it did not seem to help. She went into convulsions at the end.

He laid the body on a rock ledge and pulled the mother over to see it. The mother bent and touched the girl gently on the face and then straightened and looked at Gant helplessly. He picked up the body and walked out of the cave and down into the woods. It took several hours to dig a hole deep enough with a stick.

He hunted on the way back to the caves, and he killed a short, heavy-bodied animal that hung upside down from the lower branches of a tree. It emitted a foul odour as he killed it, but it would make a good meal. He found a large rock outcropping with a tiny spring coming out from under it. A mass of newly sprouted shoots grew in the soggy ground. He picked them all, and headed back to his cave. His wife and Dun were there and their faces brightened when they saw what he brought. His wife immediately laid out the animal and skinned it with a fragment of sharp, shiny rock. Dun watched her intently, leaning over while it cooked to smell the fragrant smoke. Gant looked at the short, thick, hairy woman tending the cooking, and he looked at the boy. He could easily see himself in the thin-limbed boy. Both his wife and his son had the heavy brows and the jutting jaw of the cave people. But Dun's body was lean and his eyes were blue and sparkling, and he often sat close to Gant and tried to go with him when he went out of the cave. And once, when the lightning blazed and the thunder roared, Gant had seen the boy standing at the mouth of the cave staring at the sky in puzzlement, not fear, and Gant had put a hand on his shoulder and tried to find the words that told of electrical discharges and the roar of air rushing into a void, but there were no words.

The meat was done and the shoots were softened, and the three of them squatted at the fire and reached for the food. Outside the cave they heard the sound of movement in the gravel, and Gant leaped for his club while his wife and Dun retreated to the rear of the cave. Two men appeared, one supporting the other, both empty-handed. Gant waited until he could see that one of them was injured; he could not place his right foot on the ground. Then Gant came forward and helped the injured man to a sitting position at the mouth of the cave. He leaned over to inspect the foot. The region just above the ankle was discoloured and badly swollen, and the foot was at a slight angle to the rest of the leg. Both the fibula and the tibia seemed to be broken, and Gant stood up and looked around for splints. The man would probably die; there was no one to take care of him during the weeks needed for his leg to heal, no one to hunt for him and give him food and put up with his almost complete inactivity.

Gant found two chips from logs and two short branches and some strips from a cured hide. He knelt in front of the man and carefully held his hands near the swollen leg so the man could see he was going to touch it.

The man's great muscles were knotted in pain and his face was grey beneath the hair. Gant waved the second man around to one side where he could keep an eye on him, and then he took the broken leg and began to apply tension. The injured man stood it for a moment and then roared in pain and instinctively lashed out with his good leg. Gant ducked the kick, but he could not duck the blow from the second man. It hit him on the side of the head and knocked him out of the mouth of the cave. He rolled to his feet and came back in. The second man stood protectively in front of the injured man, but Gant pushed him aside and knelt down again. The foot was straight, so Gant placed the chips and branches on the leg and bound them in place with the leather thongs. Weak and helpless, the injured man did not resist. Gant stood up and showed the second man how to carry the injured man. He helped them on their way.

When they left, Gant returned to his food. It was cold, but he was content. For the first time they had come to him. They were learning. He hurt his teeth on the hard meat and he gagged on the spongy shoots, but he squatted in his cave and he smiled. There had been a time long ago when he had thought that these people would be grateful to him for his work, that he would become known by some such name as The Healer. Yet here he was, years later, happy that at last one of them had come to him with an injury. Yet Gant knew them too well by now to be misled. These people did not have even the concept of medical treatment, and the day would probably come when one of them would kill him as he worked.

He sighed, picked up his club, and went out of the cave. A mile away was a man with a long gash in the calf of his left leg. Gant had cleaned it and packed it with moss and tied it tight with a hide strip. It was time to check the wound, so he walked the mile carefully, on the lookout for the large creatures that roamed the forests. The man was chipping rock in front of his cave, and he nodded his head and waved and showed his teeth in a friendly gesture when he saw Gant. Gant showed his teeth in turn and looked at the leg. He saw that the man had removed the moss and bandage, and had rubbed the great wound with dung. Gant bent to inspect the wound and immediately smelled the foul smell of corruption. Near the top of the wound, just beneath the knee, was a mass of black, wet tissues. Gangrene. Gant straightened and looked around at some of the others near the cave. He went to them and tried to make them understand what he wanted to do, but they did not pay much attention. Gant returned and looked down on the wounded man, noting that his movements were still quick and co-ordinated, and that he was as powerfully built as the rest of them. Gant shook his head; he could not perform the amputation unaided, and there was no help to be had. He tried again to show them that the man would die unless they helped him, but it was no use. He left.

He walked along the foot of the cliffs, looking in on the caves. In one he found a woman with a swollen jaw, in pain. She let him look in her mouth, and he saw a rotted molar. He sat down with her and with gestures tried to explain that it would be painful at first if he removed the tooth, but that it would soon be better. The woman seemed to understand. Gant took up a fresh branch and scraped a rounded point on one end. He picked up a rock twice the size of his fist, and placed the woman in a sitting position with her head resting on his thigh. He placed the end of the stick low on the gum to make sure he got the root. Carefully he raised the rock, knowing he would have but one try. He smashed the rock down and felt the tooth give way and saw blood spout from her mouth. She screamed and leaped to her feet and turned on Gant, but he jumped away. Then something struck him from behind and he found himself pinned to the ground with two men sitting on him. They growled at him and one picked up a rock and stick and smashed a front tooth from Gant's mouth. Then they threw him out of the cave. He rolled down through the gravel and came up short against a bush. He leaped to his feet and charged back into the cave. One of the men swung a club at him, but he ducked and slammed the rock against the side of the man's head. The other ran. Gant went over to the woman, picking as he went a half handful of moss from the wall of the cave. He stood in front of her and packed some of the moss in the wound in his front jaw, and leaned over to show her the bleeding had stopped. He held out the moss to her, and she quickly took some and put it in the proper place in her jaw. She nodded to him and patted his arm and rubbed the blood out of the hair on her chin. He left the cave without looking at the unconscious man.

Some day they would kill him. His jaw throbbed as he walked along the gravel shelf and headed for home. There would be no more stops today, and so he threaded his way along the foot of the cliff. He heard sounds of activity in several of the caves, and in one of the largest of them he heard excited voices yelling. He stopped, but his jaw hurt too much to go in. The noise increased and Gant thought they might be carving up a large kill. He was always on the lookout for meat, so he changed his mind and went in. Inside was a boy about the age of Dun, lying on his back, gasping for air. His face had a bluish tinge, and at each intake of air his muscles tensed and his back arched with the effort to breathe. Gant pushed to his side and forced his mouth open. The throat and uvula were greatly swollen, the air passage almost shut. He quickly examined the boy, but there was no sign of injury or disease.

Gant was puzzled, but then he concluded the boy must have chewed or eaten a substance to which he was sensitive. He looked at the throat again. The swelling was continuing. The boy's jutting jaws made mouth-to-mouth resuscitation impossible. A tracheotomy was indicated. He went over to the fire and smashed one piece of flint chopping stone on another, and quickly picked over the pieces. He chose a short, sharp fragment and stooped over the boy. He touched the point of the fragment against the skin just beneath the larynx, squeezed his thumb and forefinger on the fragment to measure a distance a little over half an inch from the point, and then thrust down and into the boy's throat until his thumb and forefinger just touched the skin. Behind him he heard a struggle, and he looked up in time to see several people restrain a woman with an axe. He watched to see that they kept her out of the cave and away from him before he turned back to the boy. By gently turning the piece of flint he made an opening in the windpipe. He turned the boy on his side to prevent the tiny trickle of blood from running into the opening. The result was dramatic. The boy's struggles stopped, and the rush of air around the piece of flint sounded loud in the still of the cave. The boy lay back and relaxed and breathed deeply, and even the people in the cave could tell he was now much better. They gathered around and watched silently, and Gant could see the interest in their faces. The boy's mother had not come back.

For half an hour Gant sat holding the flint in the necessary position. The boy stirred restlessly a time or two, but Gant quieted him. The people drifted back to their activities in the cave, and Gant sat and tended his patient.

He leaned over the boy. He could hear the air beginning to pass through his throat once again. In another fifteen minutes the boy's throat was open enough, and Gant withdrew the flint in one swift movement. The boy began to sit up, but Gant held him down and pressed the wound closed. It stayed closed, and Gant got up. No one paid any attention when he left.

He went along the gravel shelf, ignoring the sounds of life that came out of the caves as he went by. He rounded a boulder and saw his own cave ahead.

The log barrier was displaced and he could hear snarls and grunts as he ran into the semi-darkness inside. Two bodies writhed on the floor of the cave. He ran closer and saw that his wife and another woman were struggling there, raking each other's skin with thick, sharp nails, groping for each other's jugular vein with long, yellow teeth. Gant drove his heel into the side of the woman's body, just above the kidney. The air exploded from her lungs and she went limp. He twisted a hand in her hair and yanked her limp body away from his wife's teeth and ran for the entrance of the cave, dragging her after him.

Outside, he threw the limp body down the slope. He turned and caught his wife as she came charging out. She fought him, trying to get to the woman down the slope, and it was only because she was no longer trying to kill that he was able to force her back into the cave.

Inside, she quickly stopped fighting him. She went and knelt over something lying at the foot of his bed. He rubbed his sore jaw and went over to see what it was. He stared down in the dim light of the cave. It was Dun, and he was dead. His head had been crushed. Gant cried out and leaned against the wall. He knelt and hugged Dun's warm body to him, pushing his wife aside. He pressed his face into the boy's neck and thought of the years that he had planned to spend in teaching Dun the healing arts. He felt a heavy pat on his shoulder and looked up. His wife was there, awkwardly patting him on the shoulder, trying to comfort him. Then he remembered the woman who had killed his son.

He ran out of the cave and looked down the slope. She was not there, but he caught a flash of movement down the gravel shelf and he could see her staggering towards her cave. He began to run after her, but stopped. His anger was gone, and he felt no emotion save a terrible emptiness. He turned and went back into the cave for Dun's body. In the forest he slowly dug a deep hole. He felt numb as he dug, but when it was done and he had rolled a large stone on top of the grave, he kneeled down near it, held his face in his hands, and cried. Afterwards, he followed the stream bed to a flat table of solid rock. At the edge of the rock table, where the wall of rock began to rise to the cliffs above, half hidden in the shrub pine, was a mass of twisted metal wreckage. He looked down on it and thought again of that day ten years ago. Here, on the site of Pennsylvania State University, at College Park, Pennsylvania, was where he started and where he ended. But a difference of half a million years lay between the start and the end.

Once tears had come to his eyes when he looked at the wreckage, but no longer. There was work to do here and he was the only one who could do it. He nodded and turned to climb to his cave. There were cold meat and shoots there, and a wife, and perhaps there could be another son. And this day, for the first time, an injured man had come to see him.

The Choice

WAYLAND HILTON-YOUNG

Before Williams went into the future he bought a camera and a tape-recording machine and learned shorthand. That night, when all was ready, we made coffee and put out brandy and glasses against his return.

'Goodbye,' I said. 'Don't stay too long.'

'I won't,' he answered.

I watched him carefully, and he hardly flickered. He must have made a perfect landing on the very second he had taken off from. He seemed not a day older; we had expected he might spend several years away.

'Well?'

'Well,' said he, 'let's have some coffee.'

I poured it out, hardly able to contain my impatience. As I gave it to him I said, 'Well?'

'Well, the thing is, I can't remember.'

'Can't remember? Not a thing?'

He thought for a moment and answered sadly, 'Not a thing.'

'But your notes? The camera? The recording-machine?'

The notebook was empty, the indicator of the camera rested at '1' where we had set it, the tape was not even loaded into the recording-machine.

'But good heavens,' I protested, 'why? How did it happen? Can you remember nothing at all?'

'I can remember only one thing.'

'What was that?'

'I was shown everything, and I was given the choice whether I should remember it or not after I got back.'

'And you chose not to? But what an extraordinary thing to—'

'Isn't it?' he said. 'One can't help wondering why.'

ACKNOWLEDGEMENTS

Poul Anderson: 'My Object all Sublime' found in Martin H. Greenberg et al (eds.) *The Giant Book of Science Fiction Stories* (Avenel Books, 1986), reprinted by permission of the author's agents, Scovil Chichak Galen Literary Agency, Inc.

Steve Bowkett: 'Timestorm', copyright © Steve Bowkett 2001, first published in this collection by permission of the author.

Ray Bradbury: 'A Sound of Thunder' from *The Golden Apples of the Sun* (Rupert Hart-Davis, 1953), copyright 1952 by Crowell Collier Publishing, renewed 1980 by Ray Bradbury, reprinted by permission of Don Congdon Associates, Inc.

Fredric Brown: 'Vengeance Fleet', copyright © 1950 by Pines Publications, copyright renewed 1978 by the Estate of Fredric Brown, first published in *Super Science Stories* for July 1950, reprinted from *Nightmares and Geezenstacks* (Bantam Books, Inc., 1961) by permission of the agents for the author's Estate, A. M. Heath & Co. Ltd, and Scott Meredith Literary Agency, L. P.

Arthur C. Clarke: 'All the Time in the World' from *Of Time and Stars* (Gollancz, 1972, Penguin 1974), reprinted by permission of the author and the author's agents, David Higham Associates and Scovil Chichak Galen Literary Agency, Inc.

Ken Cowley: 'And Three to Go' from *Miscellany Macabre* (The British Fantasy Society, 1999), reprinted by permission of the author.

Nance Donkin: 'Room 409' first published in *A Handful of Ghosts* edited by Barbara Ker Wilson (Hodder & Stoughton (Australia) Pty, 1976), reprinted by permission of the author.

Harry Harrison: 'If' from *The Best of Harry Harrison* (Sidgwick & Jackson, 1976, Futura, 1980), reprinted by permission of Abner Stein and Tor Books, New York.

Wayland Hilton-Young: 'The Choice', copyright © 1952 Wayland Hilton-Young, first published in *Punch* 1952, reprinted by permission of *Punch*.

Kenneth Ireland: 'Time Shift', copyright © Kenneth Ireland 2001, first published in this collection by permission of the author, c/o Jennifer Luithlen Agency.

Garry Kilworth: 'Let's Go to Golgotha' from *The Songbirds of Pain* (Victor Gollancz, 1984), reprinted by permission of the Orion Publishing Group Ltd.

Rita Lamb: 'What Time is It?', copyright © Rita Lamb 2001, first published in this collection by permission of the author.

Penelope Lively: 'The Picnic', copyright © Penelope Lively, first published in M. R. Hodgkin (ed.): *Young Winter's Tales 6* (Macmillan, 1975), reprinted by permission of David Higham Associates.

Alison Prince: 'Fire, Fire' from *A Haunting Refrain* (Methuen Children's Books, 1988), reprinted by permission of the author and Jennifer Luithlen Agency.

Despite every effort to trace and contact copyright holders before publication this has not been possible in all cases. If notified, the publisher will be pleased to rectify any errors or omissions at the earliest opportunity.

The illustrations are by:

Martin Cottam pp 61, 69, 132, 169, 172
Ian Miller pp 48, 57, 60, 71, 77, 79, 80, 109, 116, 121, 122, 182
Brian Pedley pp 101, 108, 139, 144, 193, 204
David Wyatt pp 14, 18, 25, 39, 97, 205, 213